WHEN THE DIVINE ARE DEAD

THE DIVINER'S LEGACY: BOOK ONE

E.K. BARNES

This is a work of fiction. All characters, organizations, and events portrayed in this novel are either products of the author's imagination or are used fictitiously.

Printed in the United States of America

www.ekbarnesauthor.com

First Printing, 2020

ISBN: 9780578918891

The text type was set in Calibri Light
Cover designed by GetCovers

TO
MAGGIE
(WHO HEARD THE STORY FIRST)

TABLE OF CONTENTS

ACKNOWLEDGMENTS

"Thank you for your support, I guess," I'd written on a card meant for my parents. Mrs. Tomassi, my junior high physical education teacher and volleyball coach, chastised me. "What is this?" she'd asked, pointing out the last two words I'd written. She made me rewrite it in her locker room office. The whole time I sat there, staring at the blank card, sniveling and crying. I didn't know how to thank my parents. At this age, they were just my parents. Everything I thought to write felt like lies. "Thank you for letting me be the eighth-grade volleyball manager," I wrote, but I could never answer the 'why.' Why was I thankful? Because that way I could hang out with my friends after school. I could travel with them to their games. But that sounded selfish. What did me getting to hang out with my friends have to do with my parents? All they did was agree to pick me up from school later. So, again, why was I thankful? It's been a decade, but I still overthink this question. I'm thankful, but why?

I think part of my problem is that I'm more grateful than thankful. I'm grateful I have food to eat and books to read. I'm grateful I have a roof that doesn't leak and lungs that continue to breathe. I'm grateful to have parents who never stopped loving me and friends who grew as obsessed with my characters as I did. The "thank you" part of thankful trips me up.

For a long time, I wrote in a way that I thought would please others. "Don't write in first person," they'd say, "write like the classics." . . . "Avoid using contractions." . . . "Dialogue is hard. Don't use so much dialogue." . . . "Never use dead words." . . . "Forget putting semi-colons to use." . . . "Don't write science fiction. Everybody writes science fiction." . . . "Omit all adverbs from your writing." I let these snippets of advice from teachers and other writers destroy my natural writing voice. I filed this story away in favor of another series. My writing grew dark. There was no magic, no stories of fantastical beings, no imaginary fantasy islands to lighten the mood.

I'm grateful for a random moment of inspiration that hit me in the middle of a March day. I'm grateful for the courage it took to unzip the old files I had put away long ago, to ignore the voices that stripped my own voice away, and rewrite the story of Bradley Chambers as I saw fit. I'm even grateful for the global pandemic of COVID-19, which temporarily hindered my hours at my day job, allowing me the extra time to write. Because of all these things, I was able to write the first draft of this book in a month-and-a-half. I think that might be a new record for me.

I'm grateful to have found two amazing editors, Jessie and Rita, who also doubled as sensitivity readers, and wanted nothing more than to preserve my voice. I feel extremely lucky to have found them. Their immediate interest in the story as well as their words of encouragement filled me with the confidence needed to continue on in my pursuit of this project. I knew the second I finished writing the rough draft that I had written a great story.

I'm grateful for my best friend, Nery (*some may know her as Graylin*), for always encouraging my writing career and reading my books. I'm grateful for her attachment to several of my characters. Her enthusiasm is what has kept me going all these years. Sometimes I feel like I'm writing simply for her to enjoy. When I first told her the plot of this book, she immediately expressed her interest, excited for the historical elements that play a role in this story.

I'm grateful for those who have complimented my writing over the years, not only in my books, but in articles and posts. I'm grateful for the writing community of Twitter for continuing to be a collective shoulder to lean on.

I'm grateful for my Aunt Jen and Uncle Mike, who read the first book I published under my current pseudonym. They uplifted my confidence in my ability to portray heavy emotion in my writing. I'm grateful for the day my mom finished reading that same book. She told me she was proud of me as she hugged me. I'm grateful for the nights she spent positively comparing me to other authors as if I were in the same wheelhouse as them.

I'm grateful for my mom (again), my brother Thomas, and Dr. Hause, who, to the best of my knowledge, were the only people to read the very first book I wrote, which happened to be an early draft of the book you are now holding in your hands. It held no real plot and very few descriptive phrases, but it was the first book I wrote that explored the magical world in which the Chambers family resides. Several names have changed in this rewrite, but the characters and their personalities have remained constant.

I'm grateful for my cousin Justin, who, to my complete embarrassment, kept telling people I'd written several books. He believed in my writing at a time when I didn't. To build off this thought, I must also be grateful for former classmates like Morgan and Caitlyn, who also weren't afraid to call me out as an author. I'm grateful for Jacob, who took the time to notice and congratulate me on my first author interview. I'm also grateful for Sarah, a young fellow writer who always manages to uplift and encourage the people around her.

I'm grateful for the English professors at MidAmerica Nazarene University, professors Thomas and Blake, who both begged me to switch my major to English. I'm glad they enjoyed having me as their student. Perhaps unwittingly, they acted as confidence boosters and cheerleaders, allowing me to see my potential more clearly than ever. I was rarely, if ever, encouraged in my writing by other English teachers of the past.

I'm grateful for several of my old coworkers at Potbelly Sandwich Shop; specifically, J.P., David, and Kaitlyn, who liked to joke that one day I'd write a book about all the crazy conversations and shenanigans that took place among us. While my memories have sadly faded of specifics, I do hope to one day integrate pieces of some of those experiences at the shop into another compelling story.

I'm grateful for my current coworkers; specifically, Amanda, Tiffany, and Katie, who found a way for me to use my writing talent at a job that doesn't require such. Even if it was briefly lived, that task was what ultimately inspired me to start writing again.

I'm grateful for my best friend from high school, Megan, who is another fellow writer. We used to send our writing back and forth between the other. She was my first editor and beta reader and the first to encourage me to keep writing. I hope she continues to write as well.

I'm grateful for my cousin Curtis, whose children, Issac and Bradly, seem to have inspired my main character's name.

I'm grateful for the imagination of my youth. The original storyline of this book was the brainchild of my ten-year-old self, whom I look upon in both alarming and astonishing awe at the emotional rawness of the stories she created. As I prepared this rewrite as an adult, I continued to pause and reflect, worried about keeping the story age appropriate. I'd have to continually remind myself that a ten-year-old created the major plot points that went along with the story. I had forgotten the lack of childlike innocence that existed at a time when the media seemed to constantly be portraying violence.

I'm grateful for my childhood friend Maggie, to whom this book is dedicated to. She was the first to hear the original summary of this book back in the fifth grade. At the time, the story focused on the events that occurred in the previous year of Bradley's life. The conclusion to that story is where this one begins. Maggie was the ultimate encourager to the creation of this book and its sequels.

I'm grateful for my sister, Kaitlin, who allowed me to hire her for her first cover design job as a college graduate. She also offered me her advice throughout the process of writing and developing this story.

Lastly, I'm grateful for the people I've met who helped inspire bits and pieces of certain characters and their experiences – my cousin Jordan and former classmates Kane, Dylan, Lydia, and Selena.

I hope you enjoy this book.

CONTENT WARNING can be found at

www.ekbarnesauthor.com/contentwarning3

"Whose eyes saw us as enemies?

Whose mouth cursed us?

Do not hear them, God.

Hear us!"

— *Bronislawa "Papusza" Wajs*

PROLOGUE

I wondered if the gas would kill me quickly or if I would suffer, choking and sputtering as I gasped for clean air. I thought about what Serena had told me—how four thousand Romanies, some of them diviners, were killed this way in a single day at the Auschwitz-Birkenau death camp. Four. Thousand. People. I guess the Nazis haven't changed much since then. Was it easier for them? To not have literal blood on their hands? Easier for us to die in a room far away from them? A room far away where the only evidence of our deaths could be chalked up to respiratory failure or asphyxiation? Would they bury our bodies—our powers along with us—in the state park above, or would they dispose of us elsewhere? Maybe they would burn our remains—cremate us beyond recognition—and scatter our ashes haphazardly until all traces of us were gone. No one would be the wiser. Not even the Lawrence Police Department down the street.

They weren't planning to kill us. They were planning to destroy us.

1//MY BEST FRIEND IS A MURDERER

Jesse didn't die right away. I guess that's what's so horrible about it. He didn't die from the bullet wound in his abdomen. I watched him take a breath before choking out my name. Blood sputtered from his mouth instead, dripping down his chin. He looked like a fish out of water, his chest heaving, blood gurgling in his throat. The bullet had gone straight through his body, a trail of blood spatters marking where it had flown. Blood started to pool on the tile around his body, the back of his tie-dye shirt soaked and stained red. I wish I could say that it was the most blood I'd ever seen, but it wasn't. Chad had me pinned against the lockers, his arm pressing roughly against my chest. "Now you know how I feel, don't ya, Brad?"

I don't recommend watching someone's head get blown off. It's not like it is in the movies. There's not a single bullet hole that travels through their skull.

Chad's youngest sister, Lenora, didn't have a head when she died last October.

How did my life end up like this—pinned to a locker by my best friend so I could watch my youngest brother die? Jesse was only five. I opened my mouth to protest, to beg to be let go. Maybe I could save him. Maybe Chad would let me try. He didn't need to get back at me like this. Lenora shouldn't have had to die. Back then he had aimed for my head, and I had ducked without thinking. This was payback.

My brain was so scrambled that the words of my plea failed to reach my tongue. I know middle school is supposed to suck, but nobody had warned me that my best friend would turn into a murderer. I strained my eyes to the side, peering down the adjacent hallway. Olga was unconscious on the tile, a large bruise forming above her left eye. Chad had clipped her with the butt of his gun shortly after he lunged at me. Other than her motionless body lying to my right and Jesse's whimpering body in front of me, the hallways were empty, the school eerily silent. Following Chad's warning shot into the ceiling, the entire school had immediately gone on lockdown.

"J-J-J-Jesse?" A feeble cry came from another hallway, and I froze, holding my breath. The voice sounded like it belonged to a little girl. In a matter of seconds, my theory proved correct as one of Jesse's classmates appeared, her feet shuffling forward before planting her body in plain sight. She must have come from the bathroom. I struggled against Chad's weight, trying to shout at her to run. Chad curled his fingers around my neck, but I was able to let out a strangled cry before he tightened his grip. With his other hand, he shot blindly in her direction, missing her by an inch.

She screamed, running back down the hallway she had come from. There wouldn't be anywhere for her to hide. All the doors were locked. I tried to convince myself that Chad was only after me, that he was only trying to hurt me, but Chad was the most unpredictable person on the planet. Chad was like an IED. He could explode at any given moment.

Sirens blared from the streets as emergency vehicles made their way to the school. Jesse's eyes were closed. I couldn't tell from this distance if he was breathing or not. Chad smiled, knowing his time with me was ending. As soon as the cops saw his gun, they were authorized to shoot, and he knew it. He wanted out. I could see it in his eyes. Pulling away from me, his hands in the air, gun pointed toward the ceiling, he laughed. He laughed and he laughed as I gasped for air. I could feel the oxygen returning to my body as I slid to the ground.

"He destroys everything he touches!" Chad shouted between fits of laughter. "It's almost comical." He cocked his head to the side, crouching so that he could be within spitting distance of my face. I coughed, blood dripping from my lips. I could feel the cold metal of the gun on my temple. Grabbing a clump of my hair, he yanked my head up against the lockers, holding me there. The gun stayed trained on my face. I could feel my body tremble, despite knowing my fear would egg him on. Chad fed on fear.

"I give him a knife? He uses it. A smoke? He uses two. A gun?" He licked his lips. "Maybe you'll be his third." I cringed, closing my eyes, waiting for my end. But it didn't come. I dared to squint open one of my eyes and he laughed, stepping away and rising to his full height. "You're too easy."

Olga groaned, her green eyes fluttering open. Her hand flew to the bruise already forming on her forehead. "Ugh, my head." Chad fired a shot at the ground near her body and she jumped, barely missing the ricocheted bullet. He clearly had something against aiming a bullet directly at Olga. Her body rolled up against the lockers. Holding her head, she tried to sit up but collapsed on the ground at every attempt. Chad walked steadily toward her, his gun held behind his back. He seemed amused, humming to himself as he watched her struggle.

"Tanner," she said to him, and I flinched at the mention of an unfamiliar name. Great. Chad had hit her a little too hard. I wondered what she'd call me when she had the chance. She moaned through the pain, still struggling to sit. Squinting at our destructive friend, she forced her words out of her mouth. "Let me talk to Chad."

Chad smiled, almost blissfully. "Chad? You want to talk to Chad?" He leaned against the lockers, dangling his gun over her body. "Today is Chad's last day on Earth." A red dot appeared on the back of his black shirt, and I turned to see several members of SWAT blocking my view of Jesse. I hadn't even heard them coming. I was too busy watching Chad and Olga, my heart pounding violently in my ears. This was it. My best friend was about to die.

I lunged.

I didn't have the muscle that Chad had, but the surprise was enough to knock him off his feet. A bullet flew over our bodies, grazing my leg, before lodging itself into a locker door. We tumbled to the ground, and I rolled over his arm, loosening the gun from his grip. I jabbed my elbow into his forearm. The pain caused him to yelp, and he let go of the gun. Knocking it across the floor, I watched it spin and slide over the tile. SWAT had their guns trained on us, the barrels a foot away from our bodies. Chad's expression turned into terror and then pain. He wanted to die, and I had ruined his plan. Tears rolled down his cheeks as his chin trembled. "You should've let me die."

"That was stupid!" Officer Joey shoved my shoulder as I sat in the back of an ambulance not too long afterward. The paramedic cleaning the wound on my leg urged me to keep still.

I glared at the cop, my fists clenched. "Nobody had to die today."

Suddenly I was pinned against one of the back doors to the truck, my legs at an awkward angle due to the step. The paramedic had to dodge to keep from being hit. Tufts of my green shirt were balled up in Officer Joey's fists, his face up close and personal with mine. "You listen to me, punk," he spat. Literally spat. Saliva landed on my cheek. "That bullet could have done a lot more than graze you—do you understand me?" He jostled me by my shirt until I nodded in agreement. Letting me go, he hocked a loogie onto the concrete before looking me up and down. "What are you doing trying to save that punk, anyway?" He didn't wait for an answer, shaking his head as he walked away.

A firefighter slammed the palm of their hand against the back of the ambulance holding Chad, shouting to the driver that he was good to go. I kicked the tire of the ambulance intended for me. The paramedic held out a fresh swab and some ointment, wondering if I was ready to cooperate. Plopping back down on the tail end of the vehicle, I pondered Officer Joey's question. I didn't know what made me tackle Chad to the ground. It wasn't a logical decision. Chad was always bigger and stronger than me. He had just made an attempt on my brother's life, hoping he'd die right there in the school hallway so I could watch him take his final breath. He put Olga in the hospital with a serious concussion. She couldn't even see straight when the paramedics were checking her. Five months ago, I watched him shoot his sister in cold blood and get away with it. I should have been pissed. I should have wanted him to die. But instead, I jumped in front of a bullet to save his life. It didn't make sense. I was protecting a murderer. I was always protecting him.

"It wasn't Chad," Olga repeated as the paramedics checked her out. He had seriously done a number on her, and I wasn't the only one who thought so. I hoped she would be able to see and think straight after this.

Olga was one of those girls who loved the thrill of danger but always regretted the chase midway through any sort of crisis. She and I were always dragging each other out of ill-fated situations, most of them involving Chad. We had both been enthralled by his eclipsed views of the world, allowing him to drag us into his increasingly disorganized chaos. Chad was engrossing, a natural-born leader, but his circle was small. Only Olga and I could usually stand to be around him. We understood him and bonded over that mutual perception. We were friends, and it wasn't until Chad started to grow increasingly unwell when I thought maybe Olga and I could be more than that. But I couldn't convince her to leave him. She had to stay. She had to fix Chad.

"Bradley, Bradley, Bradley!" My sister's worried voice traveled with her as she ran across the school parking lot. Tears streamed from her brown eyes and spilled onto her cheeks. She was shaking so bad I was worried her legs would give out on her before reaching me. Is it horrible to say that I had completely forgotten about her during all this? Paige could have easily been the more obvious choice for Chad to kill. She was a whole lot closer to Lenora's age. Why he had waited until science fair day so he could shoot a kindergartner, I wasn't sure.

Paige rammed her body into mine, wrapping her arms around my neck. "I was so scared." Her voice was muffled, her arm blocking her mouth. Sobbing, she mumbled through her wails. "I heard you were shot."

"Your brother's a hero," the paramedic said, tossing the used swabs into a bag.

"Don't let Officer Joey hear you say that," I said through crushed lungs. Paige had tightened her grip on me, boa constrictor style.

"At least all the kindergartners were safe inside the gym," she said, murmuring. I stiffened. She hadn't heard.

Apparently, news didn't travel as fast as I thought it did in a middle school. Parents were starting to line up around the building to pick up their kids. I watched a few of them leave. Several students were visibly shaken, some were crying, and one guy started loudly running his mouth about how he had nearly been shot.

I could feel my anger coming back, igniting in my gut as I listened to his tale, Paige's arms still around me. The hallways were nearly empty when Chad fired his warning shot. Everybody who wasn't already in class or presenting at the science fair was quick to scatter. Chad wasn't after them. Chad was after me. Chad had his gun trained on me. Who did Chad not have his gun trained on? This random seventh grader shooting off his mouth.

Paige could feel my rage grow. Apparently, my body had started to shake. When she let go, I tried to control my breathing. It was a trick I learned in anger management class, which is how I met Officer Joey. Since then, he's been tailing my every move. He thought he could fix me, but it's been two years, and nothing's changed. I'm still the same broken, messed up person.

Paige tugged on the paramedic's sleeve, asking if he had checked my blood sugar levels. "He's diabetic, you know."

I hated when she told people that. I know she means well, but it was just another thing that I hated about myself. It's not like I asked for any of this to happen to me. It wasn't long after the discovery of my defective pancreas when everything started to go south for me.

"We need to go see Jesse," I said with a growl, watching the kid with the tall tale to tell climb into his mother's vehicle.

Paige scanned the sea of vehicles before spotting a school bus leaving the parking lot. "I think he's already on the bus back to his school."

"No," I said, grumbling. The paramedic wanted to test my blood sugar, but I refused to let him do it. Paige needed to know. I looked down at the ground. One of the legs to my jeans had been cut open, and the denim was flapping with the breeze. I watched it for a second before forcing the words out of my mouth. "He was alive when the ambulance took him." I stole a glance at Paige's face and wished I had worded it differently. I made it sound like our brother was dead. For all I knew, he could be. It's not like I've received an update on his condition. But it had sounded like he was gonna make it. The paramedics seemed hopeful—stressed, but hopeful. Did she really think I would suggest visiting a dead person?

"They probably have him in surgery right now," the paramedic said, checking his watch.

Without asking, Paige pushed past us and climbed into the back of the ambulance. "Take me to him."

2// THE NUTS AND BOLTS OF LIFE AS I KNOW IT

Standing outside with Paige was usually a safe place to be. Riding in the back of an ambulance housing pins, needles, scalpels, and other sharp, pointy objects? Not safe. Paige had a little bit of an issue controlling her powers. Yes, powers. It's a genetic gift—or should I say curse?—that was passed down to us through our mother. Paige's gift: telekinesis. And like in every sci-fi movie, her powers are tied to her emotions, so I was a little nervous sitting in an ambulance with her while our brother's life hung in the balance.

I'd give anything to have useful powers. There's a technical word for it, but basically, all I can do is make something appear out of thin air. It sounds cool in theory, but it requires a ridiculous amount of concentration and visualization. If I were any good at putting my powers to use, I would have used them to stop Chad. Instead, I'm walking around pretending to be a normal human being. I mean, most of us do that anyway, but my power is useless, so it isn't exactly difficult for me to pretend to be normal. In fact, I wasn't pretending that much at all.

Having powers doesn't necessarily make us powerful. When I first heard I was gonna develop powers when I came of age, I thought it would be so cool. I honestly believed my entire life would magically turn around when I turned ten. All I got was a massive headache and these weird light flashes when I blinked. It took a few days for my mom to figure out what my power was.

My mom's a medium, the kind who talks to the dead. She also reads fortunes. Most of it's fake, but she really can see the future. She uses her gift to counsel people. It drives the reverend nuts. He's a big believer in Deuteronomy 18. He shouted at her once, waving his Bible in the air as he paraphrased a few verses from his favorite chapter, "There shall not be found among you anyone who practices witchcraft, or a soothsayer, or one who interprets omens, or a sorcerer." He calls her detestable. She only shakes her head. Mom's been a Christian all her life, the popular religion heavily ingrained in her culture. She never intended to be detestable. She only intended to guide the broken.

Chad was the reverend's son. I've known the Micas since I was eight. Back then, Chad was unruly, but only in the mind of his father. My mother found him to be a delight, listening intently as he rambled on with his childish admirations. She and the reverend never saw eye to eye. Reverend and Mrs. Mica had four children, which is one less than my parents. Chad was the oldest, then his twin sisters, Latisha and Larissa. The youngest was Lenora. They were all close in age.

My siblings were a little more spread out.

Jesse was a surprise. He was the only one of us born here in Itasca. Blake, who is eight, was born during the short time when we lived in Niles. If our reason for leaving that town hadn't been so unexpectedly traumatic, I'd think of our house in Niles as transitional. Instead, the memory of it only haunts me. Before Niles, we lived in the capital of New Mexico. My nine-year-old sister, Rebecca, and my eleven-year-old sister, Paige, were both born there.

I was born in Franklin, Tennessee, over thirteen years ago and was most certainly not an accident. I decided early on that my parents incidentally brought some sort of curse on me by having me out of spite. They did a lot of things back in the day to piss my mother's parents off. Running off and getting married at eighteen was probably their biggest rebellion. Mom was arranged to be married young anyway but to somebody else who shared her culture. When Grandpa thought he still had a chance at breaking them up, he was sorely disappointed by my parents' decision to start their own family.

My maternal grandparents were purists, which is a sugarcoated term for, um, complete racist assholes. My dad didn't have powers. He didn't come from a powerful family lineage. He's not Romani. His ancestors were English servants before immigrating to prerevolution America. His parents have deep southern accents. His father was a medical doctor before losing his license to practice. Chastain Chambers was not the kind of man Grandma and Grandpa Anderson wanted their daughter, Clarinda, to marry. My mother's father immigrated to America from Poland as a child. His surname used to be Polish before it was changed to his stepfather's. He was forced to embrace this new culture, and he has taken his bitterness out on us. Grandpa Anderson has tried desperately to keep the flames of his ethnic customs burning. He even tried so hard as to marry a southern belle with a muted ancestry. Somewhere along her family line is a Romani who possessed great power, but even she barely knew of it. The only proof was in her abilities.

Itasca is the longest we'd lived anywhere. After all the trouble with Chad, I was surprised we hadn't moved again. We always moved after something major happened and that something major always involved me. We've lived here close to six years. I was Blake's age when we moved here. Now I'm practically grown. I'll be fourteen in July. Maybe it's the reoccurring trauma or the fact that I've attended four schools until this point, but I've always felt older than I am. Mentally, I'm an adult, though nobody else agrees with me.

It didn't take long for us to reach the hospital in Elk Grove Village. Even though the nearest hospital isn't located in town, it's still less than ten minutes away.

I've been dreading coming here. At least Paige hadn't accidentally stabbed me with anything during the trip. A pair of scissors did mysteriously lodge into the metal wall, though. It baffled the paramedic when he discovered it, and I had to stifle a laugh. If Paige hadn't been so upset, she'd have joined in on my laughter. I spotted our parents' ten-passenger van in the parking lot. It wasn't exactly hard to miss. I wondered how long our mother had been here. Dad would still be in the city, but at least he wouldn't be fighting rush-hour traffic yet.

"I want to see my son!" Mom screeched at the receptionist behind the desk. She must not have beaten us there by too much. She was a wreck, her eye makeup smeared by her tears, her shoulder-length brown hair tussled.

"Ma'am, as I told you before"—the worker said through gritted teeth—"someone will be out to update you on your son's condition shortly."

A pang of guilt twisted my insides. I needed to hide before she saw me. I couldn't bear for her to see me after this. Jesse was here because of me, whether she knew it yet or not.

"Mom!" Paige flung herself forward, falling into our mother's side. She'd blown our cover before I had time to disappear.

I looked away, staring at the near-empty waiting room. The chairs all matched, except for a random pink chair in the corner. My leg still stung from earlier. Limping, I took a seat on the far side of the room, staring straight ahead at that pink chair. My eyes didn't leave their focus, even when my mother took the seat next to me. She rested her hand on my arm, and I flinched at the touch. I always flinch. I'm a jumpy person. I always have been. My mother was silent for a moment before she lowered her voice. She has such a gentle, reassuring voice.

"You are a survivor," she whispered, amazement in her voice. "You inspire me every day." It was amazing how quickly she could go from an anxiety-ridden screaming machine to a calm, collected, and nurturing mother. That's just how she was. Most of the time, she was caring and compassionate, always attempting to lift others up. She's been like that with me for as long as I can remember. It didn't matter how many times I screwed up—she always reacted with love. I'd say I don't know how I got so lucky, but there were so many times I found myself wishing she would scream and yell.

With Jesse, she was different. She was terrified constantly. She could never see him in her visions. Ever. I think she relied too heavily on them when it came to raising us that, when the privilege was taken away, she didn't know how to react to the unknown. He was always like a ghost to her—like he was never there. Maybe that was the vision. He wasn't supposed to exist.

I still didn't look away from the pink chair as she brushed her fingers through the hair on the back of my head. She hummed. "Paige?" she said. "Could you see if you can get a nurse in here?" I was starting to feel dizzy, my hands shaking. She noticed it before I did.

My mother doesn't like hospitals. If she brushes against someone in a hallway or waiting room, she tends to envision horrible things like someone having a heart attack or a stroke. She'd make an excellent doctor since her visions tend to explain a person's illness. The problem is that it becomes too depressing for her. She can't change the main event in her visions, only the circumstances surrounding them. It's kind of like how she can't change the fact that I'm probably going to need a shot of insulin soon, but she can at least request to have a nurse on standby.

My mother was also taught to be wary of places like this because of the traditional Romani values of her household. Grandpa was always concerned with the idea of purity and cleanliness, of *wuhzo*, pureness, and *marime*, impureness. Hospitals were impure, as they were places of illness and disease. So were the Gadje, non-Romanies, who ran them. So was my mother for marrying one. So was *his* mother.

Jesse flatlined on the table. That's what the surgical intern told us when she came out to update us on Jesse's condition. He was all right for now. They shocked him back to life. The doctors were stitching him up when she told us this. It wouldn't be long before they wheeled him into a room. Our mother didn't seem too reassured. I think she needed visual proof that he was going to be okay.

Dad arrived as the doctors were giving our mom permission to see Jesse. We'd been waiting for over an hour for Jesse to get out of surgery, which meant Dad made good time weaving through city traffic. I tried to hide my face, slumping in my chair, but I could feel his dagger-like glare in my direction. I brought Chad into our lives. I did that. And now Jesse was fighting for his life. I waited for his footsteps to fade, the double doors to the ICU closing behind them, before I dropped my hand into my lap. Paige didn't say anything, but I knew her tears were far from over. My sister is an emotional person.

I think my parents forgot all about Rebecca and Blake because when I finally glanced at the clock in the waiting room, I realized both their schools would have let out. My mom usually picked us all up from school, youngest to oldest. Blake and Jesse's school was always her first stop. Our parents were still in with Jesse or the doctor or both, so I had no way to remind them of their other children. Besides, I didn't want to see my father. I was afraid he'd blow up at me. So, I sat and stared at the clock and listened to the sound of my heartbeat.

"Would you quit tapping your foot? You're driving me crazy," Paige said at one point. I looked at my leg, watching it bounce up and down, the heel of my foot creating a rapid, light tapping noise on the tile. I hadn't realized I was doing it. I knew there'd be bad news coming. Mom and Dad had been in there too long.

When Lenora Mica died, it was instant. There wasn't a question regarding her survival. Getting your head blown off is a definite one-way ticket to the afterlife. Nobody took her pulse. Nobody touched her until the rest of her body was placed in a bag. Her death traumatized half the sixth-grade class.

Paige still had nightmares.

I'm used to it, I guess. Lenora wasn't the first person I watched die, but the way she died was much worse than the others. At least nobody had to watch her suffer.

I was six when I watched an entire family die. I was five when I watched a man die by suicide by cop. Death isn't new to me. My whole life felt like it was about evading it. Death likes to come after those around me. It thinks if it can't have me, then it might as well destroy me. Maybe that's why I stopped picking good friends. I already lost the only good friend I ever had.

Dad came out first, wringing his hands. His fingers trembled, his jaw wavering. The anger I was expecting was gone, replaced with his glistening brown eyes and quivering brown mustache. Paige gasped. This was going to be bad. Keeping my eyes on the floor, I stood and headed for the exit, but my father's hand stopped me.

"Let me go!" I tried to fight against his grip. I didn't want to be here anymore. I didn't want any more bad news. I already knew I killed my brother, and I wasn't about to watch everyone suffer.

"Would you stop?" My dad resisted before he shouted, "He's alive, Bradley!" I was out the door. I didn't even give myself a chance to hear the prognosis.

It was days before my dad could drag me back to the hospital to see Jesse's forgiving smile. My brother waved at me as if the events at school with Chad hadn't happened, and for a moment, his denial erased the memories from my mind. Jesse was magic, even without powers. That's how he always was—an exemplification of our mother's usual collectiveness.

Mom wasn't calm, though. She shouted at the nurses when she wasn't praying for God to remove her curse. "It's *marime*," she dared to whisper one night before visiting hours ended. In other words, Jesse's affliction was bad fortune brought on by her "impurity." Dad spent too long trying to talk her out of that headspace.

One morning, four weeks into Jesse's extended hospital stay, Rebecca was lying at his bedside, whispering an old fairytale as she stroked his blond hair with her childish fingers. The two of us were supposed to be keeping him entertained while Mom ran to grab a few birthday balloons from a nearby shop. I could hear the story from where I stood outside the door—the story of Snow White. Jesse smiled euphorically part of the way through, interrupting Rebecca when she mentioned the magic mirror. Brushing her nose with his finger, he took over the story, quoting, "Mirror, Mirror, on the wall." His smile dwindled, his breath catching. The heart monitor began to let out a string of beeps, but Rebecca was too mesmerized by Jesse's enchanting gaze to react. He continued as I pulled away from the doorway to grab a nurse. "Who's the most powerful of them all?"

Jesse didn't die from the bullet wound in his abdomen. He never left the hospital. He stayed in bed for a month, talking and laughing and telling stories—until the tumor in his heart stopped it from beating. He died on his sixth birthday with only Rebecca there to watch him go. He was gone by the time Mom stepped off the elevator, the balloons floating to the ceiling as she let them go too.

Nobody expected this. He was just a kid. Everybody thought the bullet would kill him. After all, bullets are dangerous no matter your age. It turned out he was already dying, and Chad may have just helped him get there quicker.

My mom could never see Jesse in her visions, and she wondered if this was why. Maybe Jesse was destined to die. What she didn't understand was why God would bless her with this wonderful child only so that he could be taken away.

"God sends us down upon this Earth to make a difference in each other's lives," Reverend Mica said at the funeral, "and Jesse did just that." He choked on his words. "He put a smile on everyone's face. He was the first to get me to smile after my little girl died." He lost it right on the stage, and the entire room erupted into fits of grief. The church had experienced too much tragedy this year.

Olga stood with me in the back of the sanctuary. We pretty much never came here except to meet with Chad. We were never ones for our parents' religion. Since Jesse didn't die from the bullet, Chad wasn't being charged with murder, but he was still being held in a facility in Chicago for observation. Olga apparently spoke with the Micas all the time, which is how she continued to receive updates on Chad's condition.

"You weren't talking to Chad." Olga tried to explain this to me after she recovered from her concussion. "I don't care if you believe me or not."

I crossed my arms. Of course I didn't believe her. Chad had hit her pretty hard.

Olga huffed, frustrated in my obvious disbelief. "He has multiple personalities. You were talking to Tanner." She started speaking fast, trying to explain. "Tanner knows Chad exists, but Chad knows nothing about Tanner. He has blank spots in his memory because Tanner will take over without warning and plant him somewhere else. When Lenora died, that was Tanner who pulled the trigger. I'm sure of it."

"He looked me straight in the eyes, Olga," I said, countering. "He pointed at Jesse and looked me straight in the eyes. He told me now I know how he feels. That wasn't another personality, Olga. That was Chad evening the score."

"Obviously, you didn't notice him talking in the third person." Olga groaned. "He kept saying, 'I give him,' in regard to something he took."

I finally had to agree with her only to get her to stop talking. Olga's in love with Chad. She's always trying to fix him. At this point, I'd just as soon let him suffer.

"I'm being sent to live with a social worker for the summer," Olga said as we stood in the back of the sanctuary. "It's part of some 'troubled teens' program out of state." She held up her fingers, using air quotes around the term "troubled teens," the words dripping with disdain. I knew that wasn't at all how she expected to be spending her summer. She crossed her arms, blowing a few strands of her blond hair away from her face. "Do I look like a troubled teen to you?"

I didn't answer, rubbing my eyes.

She didn't wait too long to start ranting again.

I interrupted. "I think we're moving again."

3 // REBECCA IS COOLER THAN ME (SORRY, I WAS HACKED)

It turned out I was right. We were moving. We always did when something bad happened.

Mom made us finish the school year. By the time school let out in June, Dad had accepted a position at a new location for his company. The broadcasting company he co-operated had already been expanding to other cities, and as soon as the funeral was over, Dad jumped on the chance to relocate. He was excited. Indianapolis. As if the new city had a better rep than the big three—Chicago, New York, and Los Angeles. It didn't even make the top fifteen.

I was surprised. I always thought Dad's job would take us to one of the coasts. Instead, it kept us in the Midwest.

We were moving eerily closer to my grandparents. Sometimes I wondered if that was the big plan—if we'd eventually move back to Franklin. It wasn't like I hadn't met both sets of grandparents. Mom's parents hated us and were judgmental of how we lived our lives, so we always ended up staying with Dad's parents. I didn't mind them too much. They were kind and amicable. My dad was often that way, but unlike my mom, he was quick to anger. I sometimes think it would make more sense for his parents to have raised my mother and for hers to have raised him. My dad wasn't a horrible person, but it doesn't make sense how such horrible people raised my mother.

I wasn't excited about moving to Indianapolis. But then again, we never move under good circumstances, so moving isn't exactly a happy thing in our family.

Dad begged to differ. He'd been running around the house, cheering about the new opportunities this move would bring us. It was tough to tell by looking at him that he'd recently lost a son. That was simply the way he was, though. He depleted his emotions in the first few days of grief and moved on. He never wallowed.

Mom was different. She barely left Jesse's room. I wished her powers of mediumship were real. Then she'd be able to talk to him. Maybe he'd even help her through his death. Jesse was like that. He had this magical way of making you feel better, a trait inherited from Mom. But Mom could only see the future with the rare exception of the past. And she has never been able to see Jesse.

Paige's emotions weren't consistent. They never were. She'd be fine one moment, laughing and playing, then screaming and crying the next.

Rebecca was more composed. She and Jesse were like two peas in a pod. After Jesse's death, she sat with Mom in his room, speaking softly and making up stories about how Jesse was doing in the afterlife. She didn't cry. Her eyes would sparkle with tears, but her chin never trembled. Sometimes I wondered if she cried when she was alone and thought nobody could hear her. Rebecca is strong. Stronger than any of us.

I wasn't sure how much Blake understood. At eight years old, I would have understood perfectly. I mean, by that age, death wasn't new to me. But Blake wasn't me. Bad things didn't happen to him. He knew Jesse's prognosis, and he said his goodbyes in the hospital—multiple times. And then Jesse died. After that, Blake came home and turned on the Xbox.

I didn't know how I was doing. Very few people asked me anyway. They pretty much kept their distance from me. All summer I had nobody to talk to. Chad was still in Chicago, and Olga was in another state. I let her know not to go joining any cults while she was away, but at this rate, I wasn't sure I'd see her again before the moving truck pulled out of our driveway. I spent my birthday without them. There wasn't much to celebrate this year anyway.

It wasn't until three days before our departure at the end of July that Mom dried her tears and began carrying out all of Jesse's stuff in boxes. I noticed because Rebecca's screams made Mom drop a box down the stairs. In all the madness, we'd forgotten all about Rebecca's tenth birthday. Biology didn't.

It was early on a Friday morning. Dad had already left for the office to finish any last-minute arrangements, and I was sitting at the tiny two-person table in the kitchen, playing tic-tac-toe with myself using a napkin. Rebecca screamed from the second floor. A box of Jesse's stuff tumbled down the stairs. I jumped over it, following our mother to my sister's room. We were the only ones who saw it—if only for a split second. But he was there. He was sitting in the chair in the far corner of Rebecca's room. His mouth moved, but no words came out. Then he disappeared. And Mom collapsed.

I blinked, my heart stopping for a split second before jolting back to life. I couldn't stop staring at the corner. Neither could Rebecca. Not when our dead brother had been sitting there moments before. After a few seconds, Rebecca unwrapped herself from her pillows, having recoiled in surprise instantly at the sight. She crouched at our mother's side, and for the first time since the day Jesse had died, my youngest sister cried.

"I'm sorry," she whispered between sobs, stroking our mother's brown hair until she came to. I still couldn't stop staring, first at the corner, and then at my mother and sister. Mom blinked rapidly, rubbing her eyes as she slowly sat up. She appeared confused for a second before glancing at Rebecca, who was still apologizing. She smiled, taking Rebecca's face in her hands, and thanked her.

I blinked. What was happening here? Then it hit me. That's what my power is supposed to look like. Rebecca had rematerialized a memory of our brother. I've never been able to do that. I can barely recreate a Kleenex. It wasn't fair. Already on day one, Rebecca, who had the same powers as me, could materialize an entire person. It was like she could resurrect the dead. Except it wasn't a whole person she was creating. They didn't have a soul. They couldn't interact much. Her recreation of Jesse couldn't even talk or make noise. But he was there. He'd jumped straight out of her dreams and into her room. If things started jumping out of my dreams, I'd be constantly in danger of being sliced in half by Jason from

Friday the 13th. Maybe it was a good thing my powers didn't work.

I'd have been jealous if it weren't such a cool power to witness. I was a little jealous, kind of, but not as much as I was amazed. I wanted her to conjure something else, but Rebecca was terrified. She didn't want to try. I couldn't even convince her to try creating a paper clip out of thin air. Eventually Mom begged me to leave her alone. "She'll accept her power in her own time," she whispered softly to me. If she didn't want a power, I would've gladly traded her—my useless talents for her clearly superior ones.

The day before we left, Mrs. Burnett from down the street walked straight through our front doorway. She didn't bother knocking or announcing her arrival. She plopped her one-year-old daughter, Tuesday, right on top of the box I was holding and proceeded to walk straight back to our living room. The baby nearly toppled off the box trying to turn herself around to see me. My arms shook. The box was already heavy enough without the addition of an actual live human being. Slow but steady, I lowered the box onto the ground, Tuesday's movements making it difficult to keep her from tumbling.

"Mom!" I shouted warily before resting the box on the kitchen tile.

"I'm with a client!" she shouted back in a singsongy voice. I rolled my eyes. Of course she was. Mrs. Burnett practically lived here. With Tuesday in my arms, I walked back toward our nearly empty living room.

Mrs. Burnett had her hands in Mom's, her voice shaking with the all too familiar power of grief. "They gave him six months." There was a pause as Mrs. Burnett searched my mother's eyes. "Please, you have to tell me the doctors are wrong. They have to be. We've already been through this once before—he can fight it again. I know he can."

My mom smiled sadly, her expression giving the future away. Mr. Burnett had been in remission from cancer for two years. Their twin daughters, Sage and Seth, were best friends with Paige. I remember when he kicked cancer's butt. The whole street threw a celebration party. Less than a year later, Tuesday was born.

Mr. Burnett was a good person. He loved his three daughters with all his heart. He was kind. I once crashed my bike into a tree in front of their house when I was a kid. He fixed both me and the bike up.

I guess the years aren't ever done stealing good people away from us. Eventually, only the bad will remain.

Mom's sad smile turned into a frown, and she adjusted her grip from Mrs. Burnett's hands to her wrists. She'd seen something she hadn't expected. After a few seconds, she sighed loudly and brought our sobbing neighbor into a hug. I could see her troubled expression over Mrs. Burnett's shoulder, but she said nothing of it.

I wasn't going to be able to hand Tuesday off to them, so I turned on my heels and carried her outside. If Mrs. Burnett was here, the twins wouldn't be far behind.

Sage and Seth were saying their heartfelt goodbyes to Paige, whom they must've caught loading a few boxes into the moving truck. Unlike Chad's twin sisters, the Burnett twins are fraternal. They both have their dad's brown hair and their mom's brown eyes, but Sage is taller and has a rounder, slightly freckled face. Seth is shorter, thinner, and clumsier. It's not difficult to tell them apart.

"Your mom tried to pack the baby," I said after I cleared my throat to interrupt. I held the baby out to them by her armpits. Seth reached over and took her from me, adjusting Tuesday's signature pink hair bow, tangled in her lightened hair. Every time I see the baby, her hair is a different color. It's like it can't decide if it wants to be brown like her dad's or blond like her mom's. My brother's hair was like that. Blake's has been darkening a little, but it's still blond.

Paige's hair is dark—darker than anybody's. It's still brown, but it's like the darkest brown hair could possibly be before it's considered black. She's got Grandpa Anderson's hair. Rebecca's hair matches our parents'. Mine does, too. It's a normal brown, no added darkness or light. I guess we share a lot. First the birth month, then the hair color, now the powers.

The Burnetts have powers as well. I think that's why my parents chose to live in the northern Chicago suburbs. A lot of families live there whose ancestors were from the same group of people. Olga's family is another example, but she's mixed. Her powers come from her father's side.

Twins usually share the same power, even if they're fraternal. It never made sense to me, considering the specifics of our powers are like rolling a die. I mean, all it takes is one parent with powers to guarantee a child with powers, but the actual power itself is always randomized. There's no way to guess what powers a person will develop. Anyone with the gene can develop one out of thirteen possible powers, so there aren't infinite possibilities, but it was incredibly annoying that the twins ended up with the same power as Paige. It was like God decided to give a good portion of the sixth-grade class the gift of telekinesis.

If it weren't for the weird side effects, Olga's gift would be much cooler. Shapeshifting your body into a whole nother being is a little taxing and time consuming. Supposedly, the more she uses her powers, the easier she will be able to turn, but she once described the internal experience to me as feeling like she was "dropping acid while riding a mechanical bull that wouldn't stop bucking." Sometimes I wished she'd erupt into a full-blown tiger and eat Chad. She'd stop protecting and making excuses for him sooner or later.

Thank God Chad doesn't have powers. I'm not sure I'd still be alive if he did, especially if he had a dangerous power. I guess if he had more of a defensive power, like a force field, life would pretty much be the same. He'd still be out of control, but with the enhanced ability to protect himself.

When we were kids, I told him I'd have powers someday. I'd make up stories of how we could be a team and fight all our enemies. He probably thought all that was just child's play, that I wasn't serious. I've never been able to prove it anyway. I wouldn't be surprised if he knew about Olga's, though. I've never heard her refer to her powers in front of him, but then again, I wouldn't put it past her. If she hasn't, she will.

The house looked bigger once empty. I've always felt like this house was built backward. The front door opened into the kitchen instead of the living room. The counters were on one side, a closet and a tiny bathroom on the other. Past the bathroom were the stairs, which were skinny and steep. Past the stairs, the house opened up to a living room and dining area. There were sliding glass doors in the dining room that led to the backyard. The living room had a brick fireplace in the corner. A couch, two armchairs, and a coffee table usually took up the entire space. Two more floors were above the main floor. Each floor hosted three bedrooms, varying in size, and a good-sized bathroom existed on the middle floor. Each floor was smaller than the one below it, and you could tell that by looking at the outside of the house. The building was uneven, one side much taller than the other. I'm not sure why the house was built this way, but my parents thought it carried a unique charm, so they bought it. Now there was a For Sale sign in the yard.

I hadn't seen a picture of our new house, but apparently, it was located in East Indianapolis and much nicer than this house. Dad thought we would be pleased with the extra space. It had the same number of bedrooms, so I wasn't unsure how the new house would differ. Every time we moved, the house got bigger.

I forgot my dad made a buttload of money at this point. We didn't seem like the rich type. Our clothes weren't particularly fancy, and we didn't drive sports cars. My mom drove a ten-passenger van, and my dad drove the same car he'd been driving since we first moved to Illinois. I wasn't sure where all the money went, but I was about to find out. I had a bad feeling about this new house. I had a bad feeling I was going to start high school in a new city being known as the rich kid. Our parents had always been careful about how they raised us. They didn't want to spoil us or to heighten our privilege more than what the other parents in the neighborhood did, so they kept us on a short financial leash and usually only flashed their money during emergencies.

Jesse's death seemed to have prompted a spending spree in my father. He suddenly wanted new things. I guess the money had finally gotten to him.

4 // I CAN'T BE PSYCHIC WHEN I KEEP GETTING BLINDSIDED

Why was I not the psychic in the family? We'd become too predictable, apparently. Mom pulled the van into the Creekside Woods neighborhood, and I almost puked when I saw the houses. No way were we living here. I'd become too accustomed to being ordinary. I liked ordinary. Now I was going to have to reinvent my image and pretend that all the other rich boys had it bad when they spilled a carton of orange juice on the counter. I'd been through too much to hole up in this place.

Paige started dancing in her seat. These houses weren't mansions, but they were big and tall, just like her dreams. My oldest sister had always wanted to be rich and famous, and she was about to have one of those goals checked indefinitely. Dad had certainly gone overboard. The overcompensation was too obvious at this point.

When Mom parked the van in the driveway, I stayed in my seat for a solid ten minutes trying to avoid the inevitable. Like it or not, this was our home now. I knew I should've been grateful, but I wasn't.

"Hey, Brad!" my father yelled from the curb. "Come help me unhook this car!"

Ugh. Brad. My dad was the only person in my family who shortened my name. You know who else called me Brad? Chad. Yep, we were Brad and Chad. No matter in what order I say our names, it still sounds dumb. We should have had our own sick reality show to go with it.

I nodded to try to convince myself I was going to be calm about this and stepped out into the summer air. My dad had his car chained to the back of the moving truck. I could hear Paige's delighted squeals from inside the house. I glanced at the house across the street. It had one of those wraparound porches and a swing to match. The second floor had a small balcony, the same white-trimmed guard rails surrounding it. I noticed the house was a little smaller than ours, but it didn't stick out in the neighborhood.

Leaning down in front of the car, I examined the contraption tethering my dad's car.

Dad cleared his throat. "I know you're having a hard time with the change..." I didn't say anything, just let him ramble on. "I want this family to have some good luck for once. Believe me, we've earned it." He grunted, releasing a clasp. Well, he was right about that, but he was living in denial if he thought I didn't carry some giant curse everywhere I went. I was always the reason my family experienced pain. I'd never not been, and I doubted I'd be stopping in Indianapolis.

There was definitely more space to walk in the new house. The entrance opened onto a smaller room on the right, which in turn led into a dining room that led into the kitchen in the back. The stairs were immediately to the left of the front door, and instead of leading straight up, it curved at a perpendicular angle after the first few steps. A closet and a pantry existed underneath the stairs as well as a small built-in bookshelf. The living room was larger than our last one, with large floor-to-ceiling windows lining the back wall. The kitchen and living room shared the back of the house. The kitchen had an island with a stove built into it. At the front of the living room were two doors: one led to a full bathroom and another led downstairs to an unfinished basement. The only time we ever had a basement was when we lived in Niles. Upstairs, the hallway curved back around the front of the house and right down the middle. Six bedrooms lined the two halls, and a full bathroom, much larger than the one downstairs, was nestled in the space before the second hallway.

I heard Paige shouting cheerily from the farthest bedroom, and I hurried to see what the added excitement was all about. Blake was standing out in the middle of the backyard, waving back up at us. Paige leaned out the back window so they could jabber on. I twisted to get a better look at the room. Paige had claimed the biggest room in the house, but to be fair, the only reason it was bigger than the master bedroom was that the master had a small half bathroom taking up a chunk of space.

I ended up with the bedroom next to hers, smashed between my sisters. I wouldn't have chosen it to be this way, but it was either that one or the one with no windows directly next to Mom and Dad. I'm unsure what my parents plan to do with the extra bedroom. I hope it's not to build a shrine for Jesse. Rebecca's been putting all his boxes in there.

It took days for all of us to have a bed to sleep in. Dad had insisted on dismantling all the furniture he could so that it would fit better in the truck, which meant we all had to rebuild everything. I don't remember moving being this difficult, but I guess we also had fewer possessions the last three times. My parents don't like to hire movers. My mom is especially paranoid about strangers touching our things even though she's usually the one who invites them in every week. There was that pesky superstition of *marime* again, rearing its head. Mom insisted she didn't believe in it anymore, but then she continued to do stuff like this—avoid the unknown cleanliness of *Gadje*.

School started on Monday. The schools started earlier and weren't split by grade as much as they were in Itasca. The schools back home held, on average, three grade levels. If Jesse hadn't died and we hadn't moved, the five of us would have been split among four different schools. Now the four of us were down to three. I wanted to take the bus and save my mom the extra trip, but she insisted on dropping us all off. Just to torture me, she made sure my stop was last. I knew why she was doing this. She wanted to talk without our conversation being overheard by curious ears. Putting the van into park in front of the high school, she turned to face me.

"Bradley, I hope you know how much I'm trying to do right by you." She sighed heavily. Her words turned to tears, the van growing gradually more uncomfortable by the second. "I try so hard."

I felt bad for her. My mom's not a terrible parent. She just trusts too much and relies too heavily on her powers of precognition to guide her. I don't blame her. She grew up that way. Her parents treated their powers as gifts to be nurtured and grown as a way to be better than everybody else—better and more advanced than the "undivine," as my grandfather would put it. According to him, we were given these powers to rule over others, to defend and attack when needed. He once described Mom's gift as a way to foresee our enemies' plans of war. I'm not sure who he thinks our enemies are, but part of me thinks he means the undivine—the powerless. When my mom started to use her powers to help *Gadje*, Grandpa was furious. He called her a traitor.

Mom tried so hard to shield us from rejection on the home front. When things went awry, she spiraled into a bottomless pit of guilt. I always wished I could convince her that it wasn't her fault, that I was the cursed one, but she refused to believe it. Grandpa always told her she was the one who put a curse on the family—she had to rebel and marry a *Gadjo*.

I let her cry for a few seconds before reminding her that I was going to be late. She flapped her hand in a goodbye.

When I entered the front office, I was greeted by a police officer. He appeared to be in his mid-to-late twenties with cropped brown hair. His lopsided smile threw me off. Officer Joey would have never smiled at me. This guy's nametag read "Lantern."

He nodded at me, a manila folder in his hand. "Brad Chambers?" He lifted his eyebrows excitedly when he saw me. He looked like he was expecting me. It was unsettling. Did my reputation precede me so much that the school thought it'd be best if the resource officer introduced himself first?

Disgruntled, I corrected him. “Bradley.”

He jerked his head back toward the offices, still smiling. “Why don’t we head to my office for a second?”

I hesitated, glancing at the lady behind the front desk clicking away on a keyboard. “Uh, I don’t want to be late for class.” I would’ve left if I knew where and what my first class was, but I had to stop by the office to get my schedule. I hadn’t expected to be of special interest.

The officer tapped the manila folder he was holding. “I have all your information right here. Come on.” He started to move toward the back offices. When I didn’t follow, he spun back around. “Do you want your schedule or not?” I didn’t understand why he wouldn’t give it to me. Instead, he wanted to meet in his office. The whole ordeal reeked of suspicion. Officer Lantern walked back toward me, seeming to give up. “Okay, you want to talk out here? We can talk out here.” He gestured to a couple chairs lining the wall near the door before sitting in the one located in the corner of the room.

It took me a long several seconds before I decided to take the chair next to him. I hoped this wasn’t some sort of ploy to arrest me. Clearing his throat, he lowered his voice. “Look, kid, your mom and godparents set this up. I didn’t mean to scare you. I realize the uniform is a little intimidating.” My mom? Okay, now her speech made a little more sense. She was pulling in the big guns this time. But my godparents? I hadn’t thought of them for a long time. Hudson and Nancy Lindt were my parents’ best friends back in high school. They were all married in an elaborate double wedding. Our families used to hang out more often when I was younger.

"Here's the deal," Officer Lantern started to say.

I heard a bell ring. Great. I was going to be late on my first day. I already wasn't going to be making a good first impression.

Officer Lantern continued. "Every day between your third and fourth class, I want you to come see me. The time is blocked out on everybody's schedules for what we call success time. It's a thirty-minute time slot that's kind of like homeroom. Every student has a classroom they're assigned to be in at that time. Your assignment is my office. If you do not show up, I will hunt you down." He looked serious for a second before letting out a small laugh. "Or I will call your mother." Opening the manila folder, he snatched up my class schedule. "If a teacher marks you absent for a class, whether or not it's by accident, I am immediately notified. We all want you to succeed here"—he handed me the piece of paper—"so don't blow it." Standing, he tucked the manila folder underneath his arm and clapped his hands. "Let's get you to your first class."

"Wait!" I barely had time to glance at my schedule. Despite this fact, I knew one thing for sure. "I don't need a police escort." I wasn't about to be introduced to my new classmates by a member of the police force. That would send the rumors flying for sure.

Officer Lantern nodded, understanding my hesitance. "That's fair. If you take this hallway to your right and then turn on your first left, it should be the third door on your left."

The dude had already memorized my schedule. Great. "Thanks." I drew the word out, slipping my backpack over my shoulder.

"No problem." The officer shrugged. As I headed out the door, he shouted after me, "Say hello to Nancy for me." *Nancy? My godmother Nancy? Yeah, okay.* I wasn't sure how the two had met, but by the time I ever saw her again, I was sure I'd forget to pass the message along.

The classroom wasn't hard to find. Officer Lantern's directions were perfectly clear. I knocked on the door a second before entering. I didn't want to enter unannounced.

Nancy Lindt paused at the whiteboard, a blue marker in her hand. She shot me a smile, unsurprised by my appearance. "You can pick any empty seat, Bradley."

I paused for a second, staring at her. Her light brown hair was already starting to lose its color. She was in her thirties, but somehow, she seemed aged. Mrs. Lindt used to wear her hair in a scarf like most married Romani women, but today she looked different in slacks and a dress shirt, her hair loose around her face. I wasn't expecting to see her. Especially not like this. I mean, I knew she and her husband were teachers, but last I knew, they lived in Terre Haute, close to the Illinois border. I hadn't realized they had moved.

"Psst." I heard someone say after several seconds of standing there, staring at Mrs. Lindt. I looked at the students to find another familiar face. Mrs. Lindt's oldest daughter, Serena, tapped the desk next to her, mouthing at me to sit.

Serena and I didn't have the best relationship. She was bratty and annoying and rude and insensitive. She was older than me by nine months, which is a fact she used to throw in my face all the time. Taking the seat next to her, I whispered, "Your mother is our teacher?"

"Tell me about it," she said through gritted teeth, refusing to take her eyes off the board. After the bell rang to end class and we had made our way out of the classroom, she shoved me aside. "This is your fault, you know." Serena may have been tiny, but she was aggressive. She came up to my shoulder in height.

I rubbed the bruise that was likely to form on my shoulder. "What did I do?"

She laughed. "What did you do? Well, you just had to break the world record for who could be the biggest screwup. You know I've been assigned to be your babysitter through all this? I don't need this. I have a life to live. I have an entire high school food chain to climb and defeat." Serena didn't strike me as the kind of girl who yearned for popularity, but hey, what did I know? We hadn't spoken to each other in years.

"You think I asked for this?" I followed her through the sea of students. "I don't know if you've noticed, but bad things tend to happen around me. It's not like I ask for death and destruction to follow me—it just does. I'm cursed."

She turned around, and I almost ran into her. "You're cursed? You? What about me?" She muttered something about punishment and *marime* under her breath.

Serena clutched the shoulder strap of her backpack, her free hand flicking the straight dark brown strands of her hair back over her shoulder. Her fingernail hit a small gold hoop earring in the process, clicking as the two collided. Serena's hair used to be long and flowing. Like many Romani women, she didn't cut it. At this point, it was at her shoulders, framing her light brown face. "I thought I was going to have a normal life this year. I mean, this is my first year of high school. It was supposed to be special. Instead, I have to keep an eye on a possible future convict because somebody can't make good choices. Ugh, it's like I'm babysitting a four-year-old!" She stomped away before stopping at the end of the hallway. "We have the same schedule, doofus. Try to keep up!"

I didn't want to, but I had a growing suspicion that I was being watched. This entire situation wasn't merely a bluff. Everyone seemed to mean what they said.

Serena led us to our next class. The seats were half-full, the late bell still minutes away from ringing. Serena grabbed the sleeve of my T-shirt and hauled me to the second farthest desk in the front row. "Sit." She let go of my shirt, plopping into the seat at the end of the row. Smiling innocently at the teacher, she blinked rapidly. "Good morning, Miss Montgomery."

"Good morning, Serena," Miss Montgomery said. She was tall and slender and appeared to be in her twenties. I wondered if this was her first teaching job. Normally, I'd be glad if it were. That usually meant I could get away with more, but Serena had always been a tattletale and a suck-up. She already seemed to know all the adults even though this was also her first day at a new school.

"How long have you lived here?" I asked my bossy observer. I was curious to know just how new Serena was to the area.

Serena already had a journal out and was writing the date and hour in the right-hand corner. She answered without looking up from her paper. "Four years, give or take. My parents inherited a vineyard outside the city." That was around the last time we'd seen each other. Serena was about to come into her powers then. I don't know which power she ended up with, but I wanted to find out. Problem was, I couldn't exactly ask her point-blank while surrounded by a dozen witnesses.

We're not supposed to expose ourselves to the undivine, but as far as I knew, there weren't exactly diviners around to enforce it. It's mostly a matter of principle and better judgment. For a lot of Romanies who still lived or traveled in *kumpanias* or *vitsas*, they relied on their elders to enforce rules and administer punishments, but we didn't have that. The diviners were often looser, freer, in that sense. Several of the divine feared that outing ourselves would bring unintended consequences and create tensions between our population and the undivines. Some of us feared confrontation too much. And if they were like me, they watched too many sci-fi movies. The kids with special powers always end up running from the government in those.

The secrecy never mattered to me much. My mom used her powers to help the undivine all the time. Everyone in Itasca knew where we lived. To those who didn't know us personally, our house was known as the psychic's house. Nobody ever called the government on us, except for the time a zealot from the church called Child Protective Services. We were picketed once or twice, and sometimes nasty rumors would fly around proclaiming we were witches. Pretty much everyone else liked my mom. She was kind and her powers were therapeutic. People went to her to spill their anxieties or fears. Our house was a haven for them.

Sometimes I fed the witch rumors to see what would happen. I even pretended to put a curse on someone. Their anxiety regarding the unknowns of the curse made them break into hives. They never bothered me again. Still, I tried to respect other diviners by not outing them in public, especially if they have an offensive power. People like Olga could tear me to shreds—literally. Even if it turned out Serena had a defensive power, she could still tear me to shreds—metaphorically speaking and physically. She's strong for a little person.

The bell rang to begin class, interrupting my thoughts.

5 // I HAVE SEVERAL NEW STALKER FRIENDS

Serena was glad to get rid of me during success time. For once, she didn't escort me to my next location. I was free to breathe in peace, even if it wouldn't last long. I had to go see Officer Lantern before he started making some calls. After spending my morning with Serena, being shut in an office with a police officer didn't seem so intimidating.

I walked into the front office, nodding to the lady working the desk. I didn't exactly know where Officer Lantern's office was. Luckily, I didn't have to ask. The front desk lady pointed the tip of her pen toward the small hallway behind her. "Third door on the left."

Great. Did everyone know who I was here?

His office door was open, and I rapped my knuckles on the frame to alert him of my presence. His gaze snapped up from the papers on his desk and landed on the clock. "Must've lost track of time," he said, muttering. Beckoning me inside, he asked that I shut the door behind me. I obeyed without hesitation. After Serena, I was prepared for practically anything. Plopping myself onto one of the chairs in front of his desk, I waited for his spiel.

"I want you to trust me." Officer Lantern cleared his throat and leaned over the desk. "So, I'm going to tell you something that doesn't leave this room." He jabbed his index finger down on the desk, punctuating his sentence.

Leaning back in his chair, he smiled proudly. "Well, actually, I'm going to show you." I waited for him to move again, but he didn't. He was sitting still, his smile frozen in place. I was about to prompt him to continue with his demonstration when I saw something move out of the corner of my eye.

And then a lot of things moved at once. I nearly jumped out of my seat. Every object on his desk was suddenly in the air, rotating around us. I felt my jaw drop, amazed. It wasn't like I hadn't seen anything like this before, but it was far more controlled than anything my sister and her friends could come up with.

"You're a diviner," I said in awe. Like my siblings and me, he didn't look like one—no brown skin, no traditional Romani facial features. I stood and the objects went still, hovering in place. Studying a stack of sticky notes before moving on to a stapler, I weaved my way through the maze of objects. Why did everybody seem to have a cool power except for me? I pointed to a tape dispenser. "My sister has this power, but everything around her usually turns into a weapon."

The officer chuckled and stood, his fingers touching the desk. "Telekinesis can be tricky—especially when you're not in the right headspace. It took me years of practice to get where I am now." He let the objects float carefully back to their original locations. "I hear you have quite a power yourself."

Scoffing in disbelief at the ridiculousness of the rumor he'd apparently heard, I plopped back in the chair. "Yeah, right." Who the heck told him I had a power? My mom? Come on, she knew better than that. Mrs. Lindt?

I'm not sure she knew what my power was—unless Mom told her.

"Materialization?" Officer Lantern asked, prompting me to demonstrate.

Okay, this had to be my mom's doing. But why? I glared at the carpet. There was a line where the fabrics had come loose, and I could see the woven texture underneath it.

It took a few moments for the officer to catch on to my body language. He sat slowly back in his chair before leaning forward. "You know what I think?"

"What?" I said with a grumble, humoring him. I didn't look up from the loose threads.

"I think you're afraid."

It sounded like a challenge. I could feel my hands shake. I took in a deep breath and let it out slowly, trying to calm the tremor. I probably couldn't afford to blow up in a small room with a telekinetic police officer.

Officer Lantern leaned back in his chair, sizing me up. He didn't say anything for a long time. We both sat and listened to our breaths, mine coming out a lot louder and quicker than his. It wasn't until my breathing was under control that he spoke again. "I met with your mom yesterday, and she caught me up to speed." He opened the same manila folder he had been holding in his hands just hours before. There seemed to be more in there than my school schedule. I glanced at it, curious but also wary of what else was inside. He held a piece of paper, but I couldn't see what was on it. Letting out a huge gust of air, he rose his eyebrows at whatever words he was reading. "You've been through a lot."

"Understatement," I muttered.

"You were kidnapped?" he asked, a small hint of empathy hiding in his voice.

I glanced at the clock. Our half hour was nearly up. I slung my backpack over my shoulder as I abruptly stood to leave. "If you want to analyze every piece of my life like a freaking psychologist, *Officer* Lantern—"

"Frank," he said, calmly correcting me. "You can call me Frank."

I ignored him. "I suggest you quit while you're ahead."

He didn't stop me. I walked out of his office before the bell rang, fuming. How dare he interrogate me and then expect me to show up to my next class like nothing happened? I looked out the office windows into the hallway as the bell rang, studying the clusters of students who passed by. The lady at the front desk finally coughed, reminding me of her presence. She shot me a stern look, and I rolled my eyes, heading out into the hallway to find my next class.

When I slammed my backpack onto the desk next to Serena, she glared at me, a nail file in hand. "You act like Frank's a total monster."

"You know Frank?" I asked coldly, staring straight ahead at the whiteboard. Of course she did. She knew everybody.

"Everybody knows Frank." A guy sitting on the other side of Serena invited himself to the conversation. He had spiky black hair, freckles, and a round dark face. His broad shoulders made his arms look bigger than they probably should be. He said in a husky voice, "Dude's a legend."

Leaning in closer to us, he lowered his voice. "When my cousin went to school here, he helped them pull off the best prank on Coach Nelson. Every single item in the weight room, the gymnasium, and the sports storage rooms were on the roof. Nobody could figure out how they pulled it off. I mean, seriously, some of that stuff weighed a ton." I had a sneaking suspicion that Officer Lantern did most of the heavy lifting. The guy went on. "Coach was furious. Nobody could prove a thing. Principal Brickmore had to hire a guy with a crane to get half the stuff back down."

I narrowed my eyes. "If everybody knows he did it, why is he still working here?"

"I told you"—the guy chuckled—"nobody could prove it was him! But, hey, Coach Nelson and Frank have a whole rivalry thing going, so I wouldn't get between that if I were you."

Serena scowled, disagreeing with him. "Yes, you would, Kase. You are always getting in between things. Just like what you're doing right now."

Kase held up his hands in defense, leaning back in his seat. "I'm not going to apologize for being friendly." Serena was still obviously miffed, and it seemed to bug him. "Dammit, babe, I never get to meet many diviners."

I froze at the mention of our kind. Serena flinched before hissing through gritted teeth, "Shut up, Kase." It wasn't like he said it loud enough for everyone to hear, but it bothered me that all these strangers seemed to already know about me. I wondered how much he knew. I wondered if I could scare him with the threat of my "almighty" powers or if he would see right through the bluff. Kase didn't seem like the type of guy who scared easily.

He extended his hand over Serena's desk, introducing himself. "Kase Schwartz: mass manipulation." I studied his hand for a second. I wasn't going to shake it, but when my eyes moved to his face, his expression made it clear that his gesture was a dare. His mischievous grin told me this was a demonstration. I'd never seen this power in action before, but I had only met one other person who had it. Curious, I reached over to shake his hand but felt an isolated draft where his hand was. Withdrawing my hand in horror, he laughed loudly, drawing attention to us. "Gets 'em every time!"

Serena slapped his chest with the back of her hand, shooting him a disapproving frown, but he continued to laugh, repeatedly slamming the palm of his now solid hand against his desk. The bell rang in the middle of his fit of laughter, and he cleared his throat, struggling to control his facial expression. From time to time, throughout the class, he would randomly burst into laughter, prompting the teacher to stop her lesson to glare at him until he composed himself. After the third interruption, she banished him to the back corner of the classroom. The class let out a collective "ooh" as they witnessed his punishment. At least he was the one leaving a bad first impression this time.

I followed Serena and Kase to lunch, this time willingly. I wanted to know more of what they knew about me, about the diviners, about their powers. All day, I felt like I was ten steps behind everybody else, like I wasn't in the loop of some inside joke. I wanted in on whatever was being kept from me. To my disappointment, Serena and Kase didn't sit alone. I should have guessed by his build that Kase was a football player, which meant the two sat at a crowded table full of soon-to-be popular ninth graders. Grumbling to myself, I picked a random empty table far from the food line and sat, staring at my tray of food. I picked at the fruit with my fork.

I should have brought my lunch. I usually did. It was difficult to count carbs in food from schools and restaurants. Most places only shared their calorie count, which didn't help me when it came to monitoring my sugar intake. It's not like I have to avoid eating sugar—it's that I have to avoid eating too much sugar and, at the same time, avoid eating too little.

The cafeteria roared with conversation, much louder than my middle school back home. This school was huge. The school's population alone matched a third of the entire city of Itasca's. The table I was sitting at filled up fast, but the room was so loud, I could barely hear the conversation in front of me. Some guy was breaking up with his girlfriend. He wanted to see other people. She asked if he meant *older* people. He made the mistake of glancing at a table of varsity cheerleaders. He didn't even see the tray of food that got dumped on his head. I choked on a bite of pineapple.

Most relationships seem so mundane to me. It's like most people date just to date instead of legitimately enjoying each other's company. I can't imagine asking out someone I didn't even like. I once thought I liked Olga. She was fun to be around, but her feelings for Chad were obvious. For the sake of our friendship, I respected that.

Chad should've been in high school last year. He was a year older than me. Olga could've been too, having an August birthday and all. We were close enough in age that the differences weren't much. It didn't feel that way when we were kids. As we grew older, Chad grew stronger and tougher and meaner. I think his parents held him back in kindergarten or something. Whenever it was, it was before I met him. I kinda wish they hadn't, though. If we hadn't been in the same school in the same grade, maybe we wouldn't have been friends. Maybe he wouldn't have tried to kill my brother.

"You look like you just saw the world come to an end."

I looked up from my tray of food to find the couple gone. A guy a little shorter than me with light brown skin and dark almond-shaped eyes had taken their place. He was trying to sweep away the food the couple had left behind, but sauce ended up covering his arm from elbow to wrist. He grimaced, but let it slide. He extended his left arm, sauce-free. "I'm Jay-Jay."

I looked warily at his hand. I think Kase had ruined handshaking for me. I nodded to him instead. "Bradley."

He smiled, bobbing his head like he was rocking out to music. "*Bradley's Trip Through the Apocalypse*. I like it." My confusion must have been obvious since Jay-Jay said, elaborating, "It sounds like a great book title, don't you think?" He was ecstatic, and I wondered if he was always like this or if his mood had something to do with first-day-of-school jitters. I wasn't sure if he was serious or just trying to make conversation. He suddenly sat straight up, a new idea occurring to him. "Or a movie!" Jay-Jay spread his hands up high and apart like he was envisioning an imaginary billboard. “As gloom reigns down on the Earth, Bradley fights to see another day.” A small chunk of sauce splattered on my tray from his drenched arm. He looked back at me, proud. “What do you think?”

“Um,” I said, holding on to the word. I’m not a hero, but I wasn’t going to tell him that. No need to muddy the water. I didn’t give him an adequate answer, but he pretended I had turned the idea down.

“You’re right.” Jay-Jay nodded as if I’d given him sage advice. “It’s too lame. It needs a better hook.” He thought for a moment, tapping his chin. “Wait a minute!” He straightened up, staring directly at me. “You’re the one who saw the apocalypse! What all did you see?”

I glowered at him. I’m not the creative type, and I wasn’t about to pretend to be my mother. Once again, I was saved by the bell. As I picked up my tray to toss in the trash, Jay-Jay seemed to remember the sauce on his arm. “Aw, man.”

I should’ve known Jay-Jay would be in my next class. He eagerly took the seat next to me in time to hear the late bell. His right arm was wet, water dripping onto the desk. I rolled my eyes. What was this dude’s problem?

“I see you’ve made a new friend.” Serena smirked from the seat behind me. The teacher cleared his throat, raising his eyebrows at Serena. I realized I knew this teacher as well. It was Mr. Lindt, Serena’s dad.

I couldn’t help but laugh. “Well, this must suck!” To have one parent teach one of your classes was one thing, but both?

"Bradley." A warning tone echoed loudly in my head, and I jumped. Mr. Lindt was staring me down. I tried to collect myself. I had forgotten Hudson Lindt's power was telepathy. I swallowed. I hate mind readers and telepaths. They're incredibly invasive. Between his powers and his wife's precognition, I don't know how anyone in the Lindt household got away with anything.

The Lindts have four kids—Serena, Kevin, Mya, and Kendra. Kevin is Paige's age. I wondered how well they were getting along in the seventh grade. They used to have the biggest childhood crushes on each other. Somehow, they never believed in cooties. Mya would be in the sixth grade now. She was a grade below Kevin and Paige. Kendra's younger than Jesse. She was practically a baby the last time I saw her. She'd be in kindergarten now. The age gap between her and Mya is suspicious. I wonder if she, too, was an accident like Jesse. I know Serena was, and the thought makes me smile to myself out of amusement.

"Bradley," Mr. Lindt said aloud sternly, tapping the whiteboard to gain my attention. The equation on the board made me realize this was a math class, and I groaned. I hated math. He smiled at my expense, getting ready to torture me with questions. To my surprise, he looked away and addressed the entire class. "I love the mystery of the unknown. Many people don't, and that's okay, but here in algebra, we deal a lot with unknowns. We take those unknowns"—he points to an x in the equation he had written on the board—"and we turn into detectives trying to solve the mystery." He goes into detail regarding the equation, and he seems to drone on forever before he points back at me. “So, Bradley, if we know that this equation equals twenty-four, and we know that twelve times x equals twenty-four, then x must be…” his voice drifted off. I glared at him, but he still awaited my answer. Jay-Jay jumped at the opportunity, his hand raised. Mr. Lindt ignored him for a second before nodding. “Mr. Jones?”

“Two, obviously!”

Mr. Lindt seemed impressed by his enthusiasm. Nobody was ever like this in a math class. Nobody. “You’re correct.” Mr. Lindt said, writing the completed equation on the whiteboard.

6 // I Forgot I Wasn't Normal For a Second

Jay-Jay practically stalked me for the rest of the day. I wondered if he had any friends. Serena didn't know him. They had gone to separate middle schools. He did get her to shake his hand during sixth hour, and he had smiled creepily while doing it, holding on to her hand a little too long. She scowled and pulled it away. "Really, perv?"

He frowned for a split second before returning to his usual smile. "Sometimes we need a change in perspective." He entered back into enthusiastic writer mode, coming up with a book or movie title for Serena's name. "*Serena and Her Path of Destruction!*" She stuck her tongue out at him, and he laughed. "I'm not wrong."

I cleared my throat and tried to take Serena's side. "You should switch ours. I'm more known for my path of destruction. She's the one trying to save us from the apocalypse."

Jay-Jay laughed but didn't go along with my idea. "Like I said, perspective is everything. We don't always give ourselves enough credit. In changing our perspective"—he winked—"we change our future."

I grimaced. It sounded like a valedictorian speech. The future. I wondered how much of a future I still had left. I knew from my mother's visions that the future never changed, only the circumstances. Scowling, I replied, "You can't change the future. It's set in stone."

The classroom door opened, and a trio of ninth-grade cheerleaders glided in. Jay-Jay's smile widened at the sight of them—or, more specifically, one of them. He waved at the girl in the middle. She hadn't quite turned to see us yet—her chestnut hair nearly reached the small of her back. She caught Jay-Jay's wave, and she angled her body so that we could see her face. I thought I felt my heart stop, my breath catching in my throat. She was beautiful. Her facial features looked soft around the edges, her brown skin flawless. Her eyes were the most striking—a piercing bright blue. Her nose was small and dainty, like most of her features. She stuck out in the small crowd of cheerleaders, the perfect embodiment of beauty. Her smile was infectious. As she approached us, I felt the corners of my lips curl upward. She greeted Jay-Jay like he was an old friend, taking the seat in front of him. I found myself hoping they weren't involved, that they were just friends, like Olga and me.

Jay-Jay turned back toward me, but my eyes were staring at the back of the girl's head. I couldn't keep my eyes off her. Jay-Jay nodded knowingly, his smile sticking to his face. "You're right," he said. "Some things are set in stone."

The teacher cleared her throat, introducing herself to the class. "Welcome to world history. I'm Mrs. Scarborough, but you can call me Mrs. Scar." She flashed a smile—her teeth were perfectly straight. "I don't mind being associated with a Disney villain. However, I do think there is much to learn from pop culture." Mrs. Scar began pacing at the front of the room, rambling on about the importance of pop culture in history. I stopped listening for a second and was tuning back in when she raised an eyebrow, scanning the classroom of students. "History has a way of repeating itself," she warned.

Serena scowled. "I'll say."

After class, I wanted to follow her. My heart thudded in my chest, making my breathing unsteady. I didn't flinch when Jay-Jay shook me out of my trance. He laughed when I stumbled in the hallway, causing the crowd behind us to groan at the break in flow. The girl turned at the next intersection and disappeared. I never asked who she was, but Jay-Jay seemed to know exactly what information I wanted. "That's Savanna Huckleberry," he said as he guided me to our last class of the day. "I've known that girl since kindergarten."

Serena rushed around us and disappeared into the crowd.

"Could you...?" I stopped. I was about to ask if Jay-Jay would introduce us, but then I thought better of it. I shouldn't. I shouldn't insert myself into someone's life, especially someone as beautiful as Savanna. It wouldn't be fair. Everybody I got close to either got hurt or died.

Unfortunately, Jay-Jay finished my question and then answered it. "Introduce you? Sure." I furrowed my brows but didn't fight him. It was selfish, I know, but I also knew Jay-Jay wasn't gonna listen to me if I backtracked.

Kase was in our last class. So was Savanna. She sat in the middle of the front row, and I had to fight myself not to take the empty seat next to her. Instead, I weaved my way toward the back where Kase and Serena sat. Jay-Jay stood by Savanna's desk, shocked that I had walked right past her. Instead of following me, he sat next to her, striking up a conversation. I watched them warily.

Snorting in amusement, Kase nodded toward Jay-Jay. "Does that dude think he has a chance with her? She's nowhere near his league. I mean, she's practically a goddess."

Serena snarled at his comment, jealous, but she addressed me instead. "How'd you shake him?"

I ignored her. I don't think I did shake him. He kept glancing back at me, curious that I had chickened out. I tried to distract myself from them by turning toward Serena and her buff boyfriend. Most people were sitting on the other side of the classroom, so I thought I'd have time to ask them a few personal questions. "How...?" I stopped. Serena was glaring at the back of Savanna's head. I leaned in front of her, trying to block her view. "Did you tell Kase about me?"

"Had to." She craned her neck so that Savanna wouldn't leave her line of sight. "He's the only other diviner I know here, and I thought he'd be useful in case you tried anything." For a second, her eyes flicked to mine, a silent threat, before returning to Savanna's thin brown hair. It was a little offensive, her distrust in me, but I knew why she was reacting the way she was. Nobody trusted me anymore. Not since Jesse was shot.

I leaned back in my seat. It's like my mom had found every diviner in the area and placed them in this high school: first the officer, then Mrs. Lindt, Serena, Kase, and Mr. Lindt. I wondered if there was anybody else I should know about. I cleared my throat and addressed Serena and Kase. "You two are the only ones? Who aren't adults, I mean." They continued to stare at Jay-Jay and Savanna, one out of amusement and the other out of jealousy.

Kase raised his eyebrows, finally looking away. "My sister is telekinetic."

"He means in the high school, Kase," said Serena, murmuring, her usual tone of annoyance dripping in every word.

"Oh." He furrowed his brow, thinking. "As far as I know, but it's not like we all hang out or anything." This intrigued me. The diviners back home all knew each other.

I thought I could squeeze one more question in before the bell rang for our last class of the day. This one was aimed directly at Serena. "What's your power?"

She smiled to herself as if enjoying an inside joke. A small grin appeared on her face despite her preoccupation with Savanna and Jay-Jay. "Why? You've already seen it in action." Kase snickered, clueing me in. They had the same power. Of course they did. That's probably why they were drawn to each other. Mass manipulation. They could basically turn into ghosts—walk through walls, people, objects—literally nothing could stand in their way. To be weightless like them—I shook my head. I wondered how they didn't just float away. I stopped myself from laughing as the image of Kase, with his giant arms, floating off into the sky, never to be seen again, popped into my head. It didn't seem possible for him to be that light. It wasn't natural. But I guess that's the whole point. None of us are natural.

I returned my gaze to Savanna and Jay-Jay. They were so normal. Scratch that. Jay-Jay seemed far from normal, but nothing about him suggested he was also a diviner like the rest of us. I didn't know enough about Savanna to come to the same conclusion. All I knew was that she was beautiful, even from behind, with her long, straight hair shimmering underneath the fluorescents. Her beauty was unnatural, almost inhuman. How could one person be so attractive?

A sudden thud jarred me from my thoughts. I blinked, searching for the source of the sound until the neighbor on my right held a textbook out to me tentatively. I must have knocked it over in my trance. I grumbled an apology, taking the textbook in my hands, half the room's eyes trained on me. Even Savanna had craned her neck around to the back of the classroom. Her blue eyes appraised me for what I thought was the first time, but it didn't last long. She soon returned her attention toward the front. Serena grabbed a Capri Sun from her backpack and gestured for Kase to hand it to me. He obliged and I nodded in thanks. I usually had some kind of sugary drink stuffed in my backpack to keep my blood sugar from falling, but I hadn't come prepared at all.

When my mom picked me up after school, last as always, I was exhausted. She glanced at me as if she wanted to apologize, but I held up my hand to stop her from sputtering out the words. I found myself wanting to thank her. Not for the police officer or her role in creating my class schedule—I understood why she did it—but because her actions hadn't made the day worse. In fact, they had made them all the more interesting. For once I found myself looking forward to the next day of classes. The feeling of anticipation startled me. After the morning I'd had, I wasn't expecting to want to repeat the day's events, but the strangeness of the afternoon had balanced my disgruntled feelings into unquenched curiosity.

Paige spent the short ten-minute drive bouncing in her seat. She had made a new friend, some girl named Robin, and had apparently not expelled her day's worth of gushing about boys with her newfound friend. Paige has no shame. When she liked someone, we were all forced to hear about it, and she liked practically every guy she met. Being around her was exhausting. She didn't mention running into Kevin or Mya Lindt, and I wondered if they didn't go to the same middle school as I had expected.

Rebecca smiled meekly when asked about her first day of fifth grade. Apparently, there was a girl who wasn't so nice to her during recess, but the day had turned around when one of her classmates, Jenna, recognized her. Jenna Angel and her younger brother, Braedon, used to live at the end of our block in Itasca. They weren't diviners, but I knew them mainly because their mother was one of our mom's clients back when Jenna's dad was imprisoned. I don't know why he went to prison, I wasn't privy to that kind of information, but it didn't seem to matter now. Rebecca mentioned how Jenna had a new dad now, or she would this coming October. Her mom was expecting a baby.

Blake's first day of third grade was uneventful. Mom told him not to worry, that he'd make new friends soon, but it was a typical Mom phrase. My brother didn't pick up on the insincerity in her voice, though, and perked up at the belief that our mom had seen his future. I guess his hopefulness wouldn't do him harm, but I worried, briefly, what would happen if his hopes didn't come true. Mom seemed worried too, but these days, that was how she kept her general expression. She hardly left any room for confidence anymore.

When we arrived at the house, the phones—one in the kitchen, one in the front room—were ringing. Paige eagerly ran to answer one, hoping it was a random boy she had met at school that day. Mom and I shared an exasperated look when we realized Paige had given our home number to practically everyone at the middle school. Sometimes I wondered if my sister had any sense of self-preservation. I know it's just middle school, but I'd seen too much in my years of awkward early adolescence to not worry. After all, I had somehow befriended a murderer.

Paige groaned in displeasure when she realized the call wasn't for her, and she held the phone out in my direction. "It's for you."

I took it warily as she stomped up the stairs screaming, "Why does *he* get a call from a girl? Boys are so stupid!"

I wanted to laugh at the ridiculousness of her comment, but I was worried which girl was calling. Serena wouldn't dare—she didn't like spending time with me as it was—and I sincerely hoped Jay-Jay hadn't somehow gotten ahold of my number and given it to Savanna. I thought maybe it was Olga, having finally returned home from the summer. With that hope in mind, I raised the phone to my ear. "Hello?"

Serena's unsatisfied, nitpicky voice blared in my ear. "Before you expose us, I thought maybe you and I could clear the air."

"By all means, please." I found myself at the point of begging. I walked further into the front room, away from the rest of my family. I was glad she wasn't waiting for tomorrow or the next day or never to explain to me all that I felt I was missing today. I wouldn't be able to withstand that kind of torture.

There was a long pause on the other end and some shuffling sounds before she threw herself into her one-sided conversation. "Yes, Kase and I can manipulate our body mass as well as the mass of surrounding people and objects—although, that's much tougher to pull off. Also, please don't make any jokes about that." I wasn't sure what she meant, but I let her continue. "Kase makes enough of them as there is. How did we find out about each other, you ask? You can blame my little brother for that. He's bad at keeping secrets and his gift of power mimicry is more annoying than my dad's telepathy." Power mimicry. I was impressed. I had never met anyone with that power, but supposedly they can sense if a diviner is near and copy their gifts. I thought that'd be a useful power to have, but Serena didn't seem to share the appeal.

"Also, you really shouldn't go around talking about us all the time," she said. "People are going to start thinking you're weird. I wouldn't want you to be lumped in a group of weirdos with your new friend, Jay-Jay."

Serena sounded like she wished the opposite for me. Good riddance, I guess. "As for Frank, he's a friend of my parents. He used to be a traffic cop on the Indy police force until he transferred positions to be a school resource officer. Be nice to him and don't do anything stupid. He's not a regular cop, okay? Pissing him off could have real consequences for you." For a second, it sounded like she cared.

"It didn't seem like he was an easy guy to piss off," I said, looking out the front window at the August sun. Frank Lantern came off as slow to anger, a stark contrast from my experience with Officer Joey. He seemed happy and less concerned with exposing himself as some of the other diviners—Serena Lindt, in particular. She mumbled something unintelligible underneath her breath, and I wondered if she'd seen him in action. "What are you not telling me?"

Serena sighed a deep and heavy sigh. "You know how you haven't seen us in almost five years?"

"You told me you moved." I shrugged, thinking that was all the explanation I needed. "That your parents inherited a vineyard here."

There was a pause on the other end, but I could still hear her breathing, shallow as it was. I sat on the loveseat my parents had reassembled yesterday, preparing myself for a more personal story from my godsister. It was several moments before she spoke again. "Getting my powers wrecked everything." There was another short pause before she clarified. "Back home, back in Terre Haute." I already knew where she meant. It didn't take more than a simple deduction to understand. Annoying how much she still could find subtle ways to insult me in the middle of a serious conversation. Clenching my jaw, I waited for her to tell me the rest of her story, but she also seemed to be waiting. Maybe she had intended on me interrupting. Her next words hurried out of her mouth as if she needed to expel them before they consumed her. "We were exposed." *Click.* The phone line went dead.

7 // SERENA HAS A SECRET AND I WANT TO KNOW IT

I stared at the phone for a long time. I considered myself lucky to get that much out of her, but the information didn't at all quench my interest. If anything, I had more questions.

I stalked to the kitchen where my mom was preparing dinner and slid into one of the barstools next to the island, lost in my train of thought.

After a minute or so my mom looked up from her diced vegetables and shot me an apologetic smile. "Was that Serena Lindt?"

I drew my eyebrows together, picking at the countertop's falsified wood. Finally, I nodded slowly, still trying to figure out how Serena could've possibly ruined her family's life more than I had mine—if she had at all. Maybe she hadn't done as much damage as she thought. It wasn't like she killed her brother. I let a breath of air escape, preparing to dig answers out of my mother, but she had turned back to her vegetables, tense. I wondered if she was having another vision. She usually had to touch people to have them, but every once in a while, one would sneak up on her. When she turned to the heated pan on the stove with a handful of sliced green peppers, she looked guilty. I asked her what was wrong, but she just sighed, spreading the peppers in the pan with a wooden spoon. No matter what Mom was cooking, she always added peppers, whether it was black, green, red, or cayenne. She loved peppers.

I stared at her. I was ready to give up on finding answers when she spoke.

"She's sensitive about her powers. She's much like you in that way. And Rebecca." She tacked on, not wanting to exclude my newly gifted sister. I glanced behind me into the living room where Rebecca appeared to be using the coffee table to do her homework while Blake watched cartoons. My youngest sister still hadn't been tempted to use her powers again, and that annoyed me. It seemed like such a waste for her to have them if she wasn't going to use them. When I turned back, my mother was eyeing me critically, her hands on the counter on either side of the stove. "I think you can be just as good as your sister."

I scowled. Somehow the conversation had turned back toward me. I can't pretend that it doesn't upset me how useless my powers are, but my mom's denial infuriates me more. My nostrils flared, and my mom softened her stance. "I wish you would believe in yourself as much as I believe in you," she said. That was it. I was done with this conversation.

I didn't come down from my bedroom for dinner. I sat on the floor in my room, the only light streaming in from the south-facing window. I thought about Serena, trying not to let my mind run too wild with the possibilities of her story. I wondered how she could hang around Kase so much when she was so afraid of being discovered. Why didn't she naturally avoid the presence of other diviners?

Attempting to distract myself from thoughts of her screwup, I turned my mind's attention toward Jay-Jay. He'd approached me in the cafeteria, not in any way put off by my attitude. It was almost alarming; especially, after the morning I had had. I thought about how I hadn't come to school prepared at all. I mean, yeah, I wasn't prepared for all the people I encountered, but I also hadn't thought to pack a lunch or a drink. I usually did. It made my life a whole lot easier. I noticed my glucose meter balancing on the edge of my end table and snatched it from its perch. I hadn't brought this thing with me either, which meant I was probably in for a nasty surprise when it read my blood sugar readings for the first time in the last twenty-four hours. Pricking my finger for the millionth time in my life, I let the blood pool on a test strip and waited. My blood sugar was low, naturally, and I groaned. I would have to confront my family downstairs. I hate my pancreas.

Descending the staircase slowly, I listened for clues as to where my family was. If they were all still in the dining room, I might have had a chance to sneak past them. To my disappointment, I could hear dishes clinking and water running. Dinner was over. Plodding into the kitchen, not bothering to be sneaky anymore, I waited for my dad to chew me out for being rude to my mother. He turned, a dishrag in hand, and glared.

"Your mom made dinner for all of us," he said, gruffly. "She put all this effort"—he gestured to the island counter as proof—"into making a nice dinner for us to eat together and you—"

My mother turned abruptly, dropping a plate in the soapy water in the sink, and placed her hand on my dad's arm.

I was shaking, and I wasn't sure if it was from anger or my low blood sugar. I guess both. I pointed to a plate of cabbage rolls at the end of the counter next to my dad. "Is that mine?"

"Take it in the dining room," my mom said, smiling nervously before glancing sideways at my dad, who was still obviously furious.

I could hear them whispering as I ate my dinner alone. I tried to ignore them, but every few minutes, my dad's voice would peak before my mom would desperately shush him.

I had nearly finished my plate when Paige appeared in the seat across from me, a devilish glint in her eye. "Sooooooo, who was the girl?"

I had to stop and think about who she meant. Right. The phone call. "Serena," I said with a mouth full of food.

"Do I know her?" she asked, tugging at her pleated dark hair.

"Yes."

This stopped Paige short. She let her hands fall to the table, her mouth agape. "Serena *Lindt*?" I knew what she was thinking. Serena and I fought like cats and dogs when we were kids and had somehow spent the day making up. I could see the disbelief in her brown eyes. While I still couldn't stand Serena, I enjoyed the spiral of facial expressions my sister was making as she attempted to make sense of what I'd said. Finally, she whispered, staring at the arrangement of candles in the center of the table. "The Lindts live here." It wasn't a question, more like a realization. I raised my eyebrows, her surprise confirming my suspicion. She hadn't run into Kevin or Mya today at school. I wondered where exactly they lived to make that happen. Serena had told me they lived outside the city, but close. We barely lived in the city, smushed around Warren township and other suburbs.

My sister isn't exactly a subtle being. She nearly smashed her knee underneath the table trying to stand so fast. "I have to make a phone call." I eyed her suspiciously as she took off toward the nearest phone.

The next morning, Paige was begging our parents to transfer her to another school. Well, she didn't so much as beg than sit at the bottom of the stairs, crying, but her intention was still the same. When they didn't agree so easily, she screamed in frustration. Some of the picture frames our mom had recently nailed to the wall trembled, along with an ornate silver cross.

Dad's eyes widened at the looming threat, but he stood his ground. "Paige, you stop this nonsense right now!" A frame, the largest one in the nearest vicinity, flew right toward his face. He ducked, and when he straightened back up, his eyes held a certain type of fury that only I'd seen before. "Paige Mallory Chambers!" He lunged for her. My sister practically flew up the stairs in fear of retaliation—although, I didn't think Dad was any match against her powers. The frames all along the wall rattled as she passed them. Soon, we heard her bedroom door slam in the distance.

Mom beat Dad up the stairs, trying to block his path. "Chastain," she warned, but I could see the fear in her eyes.

He paused to breathe more calmly before sputtering, "What are we going to do with that girl?"

"She's twelve," Mom said, biting her lip. "Maybe she'll grow out of it." She didn't look convinced, but Dad nodded, seeming to accept the idea.

I was nearly late to school because of Paige's little performance. The bell rang as my foot crossed the threshold into my first class. Mrs. Lindt eyed me skeptically, silently marking me present on her attendance sheet. I took the seat next to Serena. My chest heaved, my lungs desperately searching for air. I had to run to make it on time.

Serena seemed amused, the corner of her lip twitching at the sight of me, but she appeared to be fighting it, like somehow, her reaction would betray any sort of satisfaction she would feel in watching me suffer. When I caught my breath, I whispered the first of many burning questions I had for her. "What was last night about?"

She tensed. Her teeth gritted. "Not now." I could see her hands balling up into fists underneath her desk. I'd already witnessed one emotional blowup that day. I guess I didn't need to witness another.

In Frank's office, I invited myself to sit. He wasn't at his desk nor in the room, so I took the time to study the credentials hanging on the back wall. Two graduation certificates were framed proudly side by side—one from the Indiana Law Enforcement Academy and another from

Indiana University for a bachelor of arts in psychology. Below them was a photo of him with his coworkers on the Indianapolis Police Department. He looked happy, surrounded by his friends, and I wondered why he ever transferred. I didn't understand why anyone would give up such an important career and choose to spend their time around a bunch of teenagers. Hearing Officer Lantern's footsteps, I turned to see him stop in the doorway, surprised to see me sitting so calmly in his office. It took him a minute, but he smiled when it seemed I was in a good mood. Shutting the door behind him, he said, mumbling softly, "I thought I'd scared you off yesterday."

I forced a quick smile back at him before letting my face fall back into my normal expression of apathy. "I have some questions." I felt my eagerness break the tension in my face.

"Shoot," Frank said, sitting in his chair with a small groan.

I cleared my throat. "Do you have something to do with why the Lindts moved here?" He held his hand up as if to stop me, but my lips continued to move, more words spilling out from between them. "She started to tell me an interesting story last night, but she didn't give me any of the details. I was hoping you could—"

"I'm not going to discuss another student with you, Bradley."

I couldn't read his expression. It was guarded. I knew he was serious about leaving the subject matter of Serena and her family alone, but his interruption made me curious. There was something more to Serena's story—a lot more—and Officer Lantern had something to do with it. "Kase Schwartz thinks you're cool."

He let out a snort and a small laugh. "He needs to stop telling people that story." I raised my eyebrows. I hadn't mentioned the story about his and Coach Nelson's not-so-little spat. Kase must mention it more times than Frank cared for. He leaned over the desk as he had the day before, his expression growing serious. "Bradley, we're here to talk about you and you only." I slumped back into my chair. I could tell getting information out of him was going to be difficult. For now, I would have to give in.

"Fine," I said. "You want to hear my kidnapping story? 'Cause I don't." Maybe if I told him what he wanted to hear, he would tell me what I wanted to hear. Frank leaned back in his seat, nodding subtly for me to continue. I stood and paced the small office. I wasn't sure where to start. "Nobody goes trick-or-treating anymore." I scowled. "The monsters have gotten too real."

Officer Lantern seemed to agree with my assessment. I'm sure the police always get a lot of calls on Halloween. I sat but immediately stood back up to pace, restless. "It's always colder, too, even in New Mexico." I remembered having to wear a jacket over my Batman costume. Santa Fe is close to the mountains. The Sangre de Cristo Mountains loomed over the city. I hadn't seen real mountains like that in a long time.

"There was a lady, older than my parents. She had twigs in her blond hair and a gash on the side of her face. She was limping, searching the streets and yards, but never leaving the sidewalk. She was frantically screaming somebody's name. My parents thought she had lost a kid." I envisioned every detail of that night. I stopped pacing. "In a way, she had, I guess. But that's not the point." Officer Lantern drew his eyebrows together. My side comment didn't fit into whatever version of the story was in my file.

"What do you mean by that?"

I smashed my teeth together, staring at the blank white wall to my left. "I wasn't the only one." There had been other children before me, and I had seen the proof. Too much proof, maybe. Sometimes I can still see the decaying feet sticking out underneath a bush in the wilderness. I can still see a dirty white shoe in the darkness: a kid's size twelve. I can still see everything if I want to. The memories haven't faded.

"That's not in the police report."

I sighed. I remembered the mountain lion, who smelled blood and devoured its already deceased prey. It had looked at me longingly, licking its lips. We knew in time I would be his next snack. He was tame, somehow, but still had a wildness about him. The man who had taken me had been feeding him for years. The bones were later moved and picked clean by other scavengers. That boy's decaying body could still be anywhere along the inclines. Even if his bones had been found, he would be unrecognizable. It would be impossible to connect the death to a serial killer.

I crossed my arms against my chest. I could feel my hands trembling, and I fought to keep them still. "'The blood of Christ,'" I said, sneering, translating the Spanish name of the mountains. "More like the blood of children."

8 // FRANK BRINGS UP THE BAD STUFF

There was a whole lot more to the story than Frank could manage to dig out of me in a single thirty-minute session. I was fine with that. No need to be reliving more childhood nightmares.

I sat quietly for most of my next class. The story I had told left me emotionally exhausted. Even Kase seemed wary to interrupt my brooding. I hadn't thought about the other kids for so long. The previous kid was already dead when I was led toward his body. That's how he controlled you: absolute, gut-wrenching fear. If you didn't do what he said...

I shook my head, dispelling my thoughts. I didn't remember walking to the cafeteria, but there I was, sitting exactly where I had been the day before. Jay-Jay slid a tray of food on the table and plopped down in front of me.

"I—" he said excitedly but stopped short, his dark eyes narrowing. "What's wrong?"

I straightened my posture, trying to act normal. "Nothing."

Jay-Jay would have appeared stern if not for the faint hint of a smile on his lips. "You look like someone killed your puppy." He let the full breadth of his smile return. "Yesterday, the apocalypse. Today, a dead dog. I'm sensing a pattern."

"You're sensing my life," I said, half joking, hoping my laughter would pull me from the memories. Instead, it came out as this hoarse, strangled sound. I grimaced and grabbed my water bottle.

Jay-Jay changed the subject, wiggling his eyebrows. "I think you should ask Savanna out."

I did a spit take—half of the water drenched the table, the other half sprayed Jay-Jay's face. "What." I said it like an accusation. I could hear our tablemates snickering.

He grinned, proud of himself. "I'm one hundred percent sure you two will hit it off." He didn't blink as the droplets of water and spit slid down his light brown face.

I shook my head at his ridiculous idea. "You don't even know me."

Jay-Jay's smile didn't waver. "I think she'll be good for you." I glared at him, trying to figure out how to explain my aversion to the idea. It had nothing to do with Savanna. It was all me.

"I will just hurt her," I said through gritted teeth. "I'm no good for her."

Jay-Jay pondered my claim for a moment before shrugging. "I'm not gonna lie to you. Savanna is one of my closest friends. If you hurt her, I will find a way to hurt you back, but"—he held up a finger in protest—"I think you're a better person than you give yourself credit for."

I groaned. I wanted to scream at him that I killed my brother, but I didn't think the confession would go over well in a crowded high school cafeteria. Savanna seemed so dainty and fragile, and I was a stumbling idiot bound to crash into her and burn. I wished my life were different, that I were a different person. Then maybe I could ask her out without a growing fear of destroying her.

"I rub bad luck on people," I said slowly, enunciating every word as if it were a single entity.

Jay-Jay frowned. "I don't feel unlucky."

This was hopeless.

In algebra, my new stalker friend decided to search for answers outside of my own biased opinion. He confronted Serena before class. "Do you think Bradley is bad luck?" At least he asked someone who was highly likely to agree with me. I anticipated her answer.

She scowled. "On the contrary."

I tensed. Serena wasn't going to answer how I thought she would.

She snickered. "I think anyone who comes into contact with Bradley has bad luck." I exhaled in relief. My point exactly. She continued to laugh a little, probably at all the reasons for her opinion. Serena said, "You don't know the half of it." I could see her dad's glare from the corner of my eye. She stopped laughing.

Serena waited until our next class to rat me out. I should've expected it, but I was caught off guard when she sat on the other side of Jay-Jay, whispering furiously. He listened quietly as my heart started to beat erratically. At least my stories of bad luck had little to nothing to do with being a diviner, so she didn't have to edit herself. Serena also wasn't privy to most of the details, so the stories were quick—kidnapped at five, deadly car crash at six, every other little infraction and misdemeanor with Chad, all leading to the day Jesse was shot. I ducked my face behind my hands when Savanna and her friends entered midstory and took their seats at the front of the classroom. By the end, Serena had neglected to mention how Jesse died, but it didn't matter. She'd proven my point, regardless.

Serena finished her story as the late bell rang, and Jay-Jay turned back toward me. I braced myself. Who in their right mind would still want to remain friends with a murderer? I didn't need friends anyway. For all I knew, the longer Jay-Jay stuck by me, the more danger he'd be in.

Mrs. Scar began to take roll, calling out my name near the beginning of her list. I lifted my hand, forcing a "here" out of my mouth.

Jay-Jay surprised me with a frozen expression of deep admiration. After an entire minute of this, I was beginning to feel a little creeped out. When Mrs. Scar called his name, he didn't respond. I noticed Savanna turn back toward us, eyeing Jay-Jay expectantly. My gaze flitted back and forth between Jay-Jay and Mrs. Scar as I tried to think of a rational excuse for his behavior. Finally, Jay-Jay said in a hushed tone, loud enough for virtually everybody to hear in the quiet classroom, "You are a survivor."

I started. My brain traveled back to the day Jesse was shot, when my mom whispered in the same tone of amazement, "You are a survivor."

Jay-Jay's voice wrenched me out of my memories. "You have to change your perspective."

I stood abruptly. I didn't realize what I was doing until I was through the classroom door. My hands shook violently. It took me a second to realize my teeth were chattering as well. My mom's voice echoed in my head, growing louder with intensity. "You are a survivor." I wanted to tell her to shut up, but I also didn't want to sound like a crazy person to the few students dawdling in the hallways. A new wave of frustration rolled over me when I realized that Officer Lantern would come looking for me as soon as Mrs. Scar made a phone call. I headed to the front offices to avoid spending the hour with an added feeling of uneasiness. Maybe Frank would let me sulk in his office.

I got lost in the maze of hallways, so Frank found me first. He didn't seem as mad as my father would have been, but his expression still held a hint of anger, though Frank mostly looked relieved to find me. He rambled on about added measures of security as he approached me. "I keep telling the administrators to splurge for security cameras, but they keep telling me this is a school, not a prison. It's not like I'm asking to install metal detectors at all the entrances." Frank frowned when he reached me. "Your teacher said you looked upset."

"Do I not?" I asked through clenched teeth, my hands still shaking.

The officer visually assessed me. "I think she was understating it." He paused for a second before listing the options. "Do you want to head to my office, or do you want to talk here?" I crossed my arms against my chest. I didn't want to talk at all. After releasing a puff of air, he must've decided to stay where we were because he asked me another question. "Do you mind telling me what set you off?"

"Why does he care?" My voice boomed a hundred times louder than I intended it to. A teacher down the hall poked his head out of a classroom before shutting a door.

Frank grabbed my arm and steered me back toward the offices. He'd much rather have this conversation in private. As we walked, he tried to dig for more information. "*Who* cares and about what?"

"Jay-Jay Jones." I sneered. "He refuses to believe that I am bad luck!"

Frank seemed shocked to hear me say this. His shock soon turned into concern. He stopped us just short of the main office entrance and turned so he was facing me. "Let me get this straight." He gripped my arms, ready to shake me. "You're mad because a classmate believes in you?" I didn't respond. He made it sound so simple. The situation was far from simple. Frank was trying not to laugh with his next words. He pursed his lips for a moment. "I kind of want to send you back to class for being this ridiculous." He took a step back and practically shoved me the rest of the way, slamming his office door behind us. He crossed his arms while standing in front of the door so that I couldn't leave. "Why are you bad? Tell me."

I waved my arms around the room, the answer right in front of him. Why else would my mom go to such great lengths to keep me on the straight and narrow? I was arguing with a cop, for crying out loud! She didn't want me to ruin Indianapolis. She didn't want to have to move again... because of me. Because I'm such a terrible person. Because every choice I make will continue to break my family apart. Everywhere I go, there is pain.

I didn't answer, which made Frank angrier. He stepped away from the door, scowling. "Why? Because *he* told you that you were bad?" I wasn't sure who he was referring to. We got into this argument because Jay-Jay thought I was good. "Listen to me," Frank said pleadingly, leaning over me, his hands gripping the arms of my chair. My heart had jumped into my eardrums. I could barely hear him speak. "That man was an evil, despicable..." he struggled to come up with more adjectives. "I'm not even sure I can morally call him a human being. If he told you that you were bad, you cannot take that to heart."

I realized who he was talking about. Frank was bringing up my past, my deepest, darkest past. The part that had me wishing my heart would give out already so that I wouldn't have to relive the memories. Officer Lantern had me trapped. I couldn't run. I couldn't breathe. "Stop." The word squeezed through my tight throat. I hadn't told him this part of the story. In fact, like the missing children, I hadn't told anyone this part of the story. However, unlike the missing children, this was in my file—the one Officer Lantern had held in his hand yesterday. It wasn't as much of a secret as I wanted it to be. I covered my ears, but soon Frank's hands were on mine, ripping them away. Enunciating each word, he said, "You are good."

I guess he didn't know. I guess he didn't know that good people die when bad things happen to them. The rest of us don't get the luxury of mercy.

9 // SERENA SCREWED UP, BUT THE NAZIS STARTED IT

I don't remember how I got home. I sat in the dark, curtains drawn over my bedroom window. My chest hurt from squeezing it so tightly, but I didn't want to let go, afraid my entire body would crumble into tiny little pieces. I'm not a crybaby, and it frustrates me that I can't keep the tears away. I'm stronger than this. I've had to be when every day feels like I'm walking through fire. I'm not supposed to feel scared. I've experienced such a wide range of fears that I thought I was desensitized to this feeling. I didn't expect this kind of reaction, but I also hadn't expected Frank to pull at the one string that released my greatest weakness from the depths of my mind. The painful memories replayed in my head, and I tried to keep as still as humanly possible. If I moved, even an inch, the screams of agony that would escape me would only hurt my mother further.

I could hear her breathing on the other side of the door. At times, I heard her cry, but I tried to tune it out. I could hear my own cries as well as the childish ones from my memories, and they didn't need an added chorus. I can smell the inside of that RV in my mind—the cigarettes, the musty mildew, the gasoline, the putrid stench of his breath. I can feel the carpet, coarse and rough, with little pieces of dirt hiding in the spaces between the fabric strands. I can see her, the lady with the blond hair and the gash—her injuries were real, not just for show—as she slaved away, scrubbing everything, erasing the smells for a few short hours. The bleach, oh the bleach, the smell of the chemical overpowered everything. Then there was the smell of my puke, another mess she would have to clean. She jingled when she limped, dark circular bruises marked the edge of her limbs. I didn't know her real name, only what he called her—words that my mother would scold me for repeating.

"Where did he learn that word?" Mom had asked my father, almost accusingly. We lived in Niles, and one of the other parents had heard me use it when I referred to a blond-haired woman. It was one of the few times I'd seen my mom truly angry during those first several months after the incident. She simmered back down when Blake was born on April Fools' Day.

I had been diagnosed with type 1 diabetes right before I was kidnapped. I had spent several days in a hospital earlier in October as doctors tried to balance my blood glucose levels. I was with my kidnapper for a little over two days, but it felt like at least four, and I had found myself wishing I could go back to my days at the hospital, being poked and prodded by needles and whatnot. It was a far better place to be than in his RV.

I remember the squeals of rodents he kept in a small cage. He told me they feasted on evil children, but I could've sworn I saw them feasting on each other.

Some of the trees in the mountains were tall with yellow leaves and white bark. They mingled among the evergreens. But I didn't see them much during my time there, as the small windows of the RV were covered by wooden planks and dark green fabric. I only saw them at night twice—the night he brought me to the RV and the night he took me into the woods to kill me. I watched him get shot by a police officer instead. I'm not sure how they found me. My mom's powers didn't work at the time—they don't in people who are pregnant—so being found shortly after forty-eight hours was a miracle. But I felt sad for the other children, especially the boy whose feet I'd seen under the bush. They hadn't had a chance.

I gasped in a restricted lungful of air. I was still holding myself tightly together. I could feel a string of snot running down my chin, but I didn't dare move my arms to swipe it away. I didn't dare move. Period. That's how it was in the RV. That's how it was in my room nine years later. That's how I survived. That's how I would continue to survive.

"You are a survivor." Jay-Jay's voice—and my mom's—echoed in my head. They didn't know that the words stung as bad as anything. I knew I'd survive. The fact that I had already survived—against unspeakable odds—was what decided my fate.

I am fated to live again and again in an endless cycle of misery. I will continue to live in misery.

I didn't want to die. I'd never been suicidal. The thought had crossed my mind, but it never stayed for long. I figured misery was a curse I had to live with. If I was supposed to die, I would have. No use getting myself involved.

I didn't know what time it was when I heard Serena's loud and obnoxious voice outside my door. She was speaking to my mother. Serena was telling some teenage sob story of how her parents made her come all this way to apologize. That's how many Romani families were. They valued dignity and respect. They wanted to avoid bad blood.

I didn't want to hear her apologies. They were usually insincere anyway.

Paige's voice rang above all theirs, asking if Kevin had come with her. Apparently, the whole gang was downstairs. My sister squealed in delight.

There was a knock on my door. I froze. I hadn't realized I was rocking back and forth until that precise moment. There went my no-moving policy. The doorknob jiggled, but luckily, I had locked it. Serena groaned, shouting her apologies through the door. "Bradley, I'm sorry I told Jay-Jay about you! I didn't know you would get this upset!"

This wasn't about what she'd done. It wasn't her fault I was having a mental breakdown. She hadn't said anything I wasn't expecting her to say. It was Jay-Jay's reaction that had pushed me out on a cliff and Officer Lantern's persistence that sent me over it. I couldn't believe I didn't make it through my second day of high school. This had to be a new record.

At least Chad never brought up my past. With his dad being a reverend, I'm sure he overheard all kinds of dirty secrets. For a flicker of a second, I thought about contacting Chad. Olga would be proud. Being friends with him again would be better than sinking into despair. I guess that's why it was easy being friends with Chad—the world revolved around *him*.

I wondered if I should call Olga. She was probably back home now. Her parents never liked me, but they let us hang out so she could be around other diviners. It was the same with my parents. They didn't like Olga either. Like mine, Olga's family included both Romani and non-Romani members. Her dad was full Romani, but it was difficult to know that without meeting him. Olga inherited her pale skin, blond hair, and green eyes from her mother. She stuck out in her small pack of siblings, having been the only one to inherit all the recessive genes. Her brother and sister looked like miniature versions of their dad. I guess maybe that's why Olga never really felt like she belonged.

I sighed, slowly releasing my arms from their tight grip. I could instantly breathe better now that my chest had room to move. I'd officially distracted myself with thoughts of my friends back home. They were always a good distraction.

I jumped when I saw Serena. She was sitting across from me, crisscross applesauce. Her warm round brown eyes were assessing my stance, her teeth biting into her lower lip. Quickly, I glanced at the door. I hadn't heard her come in. The bolt was still in the locked position. Damn. I forgot she could walk through walls.

Serena lifted her knee to rest under her chin as she played with her shoelaces. She did look sorry. I wanted to tell her to cut it out, to go back to being her usual unempathetic self, but she spoke before I had a chance to move my tongue. "I didn't know about some of the things"—she exhaled the breath she had apparently been holding—"you had been through." She squirmed, fidgeting her fingers.

She appeared so uncomfortable. I closed my eyes, trying to concentrate on my breathing, trying to control my thoughts—puppies, rainbows, anything other than this. I was surprised to find that my mind was already clear, other than the foggy edges where memories were sure to be lurking.

Serena shrugged, pulling her knees up, wrapping her arms tightly around her legs. "If it helps, I'll tell you about my screwup."

I blinked. I'd forgotten her cryptic phone call from last night. Frank had successfully distracted me away from pursuing that story. I didn't ask her to go on. There was no need for both of us to be crumpled messes.

She bit her thumbnail for a second before deciding to tell her story. "Has your mom told you guys that you have to be careful using your powers here?"

I shook my head. My mom hadn't set up the front room for her fortune-telling business yet. I didn't think much of it since we'd only been living in Indy a week, but now Serena had me curious. Was there another reason for the delay?

"The diviners who live here aren't as open to revealing themselves. They try to blend in with city life and often live in fear. Kase's family once described it as living like they were undocumented immigrants, like one day ICE will show up on their doorstep and rip apart the life they've been building here. Even though they had all the proper documentation, the Schwartzes weren't happy that my brother had found them out."

I wouldn't have guessed any of it, not after witnessing Kase's careless attitude regarding his gifts.

Serena sighed, a hint of a smile playing on her lips. "Kase is just excited about meeting other diviners. His family is so cut off from the culture, he feels repressed. He gets a little"—she grimaced—"rebellious about it." She paused, sadness in her eyes. "His parents don't like us. They know why we've come here and are afraid we'll bring them trouble." Serena rolled her eyes. "Don't worry." Her eyes met mine again. "Kase isn't going to tell his family about you guys. They would throw a fit." She shifted on the floor. "You know how large cities tend to have high immigrant populations?"

I nodded, surprised at the change in topic. I was familiar, though. That's why my parents moved us to the Chicago area. They had a feeling diviners would be congregating there. It was another reason why I thought it was strange that my parents chose Indianapolis to be our current home. Sure, it was large, but nothing compared to the big three.

"The Midwest is where a lot of European immigrants seeking refuge from the wars settled," Serena said. "It's not so obvious these days. Only our great-grandparents still have the accents, the heritage, the fear."

I thought of my Polish grandfather, how his mother settled them in the South. I wondered why she had chosen differently. Serena's would have been the same way, considering her parents grew up with mine.

"Kase's great-grandparents had been prisoners at the German internment camps of World War II. They weren't all for the Jews, you know." Her lip twitched as if she had thought of a joke to go along with the comment, but if she did, she didn't share it. Instead, she scowled. "That's why they were already so bitter and afraid. The existence of the Japanese internment camps really shook them. They don't want to be captured and tortured as their ancestors were." Serena shook her head. "I can't say I blame them."

I waited for her to reveal how her family came to move here, besides the generic vineyard story she gave me. I felt the minutes pass by, but, uncharacteristically, I sat patiently.

Finally, she breathed in a long breath of air and let it out in a large gust. "We were the only family of diviners in Terre Haute. We blended in easily. My parents moved us there to begin their teaching careers. My parents only used their powers to enrich the lives of their students and nothing more. They were unassuming. Well"—she corrected herself—"not too unassuming. We dressed a little differently—you remember—the long hair and the skirts and my mom's headscarf."

I did remember. The hair was the first thing I noticed about her and her mom the day before.

Serena swallowed, her eyebrows furrowing. "When October came that year, so did my powers. My body ached so bad—my dad wanted to take me to a hospital."

I remembered how my mother felt about hospitals and imagined the added level of uneasiness for the Lindts, who had, until recently, still practiced a lot of traditional rituals. That said something about Serena's pain for Mr. Lindt to have *wanted* to take her to a hospital.

I nodded, recalling how my power had given me a horrible migraine on that first day. The pain wasn't *that* bad, though.

"My mom wanted to wait it out. She thought maybe I'd shift or morph into something, and she didn't want that to expose us. She had heard that the power of shapeshifting often came with discomfort. Dad wasn't so sure. He didn't think I should have been in that much pain. He thought for sure something was wrong. After hours of me screaming, he couldn't take it anymore. He could hear my torturous thoughts. To me, my skin felt so hot it was cold. It was like I was slowly losing the sensation to feel. He carried me to the car and drove me to the nearest hospital. My dad remembers thinking I felt light as a feather, and though my skin was ice cold, sweat dripped from my pores. The nurses thought their thermometers were broken until they felt my skin through their gloves. They were horrified. I shouldn't have been alive, they thought. They got a doctor to see me right away as they covered me with as many blankets as they could find on short notice. But they were so hot." Her lips trembled. Her voice cracked.

I found myself crawling toward her. I can't stand it when people cry. It physically hurts me to hear. Draping my arm around her shoulders, I let her lean her head against my chest. I could feel her tears wetting my shirt, her breath ragged as she continued with her story. "They thought I was cold, but I was burning alive. When the doctor saw me, my lungs felt strange. I realized it was because I couldn't feel myself breathing. I thought I was dying. The monitors started screaming, an electronic chorus of panicked tones and beeps. I wasn't sure if it was because of my heart rate or if it was something else.

They kicked my dad out of the room.

I flatlined.

Or so I thought. The wires were no longer sticking to me. I felt like I was floating. The pain was gone. I thought, stupidly, that I'd become a ghost, a corporeal spirit.

"The doctor had heard the legends of the diviners. The likelihood..." She scowled, her hand gripping a handful of my shirt. "I mean, Terre Haute held no evidence of other diviners." Serena's tears slowed, and she stopped crying. She still had my shirt in her hands when she sat up. Her jaw was clenched, her voice pushing past her teeth. "We don't think of those who find the superstitions of the Romani people to be true. Especially not educated doctors! But he had noticed in my chart that it was my tenth birthday and knew that some of us Romanies were gifted with supernatural powers when we came of age. He pulled my dad back into the room and asked how we had survived the camp in Auschwitz. He called us Gypsies." She shook her head in disbelief at the memory. "Gypsies!" Serena let go of my shirt and waved her hands in the air. "As if that were an acceptable term for us!"

I knew of our genetic connection to the Romani people—to the Sinti in Europe—because of Grandpa Anderson's fixation on keeping our culture alive. For the most part, my family had chipped away at the beliefs and rituals, except for the ones ingrained in my mother's habits. That's what it was like, though, being raised in a mixed family. I was raised with dual cultures. I did know enough to understand that it wasn't just the diviners who lived in houses and attended schools and pursued careers. Other Romanies did too. It was part of our history I didn't know much about.

"My dad stood there for a long moment, studying the doctor as he prattled on over his admiration for a Nazi called Josef Mengele, the Angel of Death." She looked away from me.

"Mengele? Angel of Death?" My voice cracked from not speaking.

She dove right into the history lesson for me. "Mengele had an honorary doctorate in medicine for his research in genetics. He was the chief physician at Birkenau, the Romani camp at Auschwitz. He liked experimenting on twins especially. Some of the diviners speculate that this is why twins now share the same power—they didn't always."

I thought of the Burnett twins and how they share the gift of telekinesis, despite being fraternal twins.

"As a Nazi, he believed in racial cleansing. He killed many of the children and their mothers since he didn't want us to repopulate. He knew that they would be the easiest to kill too, as diviner children under the age of ten and those who were pregnant couldn't access their gifts." She sighed. "Noma afflicted the camp at one point. After killing the sick children, he would keep their heads and organs to study. He mainly used their bodies—alive or dead—to further his research in heredity and genetics. He had a pathology laboratory on the grounds of the camp.

Some of the children who were part of his experiments actually liked him because he seemed so nice..." When she picked up again, her voice came out hoarse. "Four thousand people—all Romani, many Sinti, and even a few diviners—were gassed and burned when the camp closed. Some of Kase's ancestors didn't survive."

Serena shook her head as if clearing her thoughts. A small frown haunted her lips. "That's why the doctor, the one in Terre Haute, was intrigued by us. He hoped we had all been killed at the camp in Poland over fifty years ago. We proved to him that we still existed. They hadn't caught us all. Not even close." Her frown turned into a scowl. "But we were Gypsies to him, flaunting our powers in his face, the powers he believed were a threat to the 'regular' human race."

I thought of my grandfather again, the one who had immigrated with his mother from Poland shortly after the war. I thought of his beliefs—the ones in which he saw our powers as superior—and nodded in understanding. My grandfather intended to be seen as a threat. He wanted others to be afraid. But truthfully, he was mostly all talk. He didn't go looking for fights.

Serena continued, interrupting my thoughts. "He chased us out of the city. We fled, hiding in motels across I-70. We didn't dare contact anyone for weeks, afraid he was tracking us. Frank found us under a bridge in the city. He guessed what we were by our looks and revealed that he was a diviner, a talented telekinetic. He knew the owner of a vineyard in Cumberland. The old man who owned it was elderly, dying. Frank was supposed to inherit the land, but instead, Frank turned it over to us.

He didn't need the space. Frank lives in the guest house. He protects us. After that, my parents used their powers more often, searching for any looming threats. We've been here nearly five years now without incident. We've relaxed, but that doesn't mean we don't fear. We try to keep out of the headlines. We don't dress so obvious anymore. Our names are kept off public records, thanks to Frank, so it's more difficult to find us."

My head spun from all the information. So that was their connection to Frank. That was why he seemed so close to them.

Serena had been staring at the wall, but now she turned back toward me. "That's why we stopped visiting you guys. We didn't want to lead a trail to you."

10 // SO, APPARENTLY, I'M "SNUBBY"

Not all Romanies possess powers as we do. Those who do renamed themselves diviners during the twentieth century following the war. It separated us from the rest of the Romani people. We wanted to stop adding to their hardships when it came to abolishing the stereotypes *Gadje* possessed of them. The Romani people weren't supernatural beings. For a while, a lot of diviners were able to live in society undetected. Many of us dropped pieces of our culture, abandoning the teachings of our heritage. I knew some of the stories due to the rare occasions when my grandfather thought he ought to fill us in, and even those stories were biased, edited by his bitterness. So, when Serena brought up our heritage, I was surprised at how much extra information she had gathered during the last several years. She had done her research and done it well.

I didn't know much about concentration camps. We hadn't gone over the World Wars in our history classes in middle school, but I also never expected to find pieces of our histories sewn into it. My grandfather spoke of massacres but was never specific. He didn't live during the Second World War. I wondered if his mother, my great-grandmother, had survived the camp at Auschwitz-Birkenau. I'd never met her, nor her husband. They'd moved on from Tennessee when my mother was a teenager. I'd never had any intention of tracking her down, but Serena's story had spurred my interest.

"I want to meet Great-Grandma Anderson," I said to my mother a week later as she was stacking a pile of clean dinner plates.

My mother froze, and I thought I saw her face cringe before she corrected it into her normal mask of calmness. "Can I ask why?"

I made up an excuse that seemed more rational than the need to satisfy my curiosity. "We're studying World War II in history this year, and I thought she might have some insider information since she lived in Poland during that time."

She eyed me skeptically. I hadn't made the story up from nothing. Mrs. Scar had mentioned that we would be discussing the World Wars by the end of the school year.

Mom glanced at the white kitchen tile, pursing her lips. "I don't think that's wise." I snorted in disbelief. Her gaze snapped up to mine. "She made a vow never to mention the specifics of the war in Poland. I think tracking her down would be a waste of our time." She turned back to the clean pile of dishes.

I was going to have to find another way.

"Don't go looking for her." Mom turned to me again, her voice serious as her caramel eyes bore into mine. "I mean it, Bradley." She grabbed my arm before I could pull away, her eyes searching my face as if something in my expression would express obedience. Her face twisted in surprise, pride flashing across her features. She let go of my arm, her lips curving into an ornery smile. "Who's Savanna?"

I stared at her in shock. Jay-Jay had stopped bringing her up, and if it weren't for the two classes I shared with her, I would have forgotten her entirely. In fact, I had shoved her to the back of my mind. She had nothing to do with my current focus. "Sh-she's..." I stuttered, trying to figure out how to explain who she was.

I hadn't said a single word to her in the week that I'd come across her. Jay-Jay would always sit with her in our last class. Finally, I said all I could say about her. "She's a friend of Jay-Jay's. I don't know her." When I realized she was asking because she had probably seen her in a vision, I immediately pushed for information. "Why? What did you see?"

"Oh, nothing," my mom said, teasing. I groaned. I was beginning to see where Paige got her sense of subtleness.

When I got to school the next morning, I searched for Jay-Jay. It was an impossible feat, trying to find one student in a sea of three thousand, especially when I didn't know his morning schedule. I ended up having to wait until lunch to confront him. As soon as he took his usual seat across from me, I slammed my hands on the table. "So, what's the deal with you trying to get me and Savanna together last week?"

He smiled, and I thought I detected a hint of relief in his expression. "Have you finally decided you're going to be nice to her? 'Cause she's currently mad at me for getting her hopes up for nothing, so this better be good."

"You"—I held up my fists, my face contorted in frustration—"told her about me?"

He looked at my fist and slowly said, "I told her that you two might be destined—"

"Why? We have nothing in common!"

A smile spread back across his face. "Why are you asking then?"

I didn't know how to explain to him that my mom had a vision of her, especially since I didn't know what that vision was. It hadn't seemed like a bad vision, judging by my mother's reaction, but both the fact that she had seen her and the fact that Jay-Jay had been pushing me toward her was highly suspicious. Sure, Savanna was pretty, and she seemed nice and I liked her, but there was no real reason to pursue a relationship with her.

When I didn't answer, he shrugged. "If we had the same lunch period, I'd walk you over to her right now and introduce the two of you, but you have to promise to be nice to her."

I wondered what made him so sure that I was a good person. I shrugged. What was the harm in letting him introduce us? It didn't guarantee we would be friends or even more than friends. "I can be nice."

"You can be 'snubby,'" Jay-Jay said in a warning tone.

"That's not even a word." Though I did tend to ignore people. I had probably unintentionally ignored Savanna. Is that why Jay-Jay had initially given up on his ridiculous idea to match the two of us together? I resolved to at least speak to her. I felt bad that I had come off as rude. I didn't mean to hurt her feelings, though that kind of proved my whole point—that I hurt people without intending to.

When we walked into world history, the only person who had beat us to class was Serena. She had her notes and pencil ready, though class wasn't bound to begin for several more minutes. Serena had a real aptitude for history, and I realized with a certain feeling of uneasiness why that was.

We were currently studying the origins of ancient societies in this class. I wasn't sure what extra information she knew regarding our cultural heritage and how it tied in with the beginning of humankind, but whatever it was, it was probably deeply fascinating. I've never had an interest in the subject before, but after Serena pointed out all the hidden ties to our history, I suddenly had a new appreciation for it.

Savanna and her two friends walked in, taking their usual seats in the front row. Jay-Jay waved and grabbed my arm, practically dragging me to the front of the class where Savanna sat. Taking a deep breath, Jay-Jay relaxed, gesturing between us. "Bradley would like to say hi to you." I so wanted to glare at him. His introduction felt so childish. But when her blue eyes met mine, I forgot about our mutual friend. My breath caught like when I had first seen her. Jay-Jay nudged me in the ribs, reminding me that I was supposed to speak to the girl, not stare at her like an idiot.

"Um, hi," I managed to say, barely moving my hand into a wave.

She smiled—her entire face lit up. “Bradley, right?” Her voice was high-pitched but somehow soft to the ears.

I felt myself nod, but no words came out.

Savanna giggled, and it amazed me how innocent it sounded. “I wasn’t sure if you were ever going to come talk to me.” Her gaze flickered to Jay-Jay before resting back on mine. “What changed your mind?”

It was a strange question, like she had already known I was going to be introducing myself. I was taken aback. It wasn’t that I had changed my mind. In fact, I didn’t recall ever deciding to speak with her *before* deciding not to. My initial decision was to ignore her, to keep her safe from my bad luck. The change to do the opposite was because of my mother, because of her vision. I cleared my throat, scratching the back of my neck nervously. “Um, that’s actually kind of a complicated story.”

She smiled, her perfectly straight white teeth showing. “You should tell me about it sometime.”

I shrugged. It was strange. I did want to tell her. Her curious blue eyes were extremely compelling. When I stared into them, all I wanted to do was fulfill her every wish. But I couldn’t. Not after the story Serena had told me. I couldn’t risk exposing us.

Savanna gave a permissive glance toward Jay-Jay. “I’m excellent at untangling complicated stories. We probably have more in common than you think.” Another strange comment. I wasn’t sure what we could possibly have in common, especially not based upon first impressions. “You can tell me all about it on Saturday.” She winked as if we already had plans.

Her friends giggled.

It threw me off guard how straight forward she was being. I wondered if she was always like this, so sure of herself. "Uh, I guess, um, do you want to meet at, uh..." I struggled to think of a meeting place.

"Don't worry." She smiled. "I know where to find you."

My heart stopped. Was this her subtle way of trying to hint that she was also a diviner? That maybe she could see the future like my mother or could read minds or communicate telepathically like Serena's dad? I found myself hoping she was. Then maybe we really would have something in common. I shook my head at my thoughts. I was getting ahead of myself, reading into things that weren't there. The likelihood that she was also a diviner was slim, to say the least.

Mrs. Scar cleared her throat, eyeing Jay-Jay and me with a stern look. I glanced at the clock. Had the bell rung? I hadn't heard it ring through my awkwardness.

Serena glared at me as I shuffled back to my desk. Jay-Jay was right behind me, grinning from ear to ear.

"Have you lost your mind?" she hissed before catching Mrs. Scar's gaze and righting her posture.

Probably, I thought, snickering. Jay-Jay and Serena were such opposites—lately it felt like they were the epitome of the devil and the angel resting on my shoulders. It was like they were fighting against my neutrality, Serena's negativity pulling me one way—Jay-Jay's optimism coaxing me the other. I was usually comfortable hanging out on Serena's overly critical, pessimistic side. She fed that normativity in me. Jay-Jay's outlook was strange to me, but it felt good to try his side for once. I've somehow walked out of it with a semi-sort-of-date with the prettiest girl in school. *Hm*, Serena's scathing expression was probably due to this.

I waited until Mrs. Scar separated us into study groups before confronting Serena. "Are you jealous?" I asked in a low, but incredulous voice.

Jay-Jay couldn't help but laugh, slapping his knee as tears sprouted from the corners of his eyes. We weren't the only ones talking, but Jay-Jay's outburst caught Mrs. Scar's attention. She raised an eyebrow, and Jay-Jay slumped over his textbook, mindlessly flipping through the pages.

Serena stuck her tongue out at me, crossing her arms. "No." Her gaze flickered back to Savanna. "She's too good for you."

I followed Serena's gaze and watched as Savanna flipped her hair over her shoulder. She was laughing at something one of her friends had said. Serena was probably right. My shoulders slumped. Why did I let Jay-Jay talk me into this again?

Jay-Jay's head snapped up. "Why are you letting the Princess of Darkness get to you?" He sneered at the new nickname he had given Serena before cracking into a smile. Serena grabbed her journal and smacked him with it, igniting more laughter.

"Do I need to separate you guys?" Mrs. Scar appeared in front of us.

Serena scrambled to smooth out her notebook, eager to take more notes on ancient Egypt. I glanced at Jay-Jay, who was smoothing his bushy black hair, his smile a permanent fixture on his face. He nodded to the teacher when he finished messing with his hair. "We're good." Jay-Jay paused, reconsidering. "Well, I am."

Mrs. Scar looked expectantly at Serena. "Miss Lindt?"

Serena nodded, ducking her face.

Serena attempted her revenge in our last class. She had her football-playing boyfriend to defend her. Jay-Jay and I had our chairs facing the back row where they were sitting. I almost didn't notice Savanna taking the empty seat on my left as I listened to Serena complain to Kase about how Jay-Jay was harassing her.

"I was not," Jay-Jay said before explaining to an angry Kase in more detail. "I called her the Princess of Darkness! That was all!"

Kase surprised us by bursting into laughter. To Serena's chagrin, he said, "You got that right!"

I glanced at Savanna. Her eyes were narrowed in concentration. She looked apologetically at Serena, who wasn't paying her any attention. Serena was too busy gawking at Kase.

Jay-Jay waved at Savanna from the other side of me. "Savanna gets my jokes. Don't you, Savanna?"

Savanna nodded warily, suddenly shy.

Kase groaned. "Does your friend not have a voice? What is she, like Ariel the mermaid? She only speaks when she cheers?" He kept rambling on, to Jay-Jay's and my horror. "What? Is that like a brand? Like, she's pretty, but that's it? She's got the body but—"

I kept myself from lunging at him—my hands gripped the back of my chair to the point that my fingers hurt.

Serena unleashed her wrath with her only weapon—her journal. She punctuated each word with a smack. "Why! Are! You! Such! A! Pig?!" I had a feeling she wasn't hurting him at all.

I couldn't look at Savanna. I didn't want to see how Kase's words had hurt her. Jay-Jay stared in Savanna's direction with an expression of dread. I heard her stand and walk away. Jay-Jay's eyes seemed to follow her to the teacher's desk and out the door. He turned back to Kase, his dark eyes flashing with anger. "What is wrong with you?"

Kase folded his arms and grinned smugly. "Now Serena's the prettiest girl in the room, obvs."

Serena stared at him wide-eyed, and for a second, I thought she was going to be flattered by Kase's comment. But she furrowed her eyebrows and snarled. "You're impossible."

"Babe—" Kase started to say, but she already had her journal and textbooks gathered in her arms. She left the room, chasing Savanna down the hallway.

"Where's she going?" the teacher asked us accusingly.

Both Jay-Jay and I swiveled around to face the front, pointing behind us at Kase. "Ask him."

11 // SERENA HAS NO CHILL (BUT I ALREADY KNEW THAT)

I found Savanna in the gym after school. She was stretching. Some of the other cheerleaders slowly trickled in to join her. I approached her cautiously. I didn't want her to see me and scatter. "I'm sorry."

She was midway through a stretch and froze at the sound of my voice. Her arms hovered over her legs. She stayed like that for several moments until she released. "Your friend is stupid."

"He's not my friend." Taking a seat on the waxed gym floor, I nodded my head and smirked. "But he is stupid—I'll give you that."

The corner of her lip twitched. Then she frowned, lines creasing her forehead. "I'm not stupid. I know that's what he was going to say—that I have beauty but no brains. Everybody thinks that at one point or another. They see the cheerleader outfit, the blue eyes, the flat stomach, and they think that's all I have going for me. I'm put in a box. As if all I could ever accomplish in life is maybe signing a modeling contract, or cheering for the Colts, or being Miss America. But I know better. I'm smart. I study hard. I get good grades. I retain information better than a lot of people. I don't mean to say that the girls who pursue those types of careers aren't smart, either, but it's not for me. I'm not who everybody thinks I am. I am better." Savanna looked at me. She still wasn't smiling, even after this proclamation of self-confidence.

I had to fight myself not to put my arm around her shoulders.

Savanna looked away again, taking a deep breath. "Serena already apologized to me." She bit her lip, an expression of concern overshadowing her face. "She made a lot of excuses for her boyfriend's behavior. I don't need excuses for his quick assumptions. I don't want to hear them. They're always lame, like, 'he doesn't think before he speaks,' or, 'he's just trying to make himself feel better.'" She made a face. "I'm sorry her boyfriend's such an asshole."

I laughed, but when I thought about what she'd said, I stopped. Her description of Serena and Kase's relationship sounded eerily similar to Olga and Chad's. There were always excuses. I guess I knew what that was like, to be friends with a guy ten times worse than Kase. I realized that I had chosen right this time—to be friends with someone like Jay-Jay. It shocked me. I stared at Savanna for a second in wonder. If I could choose Jay-Jay as a friend—that seemed like a good decision—then couldn't I also continue to make other good decisions? Savanna was a good decision, I could tell, but I was still wary. She may be a good decision for me, but was I a good decision for her?

"If I promise never to be friends with Kase, are we still on for Saturday?" I asked, hopeful.

Savanna sighed. "We're still on."

For the rest of the week, I tried to avoid Kase. I only had two classes with him, and it turned out my teachers were fine letting me switch seats with a couple other students. In our last class, I would sit next to Savanna and Jay-Jay in the front row, but the entire time I could feel Serena and Kase's death glares on the back of my head. I hardly spoke to Serena, which proved difficult when we had the same schedule. I was able to ignore most of her snide comments. It was clear she didn't like Savanna or Jay-Jay.

"I'm supposed to be watching you," Serena complained one day when I wouldn't tell her what I was doing with my new friends. "How do you think this makes me look?" She went as far as telling Officer Lantern that I seemed to be snubbing her, which resulted in an interesting conversation during success time.

"Serena shared some concerns with me," Frank said.

I snorted. "Serena only cares about herself." When Frank tried to list the reasons behind her concerns, I cut him off. "She doesn't like my new friends, and I have yet to hear a good enough explanation as to why. They're good people, better than she is, or Kase is, and whatever she said about them, she's blowing way out of proportion."

The corners of Frank's mouth turned up slightly. "You know why I have to take her word for it as opposed to yours, right?"

I scowled. Two could play that game. "Talk to Jay-Jay Jones, and then try to tell me I've picked the wrong friends."

Jay-Jay cautiously approached me in world history that same day. "Why did I spend the last hour being interrogated by a police officer? You could have at least warned me."

I cringed. I didn't know Frank was going to pull Jay-Jay from class to confront him, but that explained why he hadn't shown up to Mr. Lindt's class.

Jay-Jay squinted at me. "Did you do something?"

I shook my head. "No. He just trusts Serena's lies more than my truths. I was bluffing when I told him to talk to you. I didn't know he would actually do it."

Jay-Jay glanced back at Serena, his voice low and concerned when he asked, "Does she really have that much power over you?"

I raised my eyebrows. I could feel the horizontal lines on my forehead form. "I'm pretty sure she's the reason my parents even let me out of the house."

On Saturday morning I was flipping through television channels while my mom was baking what smelled like perogies and crepes. My mom and I are the morning people in the family. We're always awake long before anybody else.

There was a knock on the front door around nine, but by the time I stood to answer it, Mrs. Lindt had already opened it. "Knock, knock."

Mom poked her head around the corner, a childish grin taking up half her face. "I'm nearly done!" she shouted to her best friend. I gawked as the entire Lindt family poured in. Serena appeared smug as she pushed me into the backyard.

"What are you doing?" I asked as she slid the glass door closed behind us.

Serena crossed her arms, a cunning smile dancing on her lips. "My mom was too excited when I suggested we spend the day here. She never gets to see Clarinda."

I crossed my arms to mirror her. "You're spying on me."

She chortled. "You should change your perspective," she said, paraphrasing Jay-Jay. "I'm merely doing my job."

I glowered. She was taking this whole "babysitting" thing to the extreme.

Serena turned back toward the door, but I reached for the handle, holding it shut. "What?" Her voice was like acid.

"I'm trying to be good, and you're making it hard," I growled.

She guffawed. "You? Good? You're the one trying to make my life harder." She pushed my hand back and stormed inside.

"I beg to differ," I said, grumbling.

As soon as I stepped back inside, my mom asked me to wake the others. I rolled my eyes and headed for the stairs. My mom could have at least given me a heads up on the whole family get-together. I knocked on everyone's doors, announcing that the Lindts were here and hoping they'd heard me. Of course, Paige screamed when she heard. She spent forty-five minutes making herself presentable before joining us downstairs.

Mrs. Lindt had brought *manrro la smetanascas*—basically, sour cream and stewed fruit spread on bread. I chewed on one carefully as I scrutinized Serena from across the dining room table. She knew I had plans with Savanna today—that was the only explanation I could think of for her sudden appearance. Did she know that Savanna didn't like her much? She was here to stir up trouble. My family didn't know about Savanna. Only Mom knew the bare minimum I had shared when she had that vision earlier in the week.

My thoughts were interrupted by a loud, childish voice. "Who's Savanna?" The voice echoed in my head, and I nearly jumped out of my chair.

Serena snickered as I looked around the large elongated table. I found her eleven-year-old sister staring at me as she stifled a laugh. Serena hadn't mentioned Mya was a telepath like their father. I felt self-conscious. Not only could Mr. Lindt peek into my head at any given moment, but so could a sixth-grade girl. For a brief, flickering second, I realized Kevin's gift of power mimicry meant he could as well. Lucky for me, they were just telepaths. They had to focus on the person whose thoughts they wanted to hear, and they could only focus on one person at a time. Unlucky for me, Mya had chosen me as her focus. I glared at Serena. She had to have planned this. She shrugged, licking the frosting off a donut. Damn Serena and her family of telepaths.

"You haven't answered my question." Mya prodded me telepathically. "Is she pretty? What does she look like? Is she nice? Does she go to your school? Is she your"—her voice turned singsongy—"girlfriend?" Of course, as soon as she asked a question, the answer would pop into my head either with words or pictures. It was impossible not to involuntarily answer them. She would be an excellent interrogator. Better than Frank.

I left the room wondering how far I would have to go to break the connection. Apparently, all I had to do was leave her line of sight. Her questions disappeared when I did. I couldn't have been sure if that was because Mya was young and unskilled or if that was literally how it worked with all telepaths, but I didn't want to take my chances. I stepped outside to the midmorning summer air.

It didn't take me long to notice the two girls bouncing a basketball in the cleared driveway across the street. One was short with jet black shoulder-length hair. She couldn't have been older than Mya, no younger than Rebecca. The other girl—I had to look twice—was Savanna Huckleberry. They didn't have a hoop, so they were bouncing the ball between them, shouting random words. It wasn't until I reached the sidewalk in front of my house that I could hear what they were saying.

"Aqua!"

"Maroon!"

"Teal!"

"Orange!"

"Yellow!"

"Brown!"

"Amber!"

They went on like this for a while until the younger girl couldn't think of a color they hadn't already listed. The two of them still hadn't seemed to notice me standing there, watching them, even when I had reached their side of the street.

Her sister groaned. "Fine. Car brands!" She tossed the basketball to Savanna.

"Mercedes!"

"Buick!"

"Ford!"

"Kia!"

"Jaguar!"

I cleared my throat. The basketball dropped at the younger girl's feet as they abruptly turned to stare at me. The ball bounced, then rolled, down the slightly slanted driveway before stopping at my feet. "Do you mind if I join?"

Savanna smiled but didn't seem nearly surprised to see me as the other girl. "Sure! This is my sister, Ursula." It was then that I understood how much Kase's *Little Mermaid* comment had gotten under Savanna's skin. Her sister probably received the brunt of those remarks.

I waved to Ursula before I picked up the ball and bounced it back to Savanna. When her sister bounced it back to me, I was surprised when the ball disappeared the second I touched it. I jumped back in shock. My heart leaped into my throat. Had Ursula done that?

Savanna didn't seem at all shocked by the ball's sudden disappearance. "That's all right. Ursula can make another one."

Ursula stomped grumpily behind some bushes before procuring a replacement ball.

"Try not to make this one disappear this time," Ursula said, tossing the ball in my direction.

The scene was so strange, I had a vague sense that I was dreaming. I got ready to dribble the ball, but the second my palm hit the orange rubber, this ball disappeared too. Okay. Definitely dreaming. I must have passed out on my way over.

Ursula groaned. "This is hopeless! It's like playing with a newbie!"

"You're a newbie," Savanna said pointedly to her sister.

"Yes, but I don't make balls disappear every time I touch them!" Ursula crossed her arms.

I stood there confused, listening to them bicker. I also kind of hoped I would wake up soon from this strange dream. *Come on*, I thought, *wake up!* But I didn't. I was still standing at the end of their driveway.

Another basketball flew at me, hitting me on the side of my head. "Ow!" I rubbed my head where it hit.

"Ursula!" Savanna rushed to my side and pushed my hand away to inspect my head.

Ursula shrugged. "What? It was an experiment! Look. The ball's still rolling!" She pointed past me into the street.

I couldn't turn to look—Savanna was still holding my scalp, pressing her thumb to my temple. "Does this hurt?"

I winced. Then I froze. If this were a dream, I wouldn't be able to feel any of this. I yanked my head away from her grasp, sputtering. "W-what happened?"

"You hit your head." Savanna frowned.

Ursula had chased after the ball. She appeared on the other side of me, twirling it between her pale fingers. "I can control my powers better than you can, and I'm ten." She touched the basketball to the back of my hand. I flinched, but the ball stayed in her hands, visible.

"You're diviners," I said in disbelief, glancing between the two sisters.

"So are you," Ursula said, handing the ball to me. "What gives?"

I took the ball in my hands, inspecting it. "What do you mean?"

Ursula scoffed. "You don't seem to believe us! I, for one, am offended."

I tossed the ball into the air, prepared to catch it. "You girls are playing out here where anyone can see you." When the ball landed in my outstretched hands, it vanished. I shook my head. "I thought the diviners here were more secretive."

Savanna and Ursula exchanged a long glance before Ursula shot back, "You're the one making objects disappear."

Savanna grabbed my hand. "Come on," she said and lead me up the driveway, across the covered front porch, and through their front door. I barely had time to assess my surroundings. The front door opened into a square living room, the front and north walls lined with a curved sectional. A large entertainment system occupied most of the far wall. A lady, who I assumed was her mom, sat near the corner of the sectional, reading a book. She glanced from her reading when we entered, but Savanna continued to tow me through the house.

"Who do you have there?" the woman called after us.

Savanna ignored her, leading me briefly into the kitchen before turning sharply to the left to descend a short staircase. The stairs led into a wide room with tan carpet and plain white walls. Buckets of toys and other paraphernalia lined the outskirts of the room. Only a small window on the back wall allowed natural light to flow in, but the room was far from dark.

Savanna let go of my hand and began to rummage through one of the buckets. Holding up a battered Barbie doll, she spun back around to face me. "Catch." She tossed the doll into the air. I leaned forward to catch it with one hand, but as soon as I felt the plastic body touch my skin, the doll disappeared. We did this exercise several more times as she tossed random toys toward me until finally, she huffed, studying the contents of one of the buckets. "Maybe you should try picking something up."

I wasn't sure what this whole exercise was about or why she wouldn't let me keep things within my grasp. I knew it wasn't me making everything disappear no matter what Ursula said. I couldn't even make things *ap*pear. Cautiously approaching the bin in front of her, I looked at its contents. It was full of Troll dolls and My Little Ponies. I grabbed a Troll by its wild pink hair and dangled it in front of me.

Savanna stared at it for a second before snatching the doll from my hands. "Maybe this is the original," she said, muttering. She barely closed her hand around it and it too disappeared. She sighed. "Or not."

Ursula's voice came from the stairs, making us jump. "It's like you have a shield. Like you're protecting yourself."

I stared at Ursula who stood on the steps. "I'm not doing this. My powers don't work."

"Clearly." Ursula rolled her eyes.

"What do you mean?" Savanna asked.

"I mean that I've never been able to do anything with them," I said. "I can't create things, and I definitely can't make things disappear."

"Never?" Savanna pressed.

I held out my hand, palm up, and tried to concentrate on the one object I've ever been able to materialize. They watched as a minuscule speck of white fluff appeared, and then another, and another until the soft white fluff merged into a small Kleenex. It took several minutes for the entire object to form. I held it up between my thumb and index finger. "Just this."

Ursula burst into laughter, rolling down the bottom two steps. Savanna gently grasped the tissue as I let go of it. She rubbed it between her fingers until it dissolved into thin air.

"I think you're overthinking it." She pursed her lips. "In fact, why don't you try not thinking?"

I rolled my eyes. Not thinking? I was pretty sure it was impossible not to think. I could distract myself with other thoughts, but I would still be *thinking*.

"I think your brain panics." Savanna tossed a bouncy ball at me, and I barely caught it. Like everything else I had been catching today, it disappeared. She smiled, proud of her insight. "Your brain sees something coming toward you, and it immediately views it as a threat. That's why everything we throw at you disappears."

"Everything touched by magic anyway," Ursula said, muttering. She grabbed a key chain from her belt loop and chucked it at me. "Think fast!"

I barely caught it before it hit my face. This time it didn't disappear. I stared at the key chain in my hands. It was a yellow rubber emoticon with sunglasses and a cheesy smile.

"See," Ursula said with a huff, "he only destroys what we create."

Savanna squinted, studying me. "It *is* more difficult to make an original object disappear," she mused. Taking the keychain from my hands, she closed her first around it. When it didn't disappear right away, she closed her eyes, concentrating. After several seconds, she reopened her fist, her eyes sparkling with pride. The keychain was gone. She dusted her hands. "Maybe that's why you can only dematerialize objects that were created out of thin air. Even Ursula struggles with dematerializing original objects, and she's a natural."

Ursula's lips twisted as if she had tasted something sour. "I can too." She yanked one of her black sneakers off. It was too big for her to cup her hands all the way around it, so she held it off to the side, grasping the back end between her thumb and index finger. She lifted a challenging eyebrow at her sister before winking. The shoe disappeared in the same instant, prompting Ursula's haughty grin.

Savanna's jaw dropped. Her head swiveled between her sister and me. "I-I guess everyone learns at their own pace."

Ursula's smile grew. "You're jealous."

"Am not," Savanna mumbled. She focused her eyes on mine, forcing her mouth into an encouraging smile. "If we can get you to that level, though, that would be excellent."

"It would be a miracle," Ursula said, sneering.

I looked between the two of them, who were staring each other down. They both seemed hell-bent on learning as much as they could about their powers. I mean, yeah, powers were super cool and all, and if mine worked, I'd be all over testing my limits and all that jazz, but there was something familiar in their urgency.

"You don't think we have enemies out there who would try to hurt us, do you?" I asked.

Savanna broke the staring contest, her forehead lining with worry. "Do you?"

I shook my head. "No, no." I didn't mean to cause her any unease. Serena's story had occurred years ago. I doubted the one doctor from Terre Haute would wage a war against us. It was just that their obsession with growing their powers reminded me of the climate my mom grew up in. Grandpa Anderson always wanted to be prepared for hypothetical blitz attacks. Had I just stumbled in on another paranoid family of diviners?

12 // MY SISTER IS A SAINT

I had a lot to process as I crossed the street back to my house. One, Savanna Huckleberry lived across the street. Two, Savanna and her sister, Ursula, were diviners. Three, not only were Savanna and Ursula diviners, but they could materialize anything. And four, it's not so much that I can materialize things but more that I can *de*materialize things. Without. Even. Trying. I was kind of mad I hadn't discovered any of these facts sooner.

It was midafternoon when I returned home. The Lindts' minivan was still in the driveway, which meant Serena was probably going to cause a scene with my reappearance. I held my breath as I opened the front door.

"Where have you been?" Serena screamed in my face.

I hadn't crossed the threshold yet. I was pretty sure her constant frustration with everyone and everything stunted her growth. I pushed past her without answering.

She slammed the door shut and spun around. I was mildly surprised that she was the only one in the entryway. My mom must have known I would be returning safely. It bugged me that her ridiculously reliable knowledge hadn't reassured Serena in the slightest.

"Why are you so pigheaded?" I asked, stalking off to the kitchen in search of a snack. All the adults were in the living room telling stories. Mom was the only one who turned her head at the sound of my voice. She winked smugly before rejoining the conversation. Serena's face was tinged with red. "Are you okay?" I asked, not really interested in the answer. "You look like you're about to have an aneurysm."

She tried to slam her hand on the counter, and we were both shocked by the lack of noise her action made. Serena's hand had gone straight through the island and was lost somewhere inside the inner workings. For a second, she struggled to pull it out, and when she did, a can of peas was in her hand. She gingerly positioned the can on the countertop and took a deep breath. The color from her face was starting to turn back to its normal tone.

I laughed as I watched her slowly gain control. "You could benefit from some anger management classes."

"You would know," she said through clenched teeth.

I shrugged her comment off. Must she know everything? Grabbing a box of crackers from the cabinet, I tried to think of a better comeback. That's when I realized Serena had way more dirt on me than I did on her. Naturally. That's how my life is though—I'm always the bad kid. There is nothing I can say or do to backtrack that label. Even if I could go back in time...

I shook my head. No. There was nowhere I could go back in time to erase the path my life took—except for maybe New Mexico nine years ago, but I didn't want to think about New Mexico, let alone go back there. Before my brain could spiral again, I bit into a cracker, forcing myself back into the present.

"Where'd you go just now?" Serena asked. She had managed to calm her rage, her facial expression twisting in slight concern.

Ignoring her question, I glanced out the sliding glass doors at the backyard where the others were playing. I hated how she pretended to feel sorry for me. I didn't need her fake sympathy.

Mya, Rebecca, Blake, and five-year-old Kendra were jumping on the large trampoline that had been abandoned by the previous homeowners. I couldn't see Kevin and Paige from the angle I was standing. Setting the rest of the crackers on the counter, I stepped outside to investigate. They were balancing on the edge of the porch railing to my right. Kevin was leaning forward, his hands' grip on the wood was the only thing keeping him from falling forward onto the grass.

I could hear Serena behind me as she slid the door shut. Mya, her light brown hair in a ponytail, ducked under the net and leaped off the trampoline when she saw us. I prepared for another invasion of privacy, but she bit her lip.

"I'm sorry I read your mind earlier. I don't get to use my powers often, and I wanted a chance—"

Paige cut her off, nearly falling off the railing as she tried to dismount. "Wait, you read his mind?" She ran up to Serena's sister. "Oh my gosh, was it scary? Did it have actual cobwebs? You must be traumatized."

Mya eyed her, confused. "He was just thinking about some girl."

Crap. There went all my privacy. Again.

"A girl?" Paige asked before turning to me. She glared at me. "What girl?" Her index finger was pointed in my direction as she stepped up the porch steps to stand in front of me. My heart felt like it was trying to choke me.

"Um, uh, no one," I said in a sputter.

Serena rolled her eyes, stepping out from behind me. "That's where he was today, you know. He snuck off to see her."

"How?" Paige clenched her fists. She looked like she was trying to hold something back but changed her mind. "How did you end up with a girlfriend two weeks into the new school year? *You?* Of all people!"

"Oh," Serena said, her voice was dripping with satisfaction. She'd finally found someone to join in on her gossip. "Not just any girl. She's nowhere near his league. I don't even understand how it happened."

"She's really pretty," Mya said, having glimpsed Savanna in my thoughts earlier in the day.

I held up my hands in protest. "She's not my girlfriend. She's just a friend."

"Oh, right." Serena scoffed. "Girls like that don't just have guy friends."

"What are you saying?" I asked through clenched teeth. I could feel my hands shaking into fists at the accusation in her voice.

"She's a total—"

Paige cut Serena off with an agonized wail. "What's her name?" She was so close to me that I had to lean back.

"Sav..." My head swiveled, looking between Serena and Paige. "You know what? No. I'm not going to sit here gossiping. Not when you all want to stir up drama." I looked at the trampoline. Rebecca was sliding off the end, landing perfectly on her feet. I wanted to speak to her about her powers, or rather *our* powers, and I also wanted to ask her if she knew Savanna's sister, Ursula.

As I slid around Paige and jogged down the steps, I heard Serena answer Paige's question. "Savanna Huckleberry. She's a cheerleader—the totally perfect kind who turns into an evil succubus when you get too close."

Okay. I needed Serena to refrain from making assumptions like that about Savanna. But I let it slide and tuned out their conversation. I hoped she wasn't going to continue spreading false rumors.

"Hey, Rebecca. Can I talk to you for a sec?"

She looked like I had trapped her, and I immediately felt bad about that. She'd been avoiding me since her birthday. She knew I was going to bring up her powers, and she didn't want anything to do with them.

I took a deep breath. "I learned something new about my powers today, and I wanted to show you."

She grimaced, looking past me at the older girls. Rebecca wasn't one for gossip, so it said something that she was debating between joining their conversation or humoring me. Crossing her arms, she asked warily, "I don't have to use my powers for this, do I?"

I mirrored her grimace. "Well, the only way I can make them work is if someone has already materialized something."

"No." Rebecca turned to join Serena, Paige, and Mya.

I held out my hand to stop her. "Please, please, please? It's really cool! I promise."

She hesitated for a second before circling beyond my reach.

If she wasn't going to let me practice my ability, then I did want to at least know one thing. I shouted after her, "Hey, do you know Ursula Huckleberry from across the street?"

Serena heard me, her eyes bugging out of her head. "Savanna lives across the street?"

Rebecca stopped walking and half turned back to me. I could only see part of her face, but it was twisted into a full-blown frown. I barely heard her whisper, "Ursula's the meanest girl in school," before she fled, pushing past the girls as she ran into the house.

Well, that wasn't the reaction I had expected. My sister had mentioned that a girl was being mean to her at school, but I had no idea that girl was Savanna's little sister. It did make sense, though. Ursula wasn't exactly the nicest person I've spoken to today.

Serena was laughing at Rebecca's reaction, which sent a flare of anger through me. "Oh, this is great," she shouted at me. "Your girlfriend's little sister terrorizes *your* little sister!"

I felt my shoulders sag, my anger at Serena fading. She was right. Not about the girlfriend part, but now that I knew the girl of my dreams had a mean-spirited little sister who liked to make my sweet little sister's life miserable, I wasn't sure how to approach the situation. If I asked Savanna about it, I risked stirring up some bad blood and possibly losing her as a friend, but I also didn't like the fact that my little sister was being bullied at school.

I stepped back inside the house, abandoning the gaggle of family and friends in the backyard. Rebecca wasn't anywhere to be seen and neither was our mother. My dad shot me an accusatory glance from the couch. "Whoever sent your sister in here crying needs to go apologize to her right now," he said with a growl.

I knew he thought it was me. I guess he was right in this case, although it was unintentional. How was I supposed to know that Ursula was the girl bullying Rebecca? Besides, I hadn't said anything ill-mannered. I had only asked a question.

I tried not to let my dad's anger bother me too much as I ascended the stairs to the bedrooms. I could hear Rebecca's low sobs and my mother's soothing tone as I reached the second floor. Rebecca's door was open, and I could see her lying facedown on her bed, hugging a pillow, as our mother stroked her curly brown hair.

My youngest sister's walls were covered by artwork—she was a talented artist, especially for her age—and I couldn't help but marvel at the pictures. They were so realistic, like black and white photographs.

I recognized myself in some of the drawings. Everyone in the family guest-starred in at least three of the displayed sketches, but I was shocked to see how many I was in. There were drawings of Olga and me, laughing with each other as we paced the streets of Itasca. I noticed that Chad was nowhere to be seen in any of the drawings, and I wondered if she had burned the evidence. There were other sketches of me, alone, listening to music underneath the shade of maple tree or leaning against a wall with an expression that hinted that I had been lost in deep thought.

The sketch in the center of the east wall struck me the most. I remembered her sketching frantically at Jesse's bedside during his last month and figured this must have been what she was working on. Jesse sat in his hospital bed, smiling from ear to ear, the tube underneath his nose distorting his face. Mom and Dad were on either side of him, capturing a semirare moment of my dad's smile. Blake was sitting on the end of the bed, his shoes spreading dirt on the linens. Paige was standing next to Dad, but only half her face showed as she was turned to look in Jesse's direction, her lips upturned in a casual smile, her eyes lit up. Even in the limited effects of the pencil lead, Rebecca managed to highlight the slightest details. I stood casually by Mom, but there was no smile in my expression—it was blank. I was watching Blake instead, ignoring Jesse. That's when I noticed that Rebecca wasn't in the drawing. She wasn't in any of the drawings displayed on her walls. The sound of her cries brought me back to reality.

I blinked and stared at her shaking shoulders. Rebecca was usually someone who I described as strong and emotionally stable, but there she was, seeming as fragile as any other kid. My heart ached, pulsating against my chest. I wanted to strangle the monster who had hurt her, but then I remembered that it was something I had said that set her off, and suddenly, I felt like running away, far away, where I couldn't hurt her anymore.

"I'm sorry." Falling to my knees next to our mother, I started to see the world through her eyes. She'd been through so much lately—the bully, the move, the new powers, having to watch Jesse take his last breath. She was only ten. Though that was a mere four years ago for me, it felt like further. Being ten years old was so long ago for me. But not for her. Rebecca had been ten for a few weeks and everything was new to her. There was so much adversity that had wormed its way into her life, and I hoped it didn't stay there, that it didn't continue hurting her like it did me. That was something I never wanted to have in common with her—the pain of all life's traumas. I wanted her to be happy.

I knelt like that for a while, listening to her sniffle and sob. When her cries quieted a little, Rebecca's lips trembled as she turned her tear-stained face in my direction. "How do you know her?" It took me a minute to realize she was talking about Ursula.

"I... I..." I glanced at Mom and back at my sister. "I met her today. She was playing across the street. Where she lives. With her sister. Who I know..."

Rebecca sat up, sniffling and fluffing her hair. "Is her sister nice?"

I hesitated before nodding slowly. "Yeah, really nice. But I'll ask her to tell Ursula to stop being mean to you if you want." *Anything to keep the crying in this house to a minimum*, I thought.

My sister shook her head and pouted. "I don't want to cause any trouble." Rebecca, the saint, always wanting the best for others. Never wanting to add to conflict. But her expression had me making up my mind in an instant.

I never used to be afraid of causing trouble, and if I needed to risk that to keep my sister happy, I would. I never want to see that expression on my sister's face again. So, I decided. On Monday, I would confront Savanna.

13 // REBECCA SHOWS OFF HER INTERIOR DECORATING SKILLS

"Your sister is bullying my sister." The words came straight out of my mouth while I was still practicing in my head the best way to approach the situation. But my tongue betrayed me—the words came out grim and sinister—the second Savanna walked into world history. Her friends stopped walking when she did, blocking the door, all three of their faces appeared startled by my accusation. Other students groaned, trying to weave their way around them. I felt Jay-Jay tense next to me. I hadn't said anything to him regarding this matter.

Savanna looked like she was struggling to come up with a response, her mouth moving, forming half-words several times before she finally cleared her throat. "I would like to discuss this further with you, but when we have more time." And that was it. She floated gracefully to her desk, flanked by her two friends. I stared after her, shocked at how adult she sounded.

"She's my age, right?" I leaned back toward Jay-Jay.

He nodded. "More or less. Has one of those weird August birthdays." He shook his head in reverence. "Virgos, man. I've always felt like they were more mature than the other signs." Jay-Jay seemed to backtrack toward my accusation. "So, wait, Ursula's bullying your sister?"

I nodded grimly.

Again, he shrugged. "I didn't know you had a sister."

"You never asked." I flipped open my notebook to the nearest blank page.

"You're right," Jay-Jay said morosely. "I only knew about the one brother." He meant Jesse, and I knew exactly how he knew about him. I remembered what day it was too. I wasn't sure I'd ever forget.

"I have two sisters and two brothers, all younger. Paige is twelve, Rebecca is ten, Blake is eight, and then there... *was* Jesse." I paused for a split second. "He was five. Or six." I shook my head as I sifted through my thoughts. "He turned six before..." Waving my hand in the air, I didn't finish my sentence. Jay-Jay knew what I meant.

Jay-Jay's eyes were wide, his expression mirroring the one he had worn when he first learned about Jesse's death. I realized Serena had never mentioned Jesse's age in the story she told. She had said "his brother." Somehow, this knowledge always made the story sound worse. Jesse was so little, so small, so innocent. I forced my thoughts to remain on Rebecca—to focus on Rebecca—that was why I was explaining this to Jay-Jay in the first place. My littlest sister was hurt, and I wanted to stop that hurt. I clenched my teeth, swallowing loudly. Jay-Jay said nothing. He had learned his lesson the last time: silence is the best policy. Besides, Mrs. Scar was going to develop a complex if I kept having mental breakdowns in the middle of her history class.

Ever since Serena heard that Savanna's sister and my sister didn't get along, she seemed reassured that, somehow, Savanna and I wouldn't work out. She'd left me alone all day, shooting me arrogant glances every once in a while, confident that I would soon be ruining my relationship with the girl in the center of her jealous obsession.

I didn't have to look toward the back of the class to know that she was scrutinizing my interactions with Savanna, searching for the moment when we would turn on each other. Somehow, though, I didn't get the feeling that my friendship with Savanna was doomed—not yet, anyway, because she had surprised me with her response to my accusation. She didn't seem at all shocked by Ursula's behavior, but she did seem at least a little concerned by it. Maybe she would be on my side about this after all.

It wasn't until after our last class when Savanna approached me tentatively as we were packing up to leave. "So, my sister's bullying your sister?" Her eyebrows pulled together in concern, her voice softer than ever.

I nodded. "Yup," I said, stuffing a textbook into my backpack.

She sighed but didn't say anything for a while as I zipped my backpack shut and swung it over my shoulder. Following me out of the classroom, Savanna finally spoke again. "Can I meet you at your house later?"

I stopped walking. I was still waiting for an apology, but it seemed like she was going to ignore me. Savanna appeared to pick up on my anger and she quickly explained. "It's just that I have cheer practice so I can't talk long, and I want to make sure that everything that needs to be said gets said." Great. She was planning to fight.

I rolled my eyes, snorting in disbelief. "Fine."

It wasn't until I walked outside to wait for my mom that I realized I had given Savanna permission to meet my family. Crap. This was so not a good time. She wanted to fight in front of my family? How was this supposed to work?

I didn't mention Savanna's plan to meet my family. I was honestly hoping she would chicken out. The doorbell rang, though some of us were still finishing dinner. Before I could reach the door, Paige was twisting the handle. My heartbeat accelerated—my palms sweat. I could feel my hands shake at my sides.

Paige's voice sounded so surprised. It caught in her throat. "Wh—"

I ran to my sister's side, gripping the edge of the door with my left hand. I was surprised to see that Savanna had brought her sister with her. "Savanna. Ursula." The appearance of her sister left me relieved. Maybe Savanna wasn't here to fight after all. She was here to have her sister apologize. I opened the door wider. "Come on in."

"This is..." Paige's eyes were practically bugging out of her head as she stepped back to glance rapidly between Savanna and me. "Your..." She pointed at Savanna, at a loss for words.

Finally, Paige shouted, "Mom! There's a girl here for Bradley! A *pretty* girl!"

I wondered if she needed somebody else to confirm that she wasn't hallucinating.

"Rebecca!" I called for my other sister.

Mom stepped out from the kitchen. She had a plate and a dishtowel in her hands, a full smile on her lips. She wasn't surprised at all by the appearance of two girls. I wondered if this was the vision she had seen last week. "Would you girls like some food?" Mom was always trying to feed strangers.

I shut the door behind the sisters as they stepped in.

"Maybe just a bite," Savanna said politely, nudging her sister to do the same. Even though Mom wouldn't have minded their refusal to eat, it was still considered rude to refuse. It would have been rude of Mom not to offer. My grandmother, on the other hand, always let a person's refusal ruin her entire day.

Rebecca took her sweet time before ambling in from the dining room. She stopped immediately when she saw why I was calling for her.

Ursula groaned. "*She's* your sister?"

Rebecca shrank back at Ursula's question.

Savanna elbowed her sister in the shoulder, prompting an eye roll from the ten-year-old. "How was I supposed to know?"

Savanna's kind face shifted into an expression of anger and frustration. Her voice hardened as if she were chastising a defiant child. "It doesn't matter who she is. What matters is your lack of respect for strangers."

Ursula snorted. "Strangers?" She turned back toward my sister, who was half hiding behind the wall separating the front room from the dining room. "We're not *strangers*, are we Becca?"

Rebecca didn't answer, but I thought I saw her wince.

Ursula's eyes widened as she realized something. "Wait." She turned toward me. "If you have powers, then so do you." Her eyes scanned the rest of us in her line of sight. "All of you." She tilted her head as she studied Rebecca, smirking. "So, what's *your* superpower?"

I wasn't expecting what happened next. In fact, I don't think anybody was. Not when Rebecca had been pretending all this time that she was normal like me. Horror had me frozen in place as black wallpaper unrolled itself along the walls of the front room. A lit candle that was sitting on a coffee table suddenly multiplied itself by ten. The chandelier in the center of the room dripped with added crystals on strings, long enough to tickle the carpet, which changed from its boring beige color to a bright bloodred. A gold curtain rod screwed itself into the wall above the windows, and soon, solid black curtains draped from the rod, blocking the natural light from the room.

Fear and amazement bubbled up in me as small dazzling red and orange beads appeared on the fabric of the curtains, drawing several outlines of flames. In half a minute, Rebecca had redecorated the front room. She would have continued if Mom hadn't run up behind her trying to desperately break her concentration. It took a couple good shakes before Rebecca's brown eyes, burning with danger, refocused on Mom's panicked expression. The movement in the room froze, my sister blinking herself out of her trance. The rest of us remained frozen where we stood, too shocked to move. I could see my dad in the dining room, a fork of spaghetti raised halfway toward his open mouth, his expression stuck. Blake was the only one who hadn't witnessed the scene.

He was in the living room, his gaming headset tuning out any noise.

"Rebecca, honey," Mom said, worry soaking her tone. Dad dropped his fork, the clattering sound snapping us out of our individual stupors.

I was the first to speak, gasping between words of astonishment. "How can I do *that*?"

"You don't," Mom snapped at me before returning her attention to my youngest sister, feeling her forehead, studying her eyes, as if my mom had a medical degree and was searching for something physical wrong with Rebecca. My sister stood still, her breathing coming in small gasps. She was nearly as dazed as we were.

Mom whispered, "I didn't see this happen. I didn't..." Her head snapped up to look at our father, and she spoke more forcefully. "Chastain, I didn't see this coming." She sounded terrified by this thought, and it took me a while to figure out the meaning behind her reaction. Mom hadn't acted like this in a while, not since... Jesse. My breath caught in my throat. Mom never could see Jesse in her visions. Was she now not seeing Rebecca? What could that mean? I thought I remembered learning in middle school health class that certain conditions—like my diabetes, for example—were genetic. Could Jesse's heart tumor be a genetic condition?

Dad stared back at her, his horrified expression matching hers. He was on his feet in an instant, joining my mother in her examination. He held his hands on either side of my sister's face. "Hey, honey, how do you feel?"

Mom was gripping Rebecca's wrists frantically, trying to induce a vision, but clearly wasn't seeing anything in her future.

"I feel..." Rebecca scrunched her face in confusion. "I don't know." Her lips trembled. I had a feeling the waterworks were coming.

My dad immediately scooped her in his arms, speaking only to our mother. "Call Frank and Hudson, tell him to meet us at the hospital."

I remembered Serena's story and felt my heart drop into my stomach. If Rebecca were to use her powers in public, she could expose all of us. She didn't seem stable right now. "You're going to take her to the hospital?" My throat was thick with worry.

With a cell phone in hand, Mom followed Dad as he weaved around us toward the front door. Dad's voice was frantic as he answered me. "I'm not losing another kid!"

"Frank and Hudson can protect us—we'll be all right," Mom said, reassuring me before they disappeared through the front door.

The house was dead silent for several moments before Ursula finally said breathily, "What the heck was that?"

Paige stepped into the room from the hallway to get a better look at Rebecca's decorations. "And I thought *my* power was out of control."

"I wouldn't say she was necessarily out of control," Savanna murmured while examining our surroundings. "It was just excessive. I've never seen so much concentrated power before. This is pretty high-level stuff." She bent to touch the red carpet. "I'm not sure how she managed to replace the color of this carpet. Materialization doesn't usually involve replacement. If we wanted to change the carpet, we would either have to rip the carpet out and create a new carpet in our minds or layer a new carpet on top of the older carpet. But"—she ran her fingers through the fabric—"this is the same carpet."

I pointed to the black wallpaper. "She didn't do the same with the walls. I saw the wallpaper unroll itself, covering the original paint. Why would she do that if she could change the color of the walls by simply thinking of it?"

Savanna shrugged, standing to examine the wallpaper. She reached out to touch the coarse texture. "It was the first thing she did, right?" She didn't wait for me to respond. "It was like her power escalated quickly. She started with basic stuff—creating the new wallpaper and the candles." Savanna nodded toward the coffee table. "But everything she did after that was an added skill. She practically grew the chandelier, then changed the color in the carpet. The rod was added as if it were an afterthought, the curtains added just as easily. But the pattern..." She crossed the room to examine the bedazzled artwork on the curtains. "This takes precision." Her forehead creased, and she abruptly turned on her little sister. "You're lucky this is all she did, Ursula. You shouldn't taunt her."

Ursula crossed her arms, her lower lip jutting out in a pout, but she didn't argue.

Savanna was right. My sister could have gutted her with a spear if she wanted. What was I doing trying to defend her when she could clearly defend herself?

Savanna turned to me, her beautiful blue eyes full of questions. "Why did your parents take her to the hospital? This seems more like a supernatural problem, not a medical one, if you can even call it a problem."

Paige and I shared a panicked glance. "She doesn't know about Jesse, does she?" she asked.

No, she didn't. But I hadn't had a chance to spill my guts to her. It wasn't like we had a lot of alone time. Or any, for that matter. Besides, we were only friends, and I'd barely known her for a couple of weeks. And no way did I want to start our friendship with her knowing all my deep, dark secrets. But I guess Jesse wasn't a secret—at least, not the part related to this moment.

I sighed, my shoulders sagging, as I stared at the weeping crystals of the chandelier. "Our youngest brother had a heart condition. He didn't make it."

"Our mom is a precog," said Paige. "She can see our futures with the slightest touch." She poked Savanna's arm playfully. "But she could never see our brother Jesse's future. So, when the doctors found a tumor in his heart last April, she thought maybe that was why. That maybe she can't see us if our destinies lead us to the grave."

"And she panicked just now," I said, "because she hadn't seen this happening ahead of time. I think she knew you guys were coming over, but Rebecca's outburst surprised her. She'd already seen this..."

"What's wrong?" Paige asked, anxiety climbing in her voice. She clung to my arm, her nails digging into my skin.

"The future changed." I forced the words out of my mouth. They didn't make sense. That never happened. The main event was always set in stone. There was no way Savanna and Ursula's arrival was considered the main event in her vision. That was nothing compared to Rebecca's outburst. Definitely a bad omen. "I thought it was set in stone."

14 // I'M OFFICIALLY STUPID FOR NOT REALIZING THIS SOONER

"We need to call Jay-Jay," Savanna said, urgency in her voice. She whipped her cell phone out of her small black purse. The purse dangled from a long silver chain that slung around her shoulder.

I stepped forward without thinking, running into the dangling crystals of the chandelier. They clinked against each other, adding a short dazzling tune into the background of the conversation. "Why?" I asked, thoroughly confused that her mind had flown to our weird mutual friend.

She looked at me like I was stupid, her upper lip curling in disbelief. Her blue eyes narrowed as if she were trying to decide if my question was serious.

I felt like I was missing a huge chunk of information. Her stare had me feeling self-conscious.

Lifting the cell phone to her ear, she studied the confusion on my face as she waited for Jay-Jay to answer. "Hey, could you meet me at Bradley's house? Thanks." She hung up within seconds.

Did Jay-Jay somehow know where I lived? She hadn't given him an address—just expected him to show up.

Leaning against the archway that was the entrance to the front room, she sighed and looked me. "He didn't tell you, did he?" Savanna rolled her eyes. "He was probably hoping you'd figure it out on your own."

"Figure what out?" I asked slowly, narrowing my eyes.

She pushed away from the wall. "Jay-Jay's a precog like your mom. Maybe he'll be able to see something she can't."

Suddenly, everything Jay-Jay had ever said to me made sense. One conversation in particular raced through my mind. He had droned on and on once, jabbering nonsense about changing perspectives and changing our futures. I had thought he was blissfully oblivious because the future couldn't change. But now I wasn't so sure. Not when my mom suddenly couldn't see Rebecca's. He'd said this after shaking Serena's hand, holding it for too long, and saying something about her being a destructive force, even though he had just met her. But he was right. Serena was a destructive force. And then afterward, when Savanna had walked in and I saw her for the first time, he commented how maybe I was right—maybe *some* things didn't change.

"I think you two might be destined," he'd said to me at lunch on the day I'd finally decided to talk to Savanna. Did he know all this time? About me? Had he seen me coming? Is that why he approached me, a complete stranger, on the first day of school? He had plopped himself across from me at lunch and started talking to me like he knew me already, like he knew we'd be friends. When I had finally spoken to Savanna, she had said things that had me thinking *she* could see the future. But that knowledge she held had all come from Jay-Jay. My heart stuttered at the realization. I should have picked up on it, but I hadn't. I couldn't believe I hadn't.

"What could he possibly see here? Rebecca's on her way to the hospital. Wouldn't he need to touch her to get a vision?" Paige said, interrupting my thoughts.

Savanna shrugged. "Not necessarily. Sometimes he has visions of people we are close to by touching *us*. He can sense that bond, like a string of yarn on an investigation board, and he can follow it to another person. That's—" Savanna bit her tongue, stopping her sentence short. She glanced at me, a deep russet shading her cheeks, before returning her gaze to Paige.

I could feel my heart flickering rapidly in my chest, but at this point, it was background noise. I knew that look, and it made a lot more sense now that I knew Jay-Jay could see the future. "That's how he saw me coming, wasn't it?" I tried to ignore the small tremors in my hands. This was why Jay-Jay thought Savanna and I were destined. He'd seen me *through her*.

Savanna bit her lip, nodding, the color change in her cheeks refusing to go away.

How interesting, I thought, marveling at the possibility that Jay-Jay might be right. Somehow, our lives were going to entangle further, our bond strong enough that an invisible string tied us together already—a string that Jay-Jay's visions could sense before we crossed each other's paths.

It took ten minutes for Jay-Jay to arrive. Savanna let him in, and he immediately leaned over, his hands on his knees, panting.

"Did you run here?" I asked him in disbelief. I didn't know where Jay-Jay lived, but I didn't think the situation was urgent enough for him to have to run the whole way here.

Our clairvoyant friend nodded frantically as he tried to catch his breath. When he was able to talk, he slowly straightened. "I live on the other side of the neighborhood. It's no big deal." He was still breathing heavily. It clearly was a big deal. He stretched, trying to pop his back. "So, what's the sitch?" Jay-Jay stepped into the front room, taking in his surroundings. "Wow, someone went all out on this room." He ducked his head around the corner, studying the rest of the rooms he could easily see from the hallway. "It doesn't match the rest of the house."

"My sister did this," I said, waving my hand, gesturing to the room.

Jay-Jay raised his eyebrows—he seemed impressed—before meeting Paige's gaze.

Paige threw her hands in the air defensively, palms facing away from her. "Oh, not me. I wish I did. Rebecca's got a real eye for interior design. Maybe I'll ask her to redo my bedroom."

"Paige." Jay-Jay smiled, remembering the names I had given him that afternoon. He sounded proud of himself for making the connection. He turned to me. "So Rebecca did this? The ten-year-old?" Letting out a low whistle, he reexamined the features of the room. "*Rebecca and her Multifaceted Imagination*." There he went with the book and movie titles again. He ran his fingers through the chandelier's added facets. "So, where is she? I'd like to meet her."

"My parents took her to the emergency room," I said a little uncomfortably. "They might have overreacted a little bit."

"She wasn't passed out or convulsing, was she?" Jay-Jay asked, trying to gather as much information as he could. I would have to stop my bad habit of undersharing with him.

Speaking for the first time since Savanna chastised her, Ursula said, "She went into some weird trance. Mrs. Chambers freaked because she hadn't seen it coming." She rolled her eyes. "As if."

Jay-Jay furrowed his brows, his posture defensive. "Just because some of us can see the future, Ursula, doesn't mean we can see everything. We're not omniscient." He returned his attention back to me. "So, your mom's a precog?" The corner of his lips turned up into a half-smile.

I wondered if he had ever met anyone like himself before.

He pointed to the ceiling. "And this is the kind of thing that she normally sees?"

I nodded. "With Rebecca, yes. She's been watching her more carefully since she gained her powers a few weeks ago."

Ursula's shriek was as high-pitched as Paige's. "She's only had her powers for a few weeks?"

I shot her an annoyed look before continuing. "My mom's usually attentive like that. She likes to know what's going on ahead of time so she can prepare herself.

Besides, she kind of already saw this scene. She knew Savanna and Ursula were coming, but she hadn't seen Rebecca's outburst. That's when she freaked. Last time she couldn't see one of us..." I let my eyes fall to the floor. "They died."

Knowledge flashed in Jay-Jay's dark eyes as he nodded. "So that's why Savanna called me." He gestured for my sister and me to sit on the small loveseat. We obeyed, having gone through similar motions with our mother. Jay-Jay quickly blew out the ten lit candles on the coffee table and moved them to the side so he could sit on the center of the table. He held out his hands expectantly for each of us to take. "I'm guessing you know how this goes."

Nervously, I extended my right hand to place in his. I was worried about what he'd see. Paige already had her left hand in his other outstretched palm.

He closed his eyes, gripping our hands tight, and breathed slowly, searching our futures. "Is she the one with the curly brown hair?" he murmured.

"Yes," I said quietly. He was definitely seeing Rebecca through us, so that was a good sign. I tried to slow my breathing with his. We stayed like that for several minutes as he followed the invisible thread that led from us to Rebecca. His face contorted as he worked. The room had grown quiet, our breaths the only sound. Sometimes, the quiet would be interrupted by Blake shouting at whatever video game he was playing in the living room. We hadn't had a chance to fill him in. I didn't want to upset him without Mom or Dad to referee.

Finally, Jay-Jay pulled away, his eyes flying open. He was on his feet in seconds. "I have good news and bad news. The good news is that I can see your sister. She'll be fine. Ish. It's nothing big." Jay-Jay had backed up halfway through the room, getting ready to deliver the pronouncement to the rest of the room. "The bad news is that there's another threat looming. I'd only seen glimpses of it before." He shook his head, his eyes troubled. "But this time I was able to get a clearer picture thanks to you guys." He nodded to Paige and me. We all stared at him, waiting for him to elaborate, but he still looked like he was analyzing his thoughts.

"And?" Savanna said the same time I did.

Jay-Jay frowned. "We need to bring Serena and her siblings in on this." He shook his head, blaming me for his lack of foresight. "Bradley, you could have told me the Lindts were also diviners."

Savanna gasped, her blue eyes trying to meet mine, but my eyes were locked on Jay-Jay's. How had he not picked up on that before? After finding out he was also a diviner, a precog, no less, I thought he surely knew.

"Wait a minute." Savanna eyed everyone in our circle. "How 'bout we lay all our cards on the table so that we're not surprised anymore. All the diviners in the area we know, okay?" She looked pointedly at me. "The Lindts? Really?" She didn't seem pleased by the idea.

I shrugged. "The Lindts. The Schwartzes. Frank Lantern. You guys."

"I saw Frank in my vision with Rebecca, but Kase Schwartz? I also didn't see that one coming," Jay-Jay said. "There are a lot more of us than I thought."

I shook my head. "Don't tell anyone I told you about the Schwartzes. They're not keen on people knowing. I'm not even supposed to know. Serena told me that in confidence." I could feel Savanna's hurt gaze on me, but I tried to ignore it. "Anyone else you guys know?" Jay-Jay and the Huckleberry sisters shook their heads. I nodded. "Okay, so all the cards are on the table. Can we get on with the looming threat now?"

"Wait. Powers?" Savanna cut in.

Paige was all too eager to answer her question. "Serena has mass manipulation. Her brother has power mimicry. One of her sisters is telepathic. Mr. Lindt is also telepathic. Mrs. Lindt is a precog."

"And you?" Ursula asked my sister.

"Telekinetic," Paige said proudly.

"So is Frank," I said. "Kase has the same power as Serena. He also mentioned a telekinetic sister, but I've never personally met her. I don't even know her name."

Jay-Jay nodded, taking mental notes as we hashed out the details of everyone's gifts, before he said vaguely, "I don't know when it happens, but it looks like soon. They seem to be after Serena."

"Who?" Paige asked.

I swallowed. I had a bad feeling I knew exactly who was after Serena.

Jay-Jay's voice was low as he mimicked the beat of the famous Paul Revere quote. "The radicals are coming. The radicals are coming." He broke into a sly smile. "They'll see us coming, but we'll still have the element of surprise on our side."

15 // OKAY, NOW WE'RE JUST MAKING THINGS UP

"He saw Serena through you," Savanna whispered as we strolled in circles along the backyard fence. It was dark, the moon barely visible in the night sky. It was nowhere near full and yet, somehow, the night felt eerie. My parents weren't back with Rebecca yet, and Savanna offered to stay until they returned. Ursula and Jay-Jay had left for their homes an hour before. It was my job to speak to Serena in the morning regarding Jay-Jay's vision. I hadn't told them about Serena's past, but I didn't have to. The only important detail was that a group of radicals were after her in the present. Savanna didn't like me interacting with Serena. I didn't tell her it was the same vice versa. It was clear the two girls hated each other. I could hear the slight annoyance in Savanna's tone as she brought up how Jay-Jay had encountered the vision of our enemies.

Sighing, I said, "She's my godsister. I've known her my whole life. Our parents are best friends." It made sense that there was a bond there, an invisible string. I chuckled, remembering the bond had come from my sister and me. "Paige has a crush on her brother."

Savanna nodded, biting her lip. "But you think of Serena as another sister, right?"

"No, thank God." I chortled, but Savanna's shoulders drooped along with her facial expression. She ducked her head, her brown hair falling in front of her face. I was confused at first. I thought that was the answer she was looking for. Running the conversation back in my head, I assessed what I had said wrong. It took a few reruns before I realized that Savanna had *wanted* me to think of Serena as a sister.

"Wait, hey." I brushed my fingers against her upper arm. The curtain of her hair shimmered at the touch. I let my hand fall back. "I just meant that I hate being around her. She's more obnoxious than my actual sisters. I'm glad she's not my sister. That way I don't have to live with her."

"You hate her?" Savanna tucked her hair behind her ear, glancing back at me in the dark.

I shrugged. "She's a self-righteous prick, and I'm not saying that for your benefit."

Savanna tried to argue with my assessment, shaking her head in disbelief. "But why are you always hanging with her? Every time I see you, you're either sitting next to her or speaking with her—sometimes laughing. What's that about?"

I stopped walking. She was stepping dangerously close to a point that would involve my sharing things I didn't want to share yet. Serena's involvement in my life was in the outer layer of the onion of my life. No, wait. I can't go with that comparison. That makes Serena sound like some sort of protector, and Savanna would hate that analogy. But I wasn't sure what a good analogy would be for the situation because the fact remained. "Uh, she's supposed to be looking out for everyone's best interest when it comes to me." I stared at my shoes, ashamed.

"I'm not following."

This was it. This was when she would find out that I wasn't good enough for her. I took a deep breath, let it out, and said slowly and quietly, "I'm not really this great guy. I'm cursed with bad luck. Th-that's probably why the radicals are coming for her. Her life was going good until I came back into it." My voice was barely a whisper now. "Whatever string Jay-Jay senses between you and I… it can't be good. Being with me will put your life in danger."

"I'm already in danger," she said breathily, stepping in front of me.

I refused to look at her face. She was right. The pending arrival of the radicals put all of us in danger. And the common factor that ties us all together? Me. I'm friends with Jay-Jay and Savanna. I'm practically family with the Lindts, never mind the actual members of my family in Jay-Jay's vision. And I'll probably incidentally end up getting Kase involved somehow.

When I didn't respond, Savanna said gently, "Jay-Jay's been catching glimpses of this event for weeks now, before your family moved in. He knew we would be in some sort of danger eventually—he just wasn't sure what kind of danger." She shook her head. "It's because he was missing the most important pieces. You helped him put the puzzle together tonight, and it's not because you're cursed or have bad luck or are *marime*, if you believe in that. Bradley, what you did tonight was good. How can you be bad luck if you're on our side? You helped us gain the upper hand—foresight. That sounds like good luck to me."

I closed my eyes and groaned. "Not you too." I let my face fall into my hands. Savanna's blindness was all Jay-Jay's fault. He was the one overselling me to this girl. I pressed my hands against my face, sliding them up onto my scalp. "At least with Serena, I can count on her being on my side with this."

Savanna didn't miss a beat, but I did see her take a step back. "Then she's lying to you." She sounded angry. I'd given her another reason to hate Serena. She groaned. "If anything, Serena's the one who started this mess. The radicals are after *her*. We just get in the way."

I didn't want to argue with her anymore. If I tried, I'd have to share more pieces of my past that I wasn't ready to discuss with anyone. I frowned. "Serena's had people after her before." We walked the perimeter of the yard, heading west to the back doors of the house. "If the radicals are who I think they are, they've been planning this attack for a long time. Part of me wonders if they've been biding their time, waiting for Serena to lead them straight to *us*."

"What are you talking about?" Savanna asked, a new kind of panic in her voice.

I took to the three steps of the wooden porch. "They're neo-Nazis."

Savanna gasped. "The New Order."

I froze, my foot hovering over the last step. "You know of them?"

Her blue eyes were wide, the color of her knuckles lightening as she gripped the wooden railing. Her voice cracked as she spoke. "My dad..." she struggled to continue, balancing on the bottom step.

I joined her at her side. "What?"

Blood started to drain from her face, her pallor turning several shades lighter. Her eyes glistened with the coming onslaught of tears. "He grew up in foster care. He wanted to know more about his ancestry, who his parents were and all that, so he started to do some digging when we lived in Georgia." Her breaths came in quick, small gasps before her legs gave way. I caught her—barely—and gently positioned her on the steps. She was still conscious, but hyperventilating. "His research clued in the New Order. They've been hunting the descendants of their enemies. They're the ones who killed his parents when he was little." Savanna's entire body seemed to be shaking, her fingers trembling in front of her face.

I wasn't sure what to do. I put my arm around her, but it didn't seem to make a difference.

She tried to clench her teeth, but they chattered instead. "They're the ones who made him an orphan. As soon as my dad figured out who they were, we fled the country. He was sure they would kill us too. We hid in Paris for three years before returning to the States, and that was only because being Romani in France was no picnic. Bradley"—she gripped the hand I had slung over her left shoulder—"if that's who's coming, I can't be anywhere near the fight. If they find out who I am, they'll kill me for sure and they'll kill my sister."

My grip tightened around her shoulders. "Savanna, the neo-Nazis hate all diviners. Why would you and Ursula matter more to them than the rest of us?"

Tears stained her cheeks. It took a moment for her to answer. When she did, it was a quiet whisper, as if she were afraid to say it aloud. "According to the New Order, my dad's grandmother assisted in the assassination of Adolf Hitler."

I would have pulled away in shock, but she was still gripping my hand tight, refusing to let it go. My mouth gaped and I imagined I looked ridiculous, but she wasn't watching my face. Her eyes seemed to be focused on her knees.

Did she really just tell me her great-grandmother killed Hitler? Serena would have a field day with this. Diviners killed Hitler. Fantastic. I didn't know why I was laughing. It was inappropriate for the conversation's seriousness, but I couldn't stop.

Savanna let go of my hand, shooting me a panicked look. "I'm serious!"

My arm dropped behind her. "I don't doubt you," I managed to say between fits of laughter. "I was just not expecting that piece of information." She waited for me to calm down. It took several tries, but after a few minutes, I was able to keep the laughter at bay. "Savanna, if we're going to have to protect you guys, we need to make sure our powers are in perfect sync," I said.

She nodded. "In other words, you're going to have to figure out a way to trick your powers into doing what they're supposed to."

Right. Savanna and Ursula had their powers down pat. It was me who was the problem. I stood, holding my hand out for her. She took it, and I pulled her up to her feet. "Thanks to Rebecca, we have an entire room that I can practice erasing," I said.

I walked back inside with Savanna. Blake was nowhere to be seen or heard. I guessed Paige had made him go to bed. The front room still held all of Rebecca's decorations. I was so excited to have an excuse to use my powers that I didn't stop to think about it much. Gripping the black bedazzled curtain with my fists, I willed it to disappear. It didn't. Why did I think that would be easy?

"Here." Savanna tossed a candle at me. I caught it, watching it dissipate the second it was in my hands. She raised an eyebrow at my disappointed expression. "Your powers operate on raw fear, remember?"

Fear. I studied the curtain again, trying to imagine that it was somehow dangerous to me. The bedazzled flames made it a little easier. I stared at them until they blurred in my vision, feeling my heart rate accelerate as I imagined real flames licking the fabric. My powers wouldn't want me to be burned, right? *Fire*, I thought. *Flames. I'm about to touch flames.* Squinting and shaking, I extended one hand to touch the fabric. Within seconds, it was gone. I gasped in relief, opening my eyes wider. "I did it!"

Savanna hopped on one foot, throwing her hands into the air. "Yay!"

The front door opened, my mother's worried voice trailing in. "But I don't understand, Chastain. If nothing is wrong with her, why can't I see her future?"

Savanna and I froze, watching the hallway.

"I don't know, honey," Dad answered tiredly. I was sure Mom had asked the same question a million times already. They came into our view, Dad carrying a sleeping Rebecca, Mom's brown eyes frantic with her fear of the unknown. Dad strode toward the stairs. "I'm gonna tuck her into bed."

Mom nodded then turned to see Savanna and me watching her from the front room. She sighed. "You're still here." Her voice was kind. I was sure if she hadn't been so panicky, she'd have smiled at Savanna.

"I wanted to make sure Rebecca was okay before I went home," Savanna said. "I'm sure Ursula won't be bothering her anymore." She glanced out the newly uncovered window at the darkness. "I better get going. It's a school night." Mom and I said a quick goodbye to Savanna as she dashed out the door. I watched her from the window as she sprinted across the street into the safety of her home.

"I hope you two work out." Mom sighed again, clearly exhausted from the night's events.

My lip twitched as I glanced sideways at my mother. "What do you know?"

She shrugged. "I sense a strong bond between the two of you." Yawning, she dismissed herself upstairs for the night, leaving me alone with my thoughts.

I turned back to the red and black room. Savanna had theorized that my powers were tied to fear, but I was beginning to see that it was more than that. Self-preservation was what operated it. That explanation made a lot more sense. It wasn't that I was afraid an object might hurt me. I've been hurt my fair share of times. It was more like a survival instinct, like my brain didn't care too much about cuts and bruises, but about me surviving. I gasped at the thought.

"You are a survivor," Mom's and Jay-Jay's voices rang in my head. Suddenly, the mantra no longer bothered me. The clue to using my powers was right in front of me all along. I always survive. But then again, that was the problem. I may always survive, but other people always die. How was I supposed to protect Savanna when I couldn't protect Jesse, or Lenora, or my childhood friend and his family, or the other kids whose bodies are decomposing in the Sangre de Cristo Mountains? My powers only cared about me. That was the true curse I had been given. I have zero ability to protect anyone but myself. *What a selfish power.*

I sank to the ground, my reflection appearing a hundred times in the crystals of the chandelier. Somebody else was going to have to protect the Huckleberrys. Someone with extraordinary abilities outside of my realm of expertise. Someone like Rebecca. I shook my head at the thought. I wasn't going to bring my ten-year-old sister into this, even with her enhanced abilities. She was too young and fragile, and it would traumatize her further by placing her directly in the path of the New Order. I wished she were older and stronger because her powers would be a real asset to the fight. I wished I could be that powerful of an asset.

I wondered what made the New Order a threat if they didn't have any powers. They must be powerful in other ways for the diviners in Indianapolis to fear them. Serena, Jay-Jay, and Savanna hadn't shared any details regarding this, but judging by Savanna's panic earlier, there had to be something that made their death threats extra terrifying. I wondered why we never ran across them in Chicago. If the New Order wanted to seek Romanies, whether they were diviners or not, Chicago would be the best place to look for us. We didn't even try to hide much there. Mom used her gifts openly. What was so different about Indianapolis? Was it the challenge of the hunt? There were fewer of us in Indy. Most of us hid our abilities better out of fear. Almost every family of diviners I knew of in Indy had some sort of connection to the worst events of World War II. Was that it? Could we all be connected to Nazi Germany in one way or another?

My great-grandmother, Grandma What's-Her-Name Anderson. She was in Poland during the war. Was that *my* connection? Did she survive Auschwitz-Birkenau like some of Kase's ancestors? Or was she a part of Hitler's assassination like Savanna's great-grandmother? Is that why my grandmother fled to America? To escape the wrath of the Nazis? Is that why she chose an inconspicuous southern state to take refuge in? Is that why she married a man who wasn't Polish nor Romani so that her last name would change along with her son's? Is that why she fled Tennessee when my mother was a teenager? Did she think they would find her?

So many questions swirled in my head at once. Though it felt like I was getting warmer with every question that passed, the possibilities didn't leave me relieved. They escalated my fear. I brushed my hand through the crystals of the chandelier, watching each dangling gem disappear before my eyes. I wished my fears could disappear the same way.

16 // NOBODY BELIEVES ME—I'M MISTER UNRELIABLE

I don't know when I fell asleep. My mom shook me awake. When I opened my eyes, her brows knitted and worry lines wrinkled her forehead. Her eyes searched my face, looking through my grogginess for a sign that I was all right. It took me a minute to realize where I was. I must have fallen asleep on the loveseat in the front room. My legs were cramped in the small two-person sitting space, my neck aching from sleeping at an awkward angle. The room appeared to be back to normal, except for the red carpet.

"Did you do this?" my mother asked. "Did you stay up all night to put the room back together?"

I sat up and rubbed my eyes. Did I? I must have. My siblings stood in the archway, peering in with fascination. They all had their backpacks slung around their shoulders, ready to go to school. I leaped to my feet. Why hadn't they woken me sooner? I had to get to school. I had to warn Serena.

Mom frowned. "Honey, if you want to stay here and sleep a little more, that's okay. You had a long night."

I shook my head, bounding up the stairs. "No, I have to go to school today."

I made everyone late. Mom had to personally sign everyone in at their respective schools, which made us all even later. Frank was standing behind the attendance officers when Mom escorted me into school. He nodded to us in relief, and I ran off to class, leaving my mother to explain.

Mrs. Lindt didn't say anything when I walked into class twenty minutes late. She was handing out small paperback versions of *To Kill a Mockingbird*.

I slid into my seat next to Serena. "I need to talk to you."

Serena performed a double take when she saw me. "Is your sister all right? She didn't faint or have a seizure or anything this morning, did she?"

"What?" Oh. I shook my head and whispered furiously, "No, but something bad's going to happen if you don't listen to me."

"Is that a threat?" Her voice wasn't a whisper. Everybody in the room froze, all eyes on us. I glared at her. She smiled teasingly back. Now was so not the time for her antics.

Mrs. Lindt asked to speak with me out in the hall. Well, if I couldn't tell Serena, then I guessed it was time to clue in the adults.

"What's going on?" Mrs. Lindt asked as the classroom door clicked shut behind us. Her arms were crossed. She wasn't in the mood for shenanigans. Good. Neither was I.

"Something bad's about to go down," I tried to explain in a hushed tone. "One of my friends had a vision that the New Order was coming."

She raised her eyebrows at my story, but the rest of her body language didn't change. "Bradley, you cannot let what Serena told you influence your nightmares." She eyed the bags underneath my eyes. "Your mom told me you have enough of them as it is. I wish my daughter hadn't told you why we left Terre Haute. It's not our intention to traumatize you further. There's nothing you need to worry about."

I balled up my fists, frustrated that she was using my trauma to discredit me. My response was forced through clenched teeth. "This wasn't a nightmare. My friend Jay-Jay saw it."

She bent down slightly to look me straight in the eyes. Nodding her head like she was reassuring a toddler, she responded slowly, "If something was happening, I would have seen it. Now are you going to go sit at your desk quietly or do I need to call Frank?"

I glowered the rest of the morning. I would have tried to tell Frank about Jay-Jay's vision during success time, but after the way Mrs. Lindt had responded, I was worried Frank would send me home. The fact that diviners like to weigh heavily on the visions, or lack thereof, of the precogs is becoming inconvenient. My own mother couldn't see my sister's future anymore. In fact, I didn't think she could see anything accurately at all. So, what made Mrs. Lindt think that if something were going on, she'd know about it?

Jay-Jay sat across from me at lunch like he always did, except this time, he wasn't exactly his overeager self. He stared across the cafeteria at the popular table, studying Serena's body language. "She seems to be taking this well."

Serena laughed at a joke one of the football players made, slapping the back of her hand against Kase's upper arm.

"I didn't tell her," I mumbled, biting into a carrot.

"What?" Jay-Jay half stood, his hands slamming on the tabletop.

I leaned back warily. "She made a scene in English class about me threatening her, and so then I was threatened by Mrs. Lindt, who didn't believe me about any of this, by the way, and was almost sent to Frank's office for bad behavior." Dropping the rest of my carrot on the table, I groaned in frustration. "You know what? Why am I even trying to save her? Why don't we just let the Nazis have her?" I said that last part too loud, inviting some strange looks from our neighbors.

Jay-Jay waved his hand, dismissing their unwanted curiosity. "What? You guys never played Wolfenstein?" They shrugged and looked away. He rolled his eyes. I must have looked lost, because he elaborated. "It's a video game." Returning to the topic at hand, he shot me an annoyed gaze. "What Nazis?"

I hesitated, rethinking the possibility. "That's who the radicals are, right?"

He blinked. This time it was his turn to rethink. Slowly, he found the words he was searching for. "Is that who Serena has been researching?" He almost growled his next words, a fist coming down on the table. "The New Order?"

I never thought I'd see Jay-Jay angry, especially not this angry. He marched to her table, standing so that she could see him. The anger in his expression must have surprised her as much as it did me, maybe more, because she immediately stood and followed him back to our table.

She looked frightened. I never thought one glare from someone as harmless as Jay-Jay could terrify a person, but I was witnessing the oddity with my own eyes. Her voice was shaky as she stood at the end of our table, her eyes never leaving Jay-Jay. "What is it?"

Jay-Jay looked like he was having trouble speaking. He kept wordlessly opening his mouth and shutting it again, his frustration contorting his facial expression into something I didn't recognize. Finally, he gritted his teeth, and his dark eyes locked with Serena's. "The New Order?"

A slow smile crept up her face, the puzzle pieces fitting together perfectly. "I knew it! I knew you were a—" Before she could say "diviner," I stood and clamped my hand over her mouth. Her eyes were wide with excitement.

Jay-Jay didn't let her surprise dissolve his anger. He slammed his fist on the table, jolting everything on it, including a few of our tablemates' arms. "The New Order?"

I let go of her, watching her smile fade. She turned to me, fury burning in her round eyes. "You told him?"

I shook my head violently, trying to avoid her unnecessary wrath. I hadn't. The only person I had said anything to was Savanna, and all I mentioned was that neo-Nazis had been after her before. It had been just enough information to freak Savanna out. Jay-Jay was intuitive that way. Hadn't Serena noticed? He didn't know her past, but he did know that she would bring the radicals upon us because of her research. At least, that's what I was gathering from his cryptic sentences.

Jay-Jay grabbed her hand, refusing to let it go as she tugged and tried to pull away. "You have no idea the kind of danger you've put us in, Serena. Especially on Savanna. The New Order *cannot* come here." The venom in his voice was almost lethal. I barely recognized the guy in front of me. She twisted her arm, struggling against his grip. I was sure she was wishing we weren't in a public space. Then she could phase right through his grip.

Kase appeared out of nowhere, his hands separating Jay-Jay and Serena's. "Get your hands off her, freak!"

Jay-Jay stood on his chair so that he could tower over Kase. He looked like he was about to start a fight. I backed off, hoping I wouldn't end up being seen as an accomplice. Jabbing his finger into Kase's chest, Jay-Jay said with a growl, "Your girlfriend is going to get us all killed!" He was making a scene. People were starting to stare, and it wasn't the same ones who'd been listening to our conversations for three weeks—the ones nearby seemed to think our conversations were nonsense.

Kase clocked Jay-Jay, knocking him from his chair onto the ground. For a split second, I thought maybe Kase would kill him before the Nazis did. Jay-Jay was scrawny and in no way a fair match against him.

Before the fight could escalate, though, Frank came running in. "Hey, break it up!" I wasn't sure who tipped him off or if anyone had for that matter. Maybe he had been close enough to hear the change in the atmosphere. He pointed to us all individually, clearly not thrilled to be breaking up a fight three weeks into the school year. "You four, in my office!"

I should have expected this, but I didn't. Frank was the king of interventions. He didn't have enough chairs for everyone to sit, so we stood, most of our arms crossed, as he tried not to raise his voice too much. The room wasn't completely soundproof. After he yelled at us for fighting—and yes, I mean all of us—he gasped in a lungful of air before breathing it out in a long gust of wind. Pinching the bridge of his nose, Frank dared to ask, "So what is this about?"

Kase shuffled his feet. He had absolutely no idea—always throwing punches before asking questions. I glanced at Jay-Jay, who was glaring at Serena. She wasn't looking at anybody, her jaw set, eyes focused on the wall. I knew she could feel the heat radiating from Jay-Jay's eyes.

Nobody was saying anything, so I begrudgingly took it upon myself to answer. "Jay-Jay had a vision that someone was after Serena."

Serena's head shot back up, and she swiveled to meet my gaze. "What?"

Frank straightened his back at the announcement, staring at Serena and ignoring the news of Jay-Jay's diviner status.

Kase wasn't as subtle. "Dude, wait—what? You're a diviner?" He shook his head in amazement. "I totally didn't see that coming, bruh!"

Frank tried to meet Jay-Jay's gaze, but Jay-Jay was still glaring at Serena. "Tell me about this vision," Frank said.

Jay-Jay's teeth were bared. "Ask her why she's researching the New Order."

"Who's the New Order?" Kase's heavyset brows furrowed. I was surprised he didn't know.

Frank was the one who answered him. "They're a domestic terrorist organization operating as a legal political party. They have several bases here in the Midwest with members across the country. You might recognize the term 'white supremacists.'"

Recognition sparked in Kase's expression. "Like that doctor who was after Serena's family a few years back?"

Frank nodded.

A few more puzzle pieces clicked together for Jay-Jay. His expression softened the teeniest bit as he stared into Serena's fearful eyes. "You're researching them because they've been after you before? This isn't new to you?" He stepped toward her. "You can't dig into their lives, Serena!"

"Why not?" Serena said, jutting out her chin. I'm sure she meant for her tone to sound more demanding, but it sounded a little strangled. I cringed.

"Because," Jay-Jay hissed, "they'll dig back into yours."

Serena looked like she was going to pass out. Kase tried to ebb our worry, pumping himself up for a fight. "We can fight them though, can't we? I mean, between the five of us, we've got mondo power, and Serena and I are practically bulletproof—"

"Your mom hasn't had a vision about this?" Frank asked Serena.

She took a seat in one of the chairs, shaking her head and biting her nails.

"She didn't believe me this morning when I tried to warn her," I said.

Frank plopped into his chair, tapping his fingers together. He stayed like that for a long time, long enough for the bell ending our lunchtime to ring. The bell seemed to jar him from his thoughts. Frank glanced at Jay-Jay, his eyebrows raised. "Are you sure you saw a vision of the New Order coming here?"

Jay-Jay seemed to calm down in the silence, but I could tell he was still apprehensive. "I can't be sure," he said, tapping his fingers against his leg. "But they fit the description, and they're also who make the most sense. They began their hunt with Serena, and since Serena has been looking into their lives..." He trailed off, his point already made.

Frank nodded. "We're going to need to beef up security. Do you know where and when they contact Serena?"

Jay-Jay shook his head, his disappointment in himself evident by the frown on his face. "I wish I knew. All I know is that when they do get her—and they will—they keep her in a warehouse of some kind. They know we'll be coming to save her. That's the plan. They want to lure as many of us into a trap as they can."

"They're not going to hurt me, are they?" Serena asked in a small, trembling voice. "They need me, right? I'm just the bait?"

Jay-Jay ignored her, waiting for Frank's response.

"Serena," Frank said and swallowed hard. "I'm going to protect you as much as I can, do you hear me? I am going to get you back just as quickly as they take you from me."

Serena started to cry.

"You're just gonna let them take her?" Kase bellowed.

Frank held up his hand. "I'm not going to let them do anything, but precog visions are static, unchanging. Whatever Jay-Jay sees is what's going to happen."

"Then unsee it!" Kase shouted at Jay-Jay.

"Kase," Frank warned, before returning his attention back to Serena. "I'm going to let you go to class, all of you," he said, glancing at us. "I have no doubt you'll be safe with your dad this hour. I'll join you in sixth hour and stand in the back of the class. I doubt they'll try to take you here, but it's just a precaution." He dismissed us, waving us away, but Jay-Jay had one more request.

"Officer, there's something else you should know. The Huckleberrys have been on the New Order's hit list for a while. Savanna Huckleberry's a student here, ninth grade, like us. She'll also need protection."

Frank nodded. "I'll see what I can do."

17 // I THINK WE BROKE SERENA

It took a while for Serena to calm down. We left for our classes ahead of her, each with an excused late pass. Kase wasn't happy to separate from us—he didn't want Jay-Jay out of his sight. I could tell he didn't have much experience with precogs, and I briefly wondered what kind of gifts his parents had. Then I remembered that, whatever gifts they had, they probably didn't use them. The Schwartzes wanted to be normal, craved it with their entire beings—more than my sister, more than me, more than anyone I knew. Kase was probably the one person in his family willing to fight. His parents had warned the Lindts to stay away, to hide like they were. If they discovered any of this, I was sure they'd be gone in a flash.

Jay-Jay and I entered our algebra class ten minutes late.

"Where's Serena?" Mr. Lindt asked me telepathically. I could tell he was worried. Serena was unlike any girl I'd ever known—she was never late. Miss Goody Two-shoes, Teacher's Pet, and all that. She loved the charade of the perfect student.

I didn't have a chance to formulate a gentler response, his question automatically triggering the image of Serena crying in Frank's office. Have I mentioned I hate telepaths? They're impatient people. Mr. Lindt's brown eyes blinked rapidly into a squint. "Is she in ..." he brought his hand to his face, pressing his fingers against his temples. "Is that Frank's office?" His voice in my head was muffled by static, like he was an old television losing reception.

Another student asked if he was okay. To them, Mr. Lindt probably looked like he was fighting a headache. Actually, it *did* look like he was fighting a headache. Do telepaths struggle with their powers when they experience headaches? I tried to answer him back with my thoughts, but it didn't appear he was hearing me. He kept looking at me expectantly. After a painfully long several seconds, I gave up and nodded my head.

Jay-Jay and I took our seats, watching as Mr. Lindt plopped into his desk chair and dialed Frank's extension. The other students were all focused on a piece of paper on their desks, some punching in numbers on a calculator, others chewing the erasers off their pencils. I looked at my desk. Crap. I had forgotten all about the quiz. Mr. Lindt murmured quietly into the receiver. His words were impossible to hear from where we sat. I could tell when Frank mentioned Jay-Jay's vision because Mr. Lindt's eyes grew wide with terror—he positioned his head so he was staring right at Jay-Jay. I turned so I could see Jay-Jay's face, to see if I could catch the moment in which Mr. Lindt spoke telepathically to him for the first time, but his anxious expression didn't change.

"No, I don't think it's safer." Mr. Lindt said, hissing a little louder into the phone. A few students looked at him curiously. He waved their glances away, reminding them to pay attention to the quiz. I hadn't read question one, and I guarantee Jay-Jay hadn't either.

Serena was back in class before the hour was up. Her eyes held no hint that she'd been crying, but her expression was droopy and morose. Her dad watched her anxiously as she slumped into her seat. She didn't say anything to us, didn't even acknowledge that we were there. She stared at her desk, unseeing, her mind clearly somewhere else. Her behavior upset me more than I wanted it to. I couldn't help but feel her sadness, her fear, and wanted nothing more than to have the ability to take it from her. It was the same feeling I had felt for Savanna the night before and the same feeling I had felt for Rebecca the Saturday before that.

When the bell rang to end class, Mr. Lindt approached us, shaking, sweat dripping from his forehead. He placed a trembling hand on Serena's desk, his round eyes narrowing in concentration. After scrutinizing each one of us for several uncomfortable seconds, he blinked, a new worry line creasing his forehead. "Something's wrong."

Serena appeared to be focusing on keeping her mouth shut, trying to hold back any more tears that may come her way. Jay-Jay and I waited patiently for Mr. Lindt to elaborate. When he did, he choked on his words. "My powers aren't working."

My heart skipped a beat. Jay-Jay frowned, his brain forcing itself into overdrive. He started murmuring to himself, too low for any of us to hear. After a minute of this, he abruptly stood and walked out of the room.

I glanced at Serena, who was slowly gathering her books. Frank had been wrong. She wasn't safe with her dad, not when his powers were fried. I hoped the glitch in his gift was temporary. The timing was inconvenient. I followed Serena to our next class, refusing to let her out of my sight. It was strange how the tables had turned since the first week of school. *I* was now the one babysitting *her*.

Frank nodded at us from the back of Mrs. Scar's classroom. Jay-Jay was occupying most of his attention, likely hashing out theories to him in hushed tones. As I approached Savanna, who was sitting in her usual seat in the front row, I noticed Frank's eyes shift to a piece of loose paper on Jay-Jay's desk, his concern growing.

"Hey, Savanna," I said, trying to figure out how I was going to discretely catch her up to speed in front of her friends. I nodded to Frank, her blue eyes following my line of sight. "Think of him as a bodyguard."

One of her friends' eyes widened, her red hair whipping around her shoulders as her head turned toward Frank then back to me. "Is something going to happen? Was there a threat?" I froze. Did she know about Savanna's past?

Savanna shook her head, reassuring her friend. "No one threatened to shoot up the school, Marcie. At least, I don't think." She eyed the officer in the corner. Marcie didn't look reassured, but I relaxed, realizing the reason behind her concern was... normal, though just as terrifying as the real reason for Frank's presence. Lucky for her, she wouldn't be a target.

When I took my seat, Jay-Jay joined me, filling me in on his epiphany. "The adults' powers are down."

I shot a quick glance at Frank, who didn't seem bothered too much by the revelation. His composure didn't leave me any less concerned. This was not good. Serena was basically a sitting duck. We were *all* sitting ducks.

"He still has his gun, his taser, and his experience in the police force. He's hoping that'll be enough to intimidate them." Jay-Jay said, explaining Frank's lack of worry.

"He's one man," I said.

Jay-Jay shrugged. "There weren't any adult diviners in my vision. This explains why. I'm still getting my visions, so whatever is affecting their abilities, it's not affecting me, and it hopefully isn't going to affect the rest of us. You have the same power as Savanna, right? Do your powers still work?"

I hesitated. There wasn't any way for me to test them unless I wanted to embarrass myself with the one poor excuse of a Kleenex I could conjure. I recalled my reason for arriving late this morning. "They were working last night."

"Psst." Jay-Jay snapped his fingers in Savanna's direction, whispering loud enough for her to hear. "Do you have a pencil?" She rolled her eyes, stuck her hand in her bag, and pulled out a number two pencil. The pencil was passed to her friend, a neighbor, and then back a row until it reached Jay-Jay's outstretched hands. He held up the pencil, lowering his voice back to a quiet whisper. "Savanna's works."

I studied the pencil in his hand dubiously. "How do you know?"

He winked. "She never carries pencils."

I let out a sigh of relief, reaching for the materialized object. Savanna had, incidentally, given me a way to assess my powers. Cupping the pencil in my hands underneath my desk, I willed it to go away. This time I didn't have to imagine a threat. Its quick disappearance shocked me. I proudly held up my empty hands. "Still working better than ever."

Mrs. Scar asked Frank if he would like a chair, but he refused. I wondered what excuse he had given her for his presence before I realized it was probably me. I was the excuse. Bradley the security risk. Bradley the flight risk. Bradley the I-don't-even-wanna-know-what risk. It wasn't a stretch. I moved here after being involved in a school shooting. I wondered if Mrs. Scar knew that or if they had given my teachers any details at all. Maybe she just thought I was a "bad kid" and let her imagination run wild with the possibilities. Drugs? Alcohol? Fights? Gangs? Endless possibilities.

Serena was still zombie-like. History was her favorite subject, but she kept her mouth screwed shut, refusing to ask questions. She didn't even look like she was taking notes, just scribbling aimlessly in her journal. Her deviance from the norm was distracting.

In our last class, Savanna raced to meet us. Now that she was away from her friends, she could have a real conversation with us, gathering the details she had missed. When Jay-Jay and I were finished catching her up, Serena finally opened her mouth to utter one small question: "So you're one of us?" Her facial expression was blank, her words toneless. When Savanna nodded, Serena said, "When Jay-Jay said you were in danger, I thought it was because you were normal. It wasn't until he said you were on a hitlist that it clicked in my head." She paused, taking a breath. "I'm sorry."

Savanna stared at her, shocked into silence. Honestly, I was shocked too. I rarely ever heard Serena apologize, and in the times that I had, she never had uttered the words in such a sincere manner. It was strange witnessing another person's screwup. Usually, things like this happened because of me. Sure, I was still involved, but only in the rescue effort. Savanna was right. I hadn't caused this or made it worse. I knew how Serena felt. I'd been there. In fact, I was *just* there. I felt a sense of guilt and a sense of freedom. Guilt, because it seemed like I had passed on the torch, like I had handed her all my pain. I felt freedom for the same reason. For once, I wasn't the bad guy in this scenario.

"You have nothing to apologize for." Kase squeezed Serena's hand.

"The hell she does," Jay-Jay hissed, his anger returning.

Frank must've sensed the hostility between them because he ambled over to our gathering, shooting them warning glances. Jay-Jay maintained his composure, but Kase appeared ready to pounce. Frank cleared his throat, loud enough for it to gain the teacher's attention, who raised an eyebrow at our group. We were sitting where we had the day Savanna and Serena left class. He'd been keeping us separated since.

Jay-Jay changed the subject, nodding toward Kase and Serena. "Your guys' powers work, right?"

"Of course." Kase smirked, letting his hand float through Serena's. She yanked hers back in annoyance. It was clear Kase liked to use his powers without warning, a tactic that I thought might come in handy when we went up against the Nazis. Serena casually brushed her fingers through her dark hair. It was barely noticeable, but I thought I saw her fingers phase through a few strands.

Jay-Jay nodded. He didn't explain to Kase why he was asking. He never brought it up with Savanna either. I wondered if there was a reason. Maybe he didn't want to add to their fear. Something told me to play along with his silence. I was glad nobody was asking questions.

Savanna told her friends she wasn't feeling well and skipped cheer practice, but Kase refused to miss football. The ninth-grade players were getting ready for their first game this Saturday. Frank was struggling with the logistics of protecting all five of us and our families, especially when we could no longer rely on our parents to protect us. Jay-Jay refused to let Frank worry about him. His dad had left a long time ago and his mom hadn't had powers to begin with. He didn't think she would be a target.

"Besides," Jay-Jay said, "I'll be able to see if something's going to happen."

Frank thought he could stake out Savanna's and my street, but that would leave the Lindts and Schwartzes vulnerable. He mumbled something about wishing he had the power of multiplication so he could be in multiple places at once. Kase didn't want to alert his parents to the problem either, and this left Frank even more unsure of how to protect them.

"Just focus on Serena," Kase said as he headed to practice. "I can handle my family."

"What if the Lindts stayed with your family?" Frank asked me after Savanna disappeared to tell her friends she'd be missing practice.

I grimaced. "I kind of wanted to keep my parents out of this."

"Why?" Frank asked. His entire job involved maintaining the trust of our parents. He didn't like the idea of keeping secrets from them.

"Now's not the time to be selfish, Bradley," Jay-Jay said.

"I'm not being selfish." I crossed my arms in front of my chest. "It's just that my mom gets overly anxious when her powers fail her. She already knows she can't see Rebecca. I don't want to make things worse for her."

Frank waved away my worries. "The Lindts are staying with you guys. End of discussion."

Serena followed me to my parents' van when her parents left to pick up their other children. Frank was going to follow Savanna home and park between our two houses.

When the rest of the Lindts arrived at the house, it was Kevin who appeared the most confused. His parents hadn't explained anything other than the obvious—that they were staying with us for an indefinite block of time. Mya seemed to be well-informed, her powers of telepathy still intact. Kevin hadn't picked up on this fact. He was too distracted by the auras surrounding his parents.

"That's how Kevin sees our powers," Paige told me later. "We all have an aura with different colors and locations on our bodies, depending on the power. Mom and his parents don't look like they're supposed to. They're covered from head to toe in a shroud of light gray. If he doesn't look directly at them, the shroud almost looks clear, like how the undivine usually appear to him. He can't mimic it either. The auras won't budge."

"He didn't notice anything this morning?" I asked her, remembering Mom's freak-out from the night before. If it all had started then, wouldn't Kevin have seen the change in his parents' auras in the morning? Paige shook her head.

Interesting. I wasn't sure what it meant. Mrs. Lindt's powers had disappeared somewhere between when Kevin last saw her in the morning and my English class. That was a short, specific amount of time. Mr. Lindt's powers were still working when I talked to him in algebra, but they had faded fast. Frank wasn't sure when he had lost his. He hadn't noticed until world history. It was like something was blocking their abilities, like an electromagnetic pulse disrupts technology. Was there such a thing as an EMP for diviners? Could someone flip on a switch, resulting in any diviner within its radius losing access to their gifts? And why was it only impacting the adults?

I shook my head at the ridiculous thought. It didn't make sense when different diviners were losing their powers at different dates and times. Besides, our powers worked because of a gene, as far as I knew. Could a device like an EMP function as a gene inhibitor? That seemed a little far-fetched.

I hated waiting. I think we all hated waiting. I could sense the anxiousness in the house, overhearing conversations from some of the adults about leaving. My heart faltered at the thought. We hadn't lived here a month. If we moved again, well, one, that would be a new record for us, and two, who's to say the New Order wouldn't continue to track us? I didn't want to be running for the rest of my life. I didn't think anybody did.

"They can't possibly follow all of us if we separate," I overheard Mrs. Lindt say.

Her husband grumbled. "I think they outnumber us, sweetheart. This sounds like a much bigger threat than the one person from Terre Haute."

"The New Order has members all over the nation." Mom sighed in defeat. "Where would we run?"

I thought of Savanna's family, how they had fled the country the first time the New Order came after them. I couldn't imagine living anywhere outside the United States. Jay-Jay was right. We would have to stay and fight.

It was a new concept to some of us who'd been taught to avoid confrontation. The Romani people had always moved to avoid moments like these. My parents, especially, didn't like to stay in places where conflict held the potential to hurt our family. It wasn't that we were cowards. We wanted peace. The Schwartzes wanted peace. Mom and Dad wanted peace. The Lindts wanted peace. War wasn't peace. Mom always chose her words carefully, always reciting the mantra, "Fighting never solves anything." Maybe, in most cases, she was right. This time, though, we didn't see an out.

18 // WHY AM I ALWAYS THE ONE WHO SCREWS UP?

We were all still in town on Saturday. Mom kept packing our things back into boxes before changing her mind and unpacking. Dad didn't know what to do. He continued to go to work as if nothing were wrong, but I could tell he was worried. The phone would ring every half an hour so that he could hear Mom's voice to know if she was all right.

I guess I would use the phrase "all right" loosely. She wasn't exactly all right. She didn't know what to expect, and this made her behavior over the week incredibly unpredictable. One day I came home from school to a kitchen overflowing with baked goods. Another day, Mom had packs of tarot cards displayed on the coffee table, frantically searching for any supernatural clues of what the future held. I didn't think she believed in that stuff, but... Desperate times call for desperate measures.

Kase refused to skip his first football game of the season, so Frank suggested we get ourselves out of the house and join him at the game. He didn't like us in the open air, but at least we'd be in a public space surrounded by witnesses if anything were to happen. The games weren't nearly as packed as I imagined the JV and varsity games usually were. The crowd was mostly parents, family members, and friends. We were playing a school from Greenwood, their red and white uniforms sticking out in our sea of black and gold. Savanna and the other ninth-grade cheerleaders were at the sidelines in their white cheer uniforms, a gold bow displayed prominently in their varying hairstyles.

"What's your mascot again?" Blake asked for the thousandth time that morning.

"The Warriors." I lifted a bottle of water to my mouth.

The game was an early day game, like most of the games for ninth-grade players were. We were sitting in the center of the bleachers in broad daylight, Frank hanging out at the field's entrance. Kase's parents were in the front row on the far east side. It was clear they were his parents because they were wearing matching T-shirts with his name and number. I assumed the girl who was with them was Kase's younger sister. I recognized Savanna's mom near the top. She didn't seem to be paying much attention to the game. She was hunched over paperwork, a cell phone plastered to her ear. Ursula was pacing nervously beside her, her eyes flickering between us, the Schwartzes, and her sister. I wondered where Savanna's dad was and why I'd never seen him before.

"I gotta say, this is not how I planned to spend my Saturday." I whirled around at the sound of Jay-Jay's voice. He grimaced at the field. "My dad used to beg me to play sports. He got pissed every time I complained about T-ball." He took a bite of his hot dog, chewing as he talked. "I think I managed to hit the ball once."

Great. With Jay-Jay's power being practically useless in a fight, I had been hoping he'd at least have hand-eye coordination. Apparently, that was too much to hope for.

"We have to figure out the game plan." I tried not to speak too loudly in case my parents were listening. Mom would freak if she realized we were gearing up to fight alone.

Jay-Jay's mind was still on sports. "The Trojans are gonna smash us."

I rolled my eyes. "I meant the ordeal with the New Order."

"Oh." Jay-Jay frowned. "The plan is to wait for Serena to get kidnapped. I thought we were on the same page." He took another bite of his hot dog.

I groaned. "Yes, but what are we going to do after? We need to determine where they'll be taking her so we can get there before they can inflict too much damage."

The cheerleaders started shouting in synchronization, waving their pom-poms to-and-fro. Jay-Jay's lips curled into a slow smile as he watched them. When their cheer was over, he turned back to me, the same smile stretched across his face. "Did you know Savanna is a black belt?"

I flinched in surprise. I really should stop being surprised by anything these days. Savanna was growing more impressive by the minute.

"She's also taken kickboxing classes with her sister, who's a green belt. The Huckleberrys have been training their whole lives for this moment. The New Order has always been a scary story to them. Savanna was too young to remember their time in Georgia. Ursula was born while they lived in France. They have no memories of being chased or threatened. It's their dad who keeps them living in fear, who signs them up for self-defense training, who is always encouraging them to get in touch with their abilities. The first time I met him, I thought he was a crime boss." Jay-Jay snorted. "Dude's a scary guy."

I glanced back at Ursula and Mrs. Huckleberry. "So, where is he?"

Jay-Jay shrugged nonchalantly. "Probably sweet-talking a couple into buying their first home. He's a major name in real estate around here." He pondered that for a second before chuckling to himself. "He could be a crime boss."

I looked back at Savanna's mom, who was eyeing our large group curiously. When her light-colored eyes landed on my mom and Mr. and Mrs. Lindt, her forehead creased with confusion and concern. It was the same face Kevin had made the night the Lindts came to stay with us. *No way*. Immediately, I turned back to Jay-Jay, sputtering out the words as quickly as I could. "I don't think our theory about all the adults losing their powers is correct."

Jay-Jay glanced at Mrs. Huckleberry with hopeful eyes. I tapped on Kevin's shoulder. He turned and I jerked my head toward the top of the bleachers. "Can you see her powers?"

Kevin's eyes widened. His voice was shrouded in awe. "She sparkles." Holding out his arm like he was offering a fist bump, he looked at his light brown skin. "I've never met anyone like me before."

Paige turned around next to him. She looked disappointed that she couldn't also see the sparkles.

"Mrs. Huckleberry still has her powers," Jay-Jay said, watching her. "I wonder why that is?"

"We didn't tell Savanna about the adults losing their powers," I said, recalling the events from Tuesday afternoon. "She wouldn't have known to check." Mrs. Huckleberry's eyes flickered to the far bottom corner of the bleachers where the Schwartzes sat, then to the field where Kase was playing. I wondered if she was used to seeing this many diviners in one place. *Never mind,* I thought, *that was a stupid question.* Of course, she wasn't used to it. She started to look a little uneasy.

I pointed to the Schwartzes and said, addressing Kevin, "Can you see their powers too?"

Kevin's brown eyes locked on the matching trio in the front row. He nodded. "I don't know their powers, though. They won't tell me and they're the only people I've met with auras like theirs. I know that Rice is telekinetic."

Jay-Jay spit out his last bite of hot dog. "They named Kase's sister after food?"

Kevin huffed. "Don't give her any crap. People do that enough at school as it is."

"She goes to your school?" Paige asked. I could hear the jealousy in her voice. Kevin ignored it, nodding as if the truth wouldn't matter to her.

I tried to refocus on the subject at hand before Paige could make a big deal of it. "Wait, so, all the other adults have their powers except our parents and Frank?" I glanced again at Mrs. Huckleberry and back at Kase's parents. "Does anyone else find that a little suspicious?"

Jay-Jay's lips pressed into a hard line. "They're the only two families who don't know what's going on either. Savanna and Ursula never keyed in their parents, and as far as I can tell, Kase has zero intention of sharing any of this with his. You say suspicious? I say highly. They can't fight if they don't know who they're fighting. Until they became active players in this game"—he shook his head—"they still get to keep their powers."

It was a theory, but like most of our theories, it also seemed a little ridiculous. This wasn't a video game. This was real life.

I stood, nodding to Ursula and her mom. "I'm going to go say hi."

Jay-Jay grabbed my arm, hissing, "Don't bring her mom into this." He paused for a second, cocking his head to the side, his eyes zoning out.

I pulled my arm away before whatever vision he was seeing could fully manifest itself. "I just want to talk to her." Jay-Jay wasn't listening, his eyes still unfocused. I let him stay in his vision world as I walked up the steps. I heard Kevin's footsteps behind me. He must have been curious to meet another mimic.

"Hey, Mrs. Huckleberry," I said as I reached the end of the aisle that separated their row from the others.

Ursula glared at me, but her mom smiled, reaching out her hand to shake. "Bradley, right?"

I only had her hand in mine for a second before Kevin went ballistic, nearly tackling me to the ground. "No!" he shouted. I lost my balance, my shoulder blade hitting the edge of the aluminum row in front of us. Mrs. Huckleberry had let go of my hand just in time, able to steady herself.

Kevin had fallen with me, his skinny arms splayed across my chest.

I coughed. “What is wrong with you?”

Kevin glanced at Mrs. Huckleberry, who was blinking rapidly as if something had flown in her eye, before scrambling to his feet. I groaned, trying to right myself, a stabbing pain in my shoulder. Ursula was staring at Kevin in disbelief. He held out his hand, slowly approaching Savanna and Ursula’s mother. “Mrs. Huckleberry?”

She stopped blinking, her eyes focusing on him, and she gasped. Her eyes swiveled to her daughter and then to me before gazing back out at the stands where our families were sitting. “What did you do to me?”

Kevin groaned, turning back to me. I was still stuck between the rows of bleachers, trying to loosen my shoulder back up. He growled. “Don’t move.” He seemed to struggle to come up with a plan on such short notice. A plan for what, I didn’t know. I couldn’t be sure why he was acting the way that he was, but his suddenly hostile attitude made me nervous. Something was wrong. Something was very wrong.

“Mom?” Ursula asked, resting her hand on her mom’s arm. “What’s wrong?”

“I can’t see,” she whispered, her eyes still darting across the bleachers. “I can’t see the auras.”

Kevin pointed at me. “Go to Frank and stay with him. Do not go anywhere near the Schwartzes.” The commotion had attracted some of our families’ attention. They were starting to approach the scene.

I scrambled to my feet, groaning in pain as my shoulder reacted to the quick shift in altitude. I don’t know what made me listen to him, but I obeyed, jogging down the steps until I was off the bleachers and onto the grass where Frank was standing behind the ticket booth.

"You all right?" Frank asked, assessing my stature.

"Kevin." I panted, rubbing the back of my left shoulder with my right hand. "He knocked me against the bleachers."

Savanna jogged around the corner from the sidelines. She must have witnessed the altercation. "What happened?"

"Ask Kevin. He's the one who went ballistic on me."

"Well, I could see that," she said and huffed. "But what made him push you? Did you try to tell my mom about what's going on?"

Okay, see, now that theory would have made sense. Jay-Jay had warned me not to get Savanna's parents involved. If Kevin had tackled me for that reason, then sure, that was a perfectly justifiable excuse. But all I had done was greet Mrs. Huckleberry and shake her hand.

I stepped back as a new thought occurred to me. *Oh no. Mrs. Huckleberry couldn't see the auras after I had touched her.* What if Kevin had seen her aura change to the light gray that shrouded our parents? I closed my eyes. I knew this situation seemed fishy. It was all too good to be true. I mean, me not having any involvement whatsoever in the mayhem was ludicrous. I was playing my usual role, and I didn't even know it. I was hurting people. It's what I do. I'm no good.

That's when I bolted.

I wasn't sure if Frank would chase me or if he would feel a larger obligation to stay with the majority. I ran as far as my legs could take me. I ran across the concrete of the parking lot until I reached the road between the stadium and the school.

We hadn't lived here long enough for me to get to know the area too well, but I turned right, away from the direction of our neighborhood, heading west toward the city. I ran through the nearest neighborhood and headed north along Post, passing restaurants and department stores, ignoring the sounds of the parallel traffic. I didn't stop until I had crossed the bridge at I-70 and entered another neighborhood.

I'd never run so far at one time in my life, but I didn't want to stop. I'd passed bus stops for miles, but finally, the one ahead had an actual bus already loading and unloading passengers. I ran to catch it, digging for what little change I had in my pockets to pay the fare. The bus lurched forward as I took my seat to catch my breath.

The neighborhood changed the farther north we headed. Rotting wood fences, a couple white pickets. The houses were mostly one-story buildings. We passed churches and bicycle shops, schools and auto stores. The pavement changed from blank to bumpy, the crooked, curved lines of darker concrete filling in the cracks and potholes.

When we hit Thirtieth, the trees and buildings were farther apart—the city looked more like it belonged in this flat Midwestern state. The streetlights hung from wires instead of metal poles. There was a large field on my right, and a large building occupying space farther back. We hit railroad tracks, and beyond that, more large buildings—

packing plants and warehouses—their parking lots lines with semitrucks.

The roads weren't bad. Some of the buildings looked new. What appeared to be a shopping center was on my left, but it didn't look like many businesses occupied it. Another building here almost looked like a prison without the wires and the gates, a huge welcome center sign in front of it. Farther up the road was a storage facility, the buildings lined with red garage doors.

The neighborhood we entered next seemed normal, but it was hard to see much through all the trees that lined the main road. Traffic picked up at Thirty-Sixth street and soon I could see why. A much larger shopping center was up ahead, hosting several chains.

The trees disappeared again as we passed the restaurants and shops. The parking lots on my right were in significantly worse shape than the newly paved ones on my left. The lines came back on the roads, betraying the cracks and crevices that the Midwestern climate always caused.

We passed through another major intersection, the restaurants fading away into abandoned buildings and concrete. Large steel pylon signs that once held names of nearby businesses were blank. The fences turned from wood panels to chain links. There was a line of apartments for several blocks. A long one-story church building emerged past a clump of trees, its parking lot broken and crumbled, covered in patches of greenery. As we waited at the stoplight at Forty-Second, I could see the road change to the right—the cracks there not having been filled. More abandoned boarded up buildings were there.

The bus turned left instead, halting for the millionth time at another stop. I got off this time. I had studied the map that this bus route took and knew we were circling back. This was the farthest from home it could take me.

I crossed the busy intersection into the part of town that had piqued my interest. There was no curb, just patches of grass and gravel leading to a skinny sidewalk. I followed it, noting the trash lining the way. I wondered if the apartment buildings I was passing belonged to an abandoned motel. The dilapidated parking lot was blocked off, but just past the roadblocks, I could see a two-story yellow building with green doors. The building ran along the road for a while. It took me several minutes to stumble upon what I thought was a better entrance. It was gated, leading to the brick apartment buildings past the motel. I studied the motel more closely this time. Several windows on the bottom floor of the buildings were boarded up. Some of the windows on the second floor of the front buildings were broken or shattered. It was quiet on a Saturday morning, and I wondered if this was the usual for this area. I wasn't looking forward to meeting anything monstrous that could come out at night there.

I turned to head back to the main street but jumped when two lanky, heavily tattooed men appeared out of nowhere, blocking the sidewalk. I backed away, getting ready to bolt—then I felt my backside hit somebody else. I didn't turn. I could feel the larger muscled heathen breathing down my neck. The two guys in front of me smiled viciously, their teeth straight except for a few crooked exceptions.

"We've been watching you." The man behind me chuckled. His large hands wrapped around my upper arms, holding me securely where I was standing. My heart dropped into my stomach, my skin clammy with cold sweat.

It's happening again, I thought. I was being kidnapped.

19 // WHY COULDN'T THE NEW ORDER CURE DIABETES INSTEAD?

I was beginning to think Jay-Jay's visions were unreliable. I thought it was Serena's job to be kidnapped. I wasn't prepared to be kidnapped. I was prepared to fight, to play a part in her rescue, although I guess I ducked out of that plan when I ran.

But that was to protect the people I cared about. That was so I wouldn't hurt anybody else. I don't know why I didn't try to leave sooner. I'd been hurting my family and friends for too many years. I guess I snapped at the football field. I'd left Savanna's mom more vulnerable to an attack than she already was. I should have seen this coming. I leave everybody more vulnerable. It's my job. It's my nature.

The trio of men didn't take me to a warehouse. I was manhandled into a metal chair of a small office in a repurposed airplane hangar. It couldn't have been far from where I was grabbed—the drive from the back of a less-than-inconspicuous windowless white van couldn't have lasted longer than fifteen minutes. They'd had me cuffed from the get-go, like some criminal. I laughed as they attached the cuffs to the bottom of the table in the small office. The room felt more like an interrogation room than a torture chamber. Despite the lack of exterior windows, the lights in the small room were bright, buzzing overhead like a swarm of bees. The two scrawny guys who had been restraining me the entire ride continued to cuff my legs to the legs of the chair, staying silent the entire time. The larger man stepped into the room as they left, slamming the door behind him.

He was large, his hands meaty, but he was fit and muscular. At first glance, I would have assumed him to be military. His dark blond hair was cropped short, his facial features sharp and angular. He sat across the table from me, a manila folder in his hand. My breath caught. I'd been in situations like this before, being cuffed to a table in an interrogation room. I wasn't at all expecting this feeling of familiarity.

The man clucked his tongue, opening the folder to examine its contents. "Bradley Isaac Chambers. Born in Franklin, Tennessee, to Chastain and Clarinda Chambers. Subsequently lived in Santa Fe, New Mexico; Niles, Illinois; Itasca, Illinois; and now, Indianapolis, Indiana. And you're only fourteen. Your parents must have an innate interest in living a nomadic life." He paused, his harsh green eyes boring into mine. He slid a couple photographs my way. "As I said, we've been watching you."

I didn't want to take my eyes off the man, but my curiosity got the better of me. The second I glanced at the photographs, my heart felt like it had stopped beating. These were pictures of me—surveillance photos—some from years ago, some from only days ago. They'd been watching me for a long time. Vomit burned the back of my throat when I saw the oldest photograph. It was clearly taken in New Mexico; the date marked was the day before I had been kidnapped. The man who had taken me back then was standing several feet behind me, smirking his twisted, sickening smile. He'd found his next target, a target that would unknowingly be his last.

The man in front of me looked with distaste at the photograph I was staring at. "I was never fond of Garrett. He was more trouble than he was worth."

I jerked at the sound of his name, forgetting for a second that I was shackled in place.

The man sighed mournfully. "But he was a brother, nonetheless." His left hand instinctively flew to his upper right arm, where a red tattoo of a strange deformed *A* existed. The *A* almost looked like a star the way it was drawn. I gasped. I knew that tattoo. Glancing back at the photograph, I could see it plainly on Garrett's arm.

The man cocked his head to the side, an amused smile curled his lips. "Oh yes, Bradley, we've been after you for a while, waiting for you to leave the safety of your home in Chicago. You diviners really love that city, claim it as your own. It's difficult to separate you there, to disempower you. So, we've been waiting, biding our time, and then we saw your father's name pop up on a mortgage loan for a home in sweet home Indiana." He placed his heels on the desk, leaning back in his chair. His black combat boots were caked in mud.

"Oh yes, Bradley"—he flashed a smile—"we've been waiting for you." He stayed like that for a long time, watching me, studying me. I tried to stay as still as possible during his quiet assessment, which proved to be difficult. I wanted nothing more than to rip his head off—not that I thought I could.

Finally, the man restored his posture, taking his feet off the table to lean forward, interlocking his fingers. "I have to say, I'm glad Garrett didn't manage to kill you. Your powers have proven to be quite..." he hesitated, seeming to search for the right word. "Useful to us." He smiled menacingly. "It would have been too easy to kill you, what, with you being diabetic and all. We literally could have locked you in a room until you went into diabetic ketoacidosis. Your cause of death would be easy to determine—no foul play suggested. We'd get none of the credit."

Stupid, I thought. He was right. It wouldn't be hard. Mornings were almost always the worst too. That's what happens when I deprive my body of medication at night, lying unconscious for however many hours I could make myself sleep. It may be long and painful, but not hard. Not for him anyway.

I didn't have one of those fancy insulin pumps to counter the effects. The adrenaline wouldn't have helped either. I had run I don't know how many miles, allowing the hormone to boss my liver around.

"Release the sugar!" Adrenaline likes to laugh maniacally as my liver does what it's told, releasing all my stored energy into my bloodstream. This isn't a problem for most people, but *my* pancreas can't produce insulin. It can't tell my cells to absorb the glucose, so the sugar aimlessly floats around in my bloodstream. It acts more like a poison than anything. If there's too much glucose with nowhere to go, fat starts to break down, turning into ketones. My blood would literally become acidic. If nobody found me, I would die. The stress would only make it worse. I lived for the two days I was in Garrett's RV, but my diagnosis was new then. I still had some residual insulin being produced by my uncooperative pancreas, but at this point, after nine years of insulin dependency, it might only take days. I could already feel my mouth dry, my throat pricking with thirst. If I were lucky, I'd maybe last a week. Actually, the longer timeframe wouldn't be that lucky at all. Not if nobody found me. I'd be suffering longer, pain and delirium overtaking me. Would my family know I'd been kidnapped, or would I be labeled a runaway? Amber Alerts weren't issued for runaways. I had to run.

"I'm a survivor," I whispered the words of my mother and Jay-Jay underneath my breath, my voice hoarse. I wanted it to sound like a threat. I had survived attempts on my life before.

"That you are—which is why we chose to *use* you instead."

Maybe I should have been relieved. They weren't going to kill me after all. But as the large window behind him lit up when the rest of the hangar lights flipped on, I wasn't exactly put at ease. Half of the large space was occupied by lab and science equipment, the other half repurposed into some kind of gymnasium or arena. Only a few people were dallying in the space—a couple scientists and the two goons who had helped capture me.

The man dug in his pockets, pulling out a couple small vials of clear liquid. "Recognize these?"

If it were possible to jump out of my seat, I would have. The vials looked exactly like my insulin vials did.

He chuckled. "Dr. Sauer came up with this little concoction."

I recognized the name, but I wasn't sure why. I racked my memory of recent doctors and pharmaceutical visits, but we hadn't been in the area long enough for names to stick.

The man flipped a photo from the bottom of the stack—another surveillance shot. This one was from the pharmacy closest to my house. My mother was speaking to a pharmacist as my siblings and I browsed the shelves out of boredom. Was that where I knew the name? I couldn't be sure.

"Very ingenious," the man said. "It still provides you your insulin but with a little added kick for good measure." He winked at me. "Don't worry—it has no effect on you whatsoever. It just enhances your ability—you can dematerialize the other abilities around you. It's a genius sleight of hand. No one would be the wiser as it slowly incapacitated the other diviners." The man cocked his head to the side. "Tell me, Bradley, you must have noticed the changes around you."

I gritted my teeth. This was why Mrs. Huckleberry had lost her powers when I shook her hand. I dematerialized them. It would have been a fascinating trick if it hadn't been in the bad guys' favor. It all was starting to make sense. Mr. Lindt had lost his when I walked into his classroom. Same with his wife. Frank's probably disappeared during success time that same day. My mom could have lost hers any time before that.

Whatever Dr. Sauer tainted my insulin with, it was causing me to dematerialize the adults' powers. I wondered if that was the plan—to only incapacitate the adults—or if the serum hadn't worked exactly the way they had planned. I hoped for the latter. That would mean they'd be in for a surprise when the rest of us fought back. The problem was that Jay-Jay was probably searching for a warehouse, not an airplane hangar. I didn't think they had Serena here, not yet. But if they *did* have her and were holding her somewhere else, would my friends and family be wasting their time searching for *me*?

"That's what I thought." The man leaned back in his chair, looking smug. He crossed his arms, and said, rambling, "The diviners have had the advantage for far too long. It's time we made our move, fight to rid the world of your disease."

I glared at him. If he had said, "rid the world of diabetes," I'd take him up on his offer in a heartbeat, but I knew he meant our divinity—our powers, our abilities, our gifts, and he was using me to do it. I was the catalyst. I was the one they were using to lead my people into extinction. They'd been planning it this way all this time.

The idea didn't sit well with me. I'm used to thinking of myself as someone who destroys things, but this current situation was especially maddening because I knew I wasn't the one to blame. It was the New Order and their scientific trickery.

It pissed me off that they had thought to taint my insulin.

It pissed me off that my diabetes had made me their easiest target.

And it pissed me off that they'd been pulling the strings this entire time.

This anger didn't make me afraid of them at all. I wanted to end them. I wanted to reach across the table and strangle the pompous man in front of me with my bare hands. I wanted to find a way to destroy this place, destroy the lab, destroy any trace of the New Order.

He checked his cell phone, seeming pleased by whatever message he had received. He dialed a number, his booming voice jarring me from my fury. "Brothers!" His voice echoed from speakers hidden throughout the hangar. The few men who were within my sight stood straight up, held their right arms at chest level, palms facing downward as if every person other than themselves was below them, and thrust their hands up at a diagonal, far out into the distance at forehead level, as if to say, "We are bigger and better than you." I'd seen the salute before in old footage. It was the Nazi salute. I swallowed, a small portion of my fear returning.

All the men chanted in unison, but I could barely hear them through the glass. "We are the Aryan Brotherhood of the New Order! We defend the blood within against the blood without!"

I shuddered. It was like I was at a KKK meeting, but without all the white robes and the plumes of fire. I hoped that wasn't how I was going to go down. I preferred not to be burned at the stake. A quick bullet to the brain would do it. Easy. Painless.

The man continued his speech. "Phase two in our plans to rid the area of diviners is about to commence." His voice turned into a snarl. "It's time we get the girl."

The lights dimmed as he left the room. It wasn't long before I was left alone in the darkness. I sat there for a second, processing what had happened. They were after Serena for sure—that had to be what he meant by phase two. At least, I hoped it was Serena. If it were, that would mean everything on our end would be happening as planned. A small part of me worried they were after Savanna, though. Surely, they had realized the Huckleberrys were in the area, and from what I'd heard, she and her sister had the bigger targets on their backs.

I tried to move my legs a little bit, to test how tight the restraints were. I couldn't see anything in this blackness, but I could feel the little wiggle room I had. Blood seemed to be flowing to my feet, so at least they weren't cutting off my circulation. I'd hate to lose a foot more than I'd hate to be killed by the Nazis. It was another thing I had to worry about daily. High blood sugar levels damage blood vessels, which often means poor circulation to my hands and feet. The restraints seemed to be made of iron. The cuffs that bound my wrists to the table were standard issue and seemed to be less sturdy than what was binding my legs.

I thought about how normal materializers could dematerialize anything they wished if they had enough focus and practice, but I was still stuck at a beginner's level with my skills—I could only dematerialize objects that had been produced by other diviners. Still, I curved my hand inward just enough to grab the chain connecting the cuffs and willed with all my might for it to disappear. It was easy to visualize since I couldn't see anything to begin with.

Come on, come on, come on, come on, come on.

Nothing. Rather, if I had succeeded, there would be nothing in my hand but air. But all I had was a handful of something. *Damn.* I let go of the chain.

I sat there for a while, listening for a sign of their return. The chair was growing increasingly more uncomfortable by the second. Parts of my body grew numb from the lack of movement. My heart sped up at the thought that I might die there. Alone. In the dark. Tied to a chair. I wasn't a friend to death, though I'd been so close to meeting him several times. I could hear my breathing speed up, and a new sensation of coldness began to drift near my calves. My eyes had adjusted a little to the dark, but not by much. I leaned over to see if I could make out the silhouette of my feet and was surprised that at least one of them seemed to be free. It inched forward to prove its freedom, the restraint gone. I glanced at my other foot and thought I could barely make out the shackle, until suddenly, the shape of it was gone, leaving both my feet free to move.

I stood too fast in my excitement, needing to lean on the table for support. My hands were still fastened securely by the cuffs, but at least I didn't have to sit in the hard metal chair anymore.

Gravity reminded me of how much I needed to pee. I tugged on the chains, trying to break free. They wouldn't budge. I wondered how long I'd been in here. It felt like hours. They still hadn't returned.

"What if I die?" I shouted aggressively at the chains, glad for a moment I was alone. I shouted at the inanimate object, "You want to see that happen? Then keep me chained here for all I care! I'll just rot and—" I didn't get to finish. The chain disappeared, along with the cuffs. Maybe I was making this whole dematerialization thing too hard. I stared at my wrists for a second, blinking in disbelief. It only took a second for me to process that I was free. I bolted.

It was still daylight outside. The sudden burst of light blinded me for a second, but I couldn't let it stop me. Guards stood a few feet from the exit, but if there was anything I was good at, it was running. I darted around the corner of the building before they could see me, but it was clear they heard my footsteps. I could hear shouting as I ran across the empty runway toward the first road I could make out in the distance.

I wasn't sure which way I was running. Glancing at the sun's position in the sky, I guessed it was two or three in the afternoon, and since the sun set in the west, I was heading west. I was sure of it. Speeding up, I sprinted along the main road, assessing my surroundings as I passed them, searching for anything familiar. I wished I knew Indianapolis better. The area didn't look too different from where I'd been taken.

The first street sign I recognized was Mitthoeffer Road. It was several more blocks of endless running as I followed the road south, happening upon a high school that wasn't mine. The parking lot was fenced off. I kept running, my breathing uneven. After all the running I'd done that day, I briefly considered joining a marathon if I survived this. There was a bus stop a little ways down the road, and I gasped in relief when a bus passed me only to brake at the stop. When I stepped onto this bus, I realized

I had spent all my change on the ride up Post and didn't have enough for the fare.

"I've got him covered," somebody said, swiping his bus pass. I looked at the guy's face to thank him, but my breath caught in my dry throat when I realized who it was. "Jay-Jay."

The corner of his lip curved into a half-hearted smile before returning to a hard line. I followed him to his seat near the front, plopping down in exhaustion.

"Took you long enough," Jay-Jay mumbled. He stared cautiously out the window. "I've been riding this thing for an hour, waiting for you to show." He paused his assessment of our surroundings to grab a water bottle from his backpack. He handed it to me. "You're lucky I knew where to find you. If I hadn't grabbed your arm earlier, I wouldn't have seen you get on this bus."

I blinked. I had forgotten all about Jay-Jay's vision—the one he had right before I had spoken to Mrs. Huckleberry at the stadium.

Still, he didn't seem happy to find me. Jay-Jay turned back to the window. "Serena's the one missing now." He grimaced, pulling a piece of folded notebook paper from his jeans pocket. "She turned herself in."

20 // DON'T MIND ME—I'LL JUST LEAD US TO OUR DOOM

The bus took us as far as the Walmart north of our neighborhood. We walked the rest of the way, passing Jay-Jay's house before weaving through the streets until we could see my house and Savanna's in the distance. Frank's car was parked at the curb in front of my house. He was the first to see us strolling down the sidewalk.

He looked relieved and angry as he met us halfway. Crossing his arms, he stopped me from walking any further, only letting Jay-Jay pass. It was seconds until we were alone. I knew he wanted an explanation for my behavior. His voice was gruff as he tried to stay calm. "Why did you run?"

I ran 'cause I always run when something crazy happens. I was sure that fact was in the file he kept in his office at school. He would know that already. But he wanted specifics. Too much had happened in the few hours I had been gone. What had happened to make me run again? Oh. Yeah. Actually, according to the Aryan Brotherhood or the New Order or whatever they were calling themselves, there was a lot more to the story than the small reason I had run in the first place. I ran because I knew I had hurt Savanna's mom somehow. I had taken her powers. But now I knew more. I knew *why* that happened.

I stepped back from Frank, trying to protect him from me. It was probably a useless attempt. I'd already stolen his powers. Still, I didn't want to take any chances. "I'm cursed."

He rolled his eyes. "Not this again. We've talked about this."

"No." I shook my head, taking another step back. "I mean, the New Order did something to my medication. I'm the reason your powers are missing. I've been taking them away somehow." Frank stared at me for a second. I knew what I was saying sounded ridiculous, but it must have matched the story Kevin told him because he harrumphed before leading me back to the house.

I was surprised to see Savanna's family in our house, including a guy built much like Mr. Lindt with dark hair, dark eyes, and a mustache—he must have been Savanna's father. I could see where Ursula got her looks. Plus, Jay-Jay was right. The guy definitely looked like he could have been a crime boss.

Remembering my extraneous ability, I stumbled back, trying to put a good amount of distance between me and him. He was the only adult here I hadn't already infected. Kevin seemed to understand my fear and urged Mr. Huckleberry to another portion of the house. The man grumbled something unintelligible under his breath as he obeyed, leaving my line of sight. I stood where the stairs curved, just in case.

Mom was happy to see me. She cried in relief, skipping the first three steps to throw her arms around me. I stiffened, wishing I could give her powers back, wishing I could do anything to ease her anxiety. No one seemed to realize I'd been kidnapped and held against my will for a couple hours. I guess they all thought I'd run away, which was partially true.

Mya was the first to bring it up. "They just let you go?" she yelled. She apparently read my thoughts.

"What? Who let you go?" Mom asked, pulling away from me to study my face. I held up my shaking hands, revealing the new bruises that had formed around my wrists from all the pulling and tugging I had done to try to free myself from the handcuffs. It was the only physical proof I had. Their plan wasn't to torture me—yet. She gently held my hands in hers, gasping. "Oh, baby..."

I could feel several pairs of eyes on me, including Savanna's, but I didn't dare meet them. Pulling my hands from my mom's grasp, I tried to squeeze around her. "I need to use the bathroom," I said, mumbling. I know she followed me up the stairs. I could hear her footsteps and her breathing as I closed the bathroom door. I had to pee. I'd been holding it in longer than I thought was humanly possible.

When I left the bathroom, I was surprised to find Savanna standing there instead of my mother.

"You ran from me," she said, pouting.

I rolled my eyes, trying not to let her emotions alter my own. "It's what I do." I tried to place a hand on the stair railing but missed. My heartbeat still hadn't slowed from my run. My lungs ached. I knew this feeling. I had too much glucose. I'd been running too long and too fast, and it had sped up the process.

"Crap." I moaned, bending to rest my head on the railing. My head spun and I closed my eyes, trying to breathe through the nausea.

"What's wrong?" Savanna asked, her tone growing worried. I could feel her hand on my back. I shook it off.

If they had messed with my insulin, then surely I couldn't take any of it. That's probably why they'd let me escape, so I could run myself to death. They knew I'd be afraid to trust anything I had on hand. I'd have to run to a pharmacy to restock. Would they be waiting for me at the nearest one? The one Dr. Sauer was at?

I stumbled past Savanna down the hall to my bedroom. I kept a stash of supplies in the top drawer of my end table. I thought maybe I could find an old vial of insulin—one that was still left over from our days in Itasca. It wasn't common for me to have old vials, since Mom usually swept the whole house for them before deciding to buy more, but I was hoping just this once she had missed one. Yanking the top drawer open, I stuffed my hand into the mess of bottles and needles until I felt a familiar round cylinder. Pulling it out, I examined the contents. There was still some liquid in the vial from late July. The date I had first used it was scrawled in permanent marker on the glass—August first. Open containers of insulin only lasted twenty-eight days before they had to be disposed of. It was the twenty-sixth. I sighed in relief.

Plopping onto the floor and leaning against my bed, I grabbed my glucose monitor from the top of the end table, checking to see how high my blood sugar really was. I needed to know how much insulin to inject. I tried not to suck in too much air as the number climbed far into the two hundreds. This was not good. I filled a syringe with the clear hormone, lifted my shirt, pinched a portion of skin on my stomach, and sucked in a lungful of air as I jammed the needle into it. I released my skin, and slowly injected the insulin, counting to five after I had finished before pulling it out. *Damn.* I closed my eyes. *I freaking hate this part.*

When I opened my eyes, Savanna was standing in the doorway, watching me, confusion drawn on her face. I knew I'd have to explain my behavior. I tried to do it lightly, with as much of a sense of humor as I could muster.

"I'm not into drugs, I promise." I tried to chuckle, but it sounded off. It was a bad joke anyway. I tossed the syringe into a nearby trashcan. I wasn't supposed to toss them in like that, but whatever. "In middle school, one of my old friends told people I was, though. He thought it made me seem cool. My mom was not happy when she heard it from a few concerned parents." I tried to laugh again, but I snarled instead. "Did you know running heightens blood glucose levels? If I'm not careful, I could run myself into hyperglycemia or ketoacidosis." That was only true if I ran without any insulin in my system, but I didn't tell her that. My head was pounding. It always took a while before the insulin started to work. I'd still be stuck with the symptoms until my blood sugar lowered. I hoped my glucose levels weren't so high that the amount of insulin I had just injected wasn't effective. If my levels were to get above three hundred, well, I didn't have time for a hospital stay. We had to find Serena first.

"You're diabetic?" Savanna asked.

I didn't answer. Instead, I changed the subject. "So, what's up with Serena leaving? Is there a plan to get her back?"

She entered my room to sit on the floor next to me. "She's been missing for a couple hours now. It took us a minute to realize she was gone. She left a note in the stadium bathroom saying she couldn't wait any longer, that she had contacted the people who were after her, and she was going to meet them at the library to quietly turn herself in. Frank tried to chase after her, but by the time he got there, she was gone. We've been running through different scenarios and tactics ever since. I think Jay-Jay's trying to hack into Serena's emails for clues as to where they could have taken her."

"They probably took her back to where they took me."

Savanna shook her head. "Jay-Jay doesn't think so."

"Jay-Jay doesn't know where I was." He hadn't asked, and I hadn't told him.

"Serena left only an hour or so after you did. You would have seen her if they had taken you guys to the same place. Jay-Jay and Frank think the New Order owns or leases multiple buildings. They're trying to narrow down the possible locations they could be keeping her," Savanna said.

Mya knocked on the doorframe, interrupting our conversation. "Jay-Jay has some questions for you."

I groaned. *Time to get up.*

We followed Mya down the stairs and into the living room. I tried to keep as close to the wall as I could, to keep my distance from Mr. Huckleberry, who stood on the far side of the kitchen so he could still hear the conversation. I didn't know how long the drug that Dr. Sauer had inserted into my newer insulin vials would last. I wasn't sure injecting an old one immediately solved the problem.

Jay-Jay had a map of the Indianapolis area splayed across the dining table. It was a little too large for the skinny table, but that didn't seem to bother Jay-Jay too much. He was marking certain locations with a red marker, pausing every few seconds to check his accuracy on Frank's laptop.

As I leaned against the far wall, Jay-Jay explained what he was doing. "We're lucky Serena kept all her research backed up on an online server. Not lucky because that's probably what led them to us in the first place, but lucky because it was easy for me to access. She actually identified a couple prominent, local members of the New Order." He marked a spot near Sixteenth and Ritter. "A doctor, Clayton Sauer, mainly operates out of a hospital here, even though he does volunteer pharmaceutical work in various locations."

I bristled at the mention of the doctor's name. Mom, who was much better at remembering names, gasped.

Jay-Jay tapped the map in a different location. "She tracked another member to a church near Emerson and Forty-Second." He marked another spot on the map. "They took Serena from the library across from the school." Glancing at the crowd of people surrounding him, he said, "It looks like they've been establishing themselves in East Indianapolis for a while. It's their comfort zone." He looked at me. "Bradley, do you know where they took you?"

I hesitantly stepped forward to study the map. "An airfield several miles east of Mitthoeffer." It looked farther on the map than I thought it was, but Jay-Jay marked it anyway.

"It looks like a square almost." Jay-Jay pointed to an area in the middle of the four dots. "We should probably be searching somewhere around Four Sixty-Five and Thirty-Eighth."

Frank shook his head from behind Jay-Jay. "There's a lot of businesses right in there. I don't know about any warehouses."

I stared at the map. Something was bothering me about it. It blurred a little. I blinked, trying to refocus my eyes. The square wasn't really a square, more like a trapezoid. It didn't feel complete, like we were missing a location. *Maybe it wasn't a square or a trapezoid that we were looking at. Maybe it was—*

I gasped, lunging toward the map, my knees hitting the carpet. "Give me that." I motioned for the marker in Jay-Jay's hand. I started at the airfield, drawing a line from it to the church. I continued the line from the church to the library, as if I were drawing a star. The only point that didn't connect to the shape in my mind was the hospital. I pointed to a patch of green on the map north of all the dots. "What's here?"

"Fort Ben." Jay-Jay shrugged.

Frank stiffened. Speaking slowly, he asked Jay-Jay, "Are you sure you saw Serena in a warehouse, or could it have been a bunker?"

Jay-Jay tilted his head to the side, reimagining the vision. "I guess it could have been..."

I quickly marked a dot in the middle of the state park, drawing a line from it to the library and another from it to the hospital. I didn't complete the star by connecting the hospital to the airfield, because it wasn't a star I was drawing. "The guy who took me had this symbol tattooed on his arm."

Frank was the only one who recognized it. He didn't sound happy. "That's the symbol for the Aryan Brotherhood. It's a white supremacist gang. They've got chapters all over Indiana."

"You said there are bunkers at this park?" I asked Frank, pointing to the patch of green I had marked.

He nodded. "The general population doesn't know about it. They were sealed off when they converted one of the buildings into a museum for twentieth-century warfare. The bunker runs underneath a good length of the park. It's fairly elaborate."

"It's the perfect place to set a trap for us." Jay-Jay glanced at me. "I see now why they let you go. They knew you'd lead us right into their trap."

His comment made me sick. Of course I played an even bigger part in their entire elaborate scheme. First, they needed me to dematerialize everyone's powers. Second, they needed to reveal one of their locations to me. Third, they needed my knowledge of that location and the shape of their tattoo to lead us all into the bunker at Fort Ben. But there was one thing they didn't know or weren't expecting: only the adults were affected by my touch or my nearness. If Serena went with them willingly, she may not have revealed her powers to them. We could use this to our advantage.

I straightened up, again trying to breathe through the nausea. "They think we're all powerless except for me. Their plan was to enhance my powers of dematerialization—through a tainted serum of my insulin—so that I could unknowingly take your powers. But it didn't work the way they think it did. It only affected the adults I encountered." I thought I saw Mr. Huckleberry take another step back in the kitchen.

Mom knew what I was getting at. "No." she shook her head, her voice adamant. "You kids are not going in there alone."

"We won't be alone," I said. "There's, what?" I quickly counted our numbers in my head. "Nine of us, not including Serena?"

Mom looked to Jay-Jay for reassurance. He shrugged. "It's the way I saw it."

Tears started to stream down my mom's cheeks. Her voice shook as she asked him, "Are you all going to come back?"

There was a horribly long silence on Jay-Jay's end. I cringed in anticipation of his answer. Mom was gonna lose it if he didn't make something up to quench her fear. He decided to be honest instead. *Idiot.* "I don't know."

21 // AND THE HOLOCAUST COMES FULL CIRCLE

We all stood at the entrance of the 1,700-acre state park a few hours later, with Frank flanking us on one end, Mr. Huckleberry on the other. I tried to stay on Frank's side of the line, keeping my distance from the only adult diviner who still had his powers intact. Mr. Huckleberry had the gift of quantity manipulation, which meant he could make several copies of an object at once. His powers worked similarly to his daughters', except that he could also multiply copies of himself. He just had to be sure to keep any of those copies away from me, which meant he couldn't offer me his protection. We positioned Jay-Jay near him instead as he was the only one of us with a passive power. His gift of precognition wouldn't help him too much in a fight.

"Sunset's in three hours," Frank said to us as we followed him on foot along Shafter Road. "The park closes then. We're going to have to walk the rest of the way." He'd already warned us of that part of the plan, but the reminder sent a new wave of groans through the line. Frank thought we'd have a better chance of sneaking up on them if we were on foot, and since the park closed at eight, he didn't want the two vehicles we brought to get towed or trapped. Everyone had a backpack slung around their shoulders, each full of survival gear—bottles of water, compasses, flashlights, and so forth. Frank handed us each a map in case we somehow got separated—although, I wasn't sure how it was at all possible to lose a line of eleven people.

The road split at a gatehouse, which was our cue to head southwest into the forest. The trail wouldn't be too far from the road. The Schoen Creek Trail was skinny and winding as it wove through the trees. The entire trail was three miles long, but Frank assured us that we would be leaving the trail after about a mile.

The sun made its descent in the sky as we followed each other on the winding path, but it was still too bright outside to obscure our vision. I had to stop a couple of times to check my blood glucose levels. After the day I had, I was surprised I wasn't in a coma. I didn't have any more untainted vials if I needed to inject more insulin, and that made me nervous.

Paige started complaining loudly about five minutes into our hike. She hated anything outdoorsy.

It wasn't long until a few small buildings were in our sights. Frank nodded from the back of the line to give us the go-ahead. "We're tourists," he said as a reminder to us, "so please don't draw suspicion to yourselves." We'd all dressed according to this facade. Frank was even wearing khakis.

Our plan was to head to the visitor's center and pretend to gather information about the park as we casually assessed the building for secret passageways. Some of the girls needed to use the restrooms, so we mostly just dallied in the main entrance, looking at brochures and reading plaques.

"This building used to be part of the POW camp," Frank said in a low voice as he and I stood by the windows. "They would bring in prisoners of war here to Camp Glenn during World War II. Mostly Germans and Italians. If the entrance to the bunker isn't in this building, then it's likely in the museum a few buildings over. These men are obsessed with the Second World War. It was a time when Nazis reigned and white supremacist ideals ran rampant. It would make sense for the entrance to be here somewhere."

A cheer broke our focus. Kase had his arms up in the air, a huge smile plastered on his face, as he rounded the corner. His smile quickly disappeared when he realized how conspicuous he was being. He glanced at Mya, who was frowning at him from a stack of postcards. She must have yelled at him telepathically. Quietly, one of us at a time rounded the corner to see what he had found. When it was my turn, I crouched and looked at the part of the floor he was pointing to. There it was, etched in the wood: the symbol for the Aryan Brotherhood. He hopped on the nearby heavy rug. The sound was noticeably different than walking on the rest of the floor in the room, and not because of the rug. There was a hollow spot underneath—we were sure of it.

"Ready?" He eyed me, his surreptitious smile growing.

"For what?" I whispered back, unsure what he meant.

Grabbing my arm, Kase squeezed it as hard as he could. My entire body went cold, the floor giving out underneath me. "Wha—" I shouted in surprise as I fell through the floor. The only thing keeping me upright was Kase's tight grip on my arm. It was dark where I was, but I could see dim lights several feet down. Something cold and metal scraped against my free arm, and I reached to grab it. A ladder. Kase must have been able to tell when I had grabbed hold of the bars because he let go, his arm disappearing through the ceiling of the pit I was in.

Half of our group was already waiting at the bottom. I waited quietly with them, continuing to keep my distance from Mr. Huckleberry while the rest arrived. Once Kase slammed his feet down on the concrete floor, we followed the path of the dimly lit hallway, searching for clues, listening carefully for any sounds other than our own footsteps. Every movement we made seemed to echo throughout the chamber. I figured they knew we were here. I wasn't absolutely sure, though, until I heard Serena scream.

Kase lost his cool. "Serena!"

Frank and Mr. Huckleberry grabbed Kase, slamming him against the cold wall and covering his mouth. I didn't see what use it was. He'd already given away our location.

"Guys," Savanna said, pointing in the direction of heavy footsteps of men hurdling toward us.

Paige ran out in front of her, hand extended. The second someone came into her view, she bent her elbow and jerked her hand forward, sending the men flying backward into a wall. She screamed when another guy appeared. "Kevin!"

Kevin appeared at her side, channeling her powers, continuing to fling men dressed as soldiers against the concrete. They couldn't keep it up for long, though.

Frank let go of Kase, drawing his gun. The men had much larger weapons—military style—to counteract Frank's standard issue. He managed to get one bullet out before one of the men started shooting.

"Get down!" Frank shouted urgently as we all threw ourselves to the floor. The bullets ricocheted off the walls. I hoped the stray bullets weren't managing to hit any of us. Kase was the only one who was practically bulletproof. I could hear Rebecca crying from behind me. She was too young for this. We shouldn't have brought her with us.

I looked ahead at Ursula, whose face said she had other ideas. An assault rifle started to form in front of her. It was unsettling to see a little kid with such a big gun. I was glad when she slid it forward at Frank's feet. He took it in his hands as Ursula started to make another one. The second gun she slid toward her dad. She was making the fight fair. Frank and Mr. Huckleberry were able to move forward a few feet, shooting a few of the soldiers down as they did.

"Go, go, go!" Frank shouted, motioning for us to run down an adjacent hallway. Quickly, we scrambled to the new hallway until all of us were safe from the gunfire. We kept running, leaving Frank and multiple Mr. Huckleberrys to cover.

"Where do you think Serena's voice was coming from?" Kase asked frantically as we reached a fork. Doors were all along the corridors, leading to rooms that contained the unknown.

"We have to split up," Jay-Jay said. He quickly made the decisions for us, pointing at each person as he spoke their name. "Kase, Paige, Ursula, and Mya are with me. We'll take the right corridor. The rest of you go left."

I quickly turned into the left corridor, hoping Savanna, Rebecca, and Kevin followed. Most of the doors didn't have windows, making it hard to tell what was going on behind them. We heard Serena scream again. We were definitely heading in the right direction.

Kevin sped up ahead of us, following the sounds of his sister's cries. Several twists and turns later, he stopped in front of a door. "It's this door, I swear it." As if on cue, Serena's shrieks confirmed his theory. Kevin twisted the door handle, but it didn't budge. "What are they doing to her in there?"

I banged my fist on the door. "We need Kase to get through this." At my suggestion, Kevin bolted back down the way we had come.

"They're watching us," Rebecca said, her voice shaky and her eyes on a security camera above the door.

A slow clap boomed from down the hallway as a man came into view. It was the same man who had taken me earlier. I instinctively positioned myself in between him and the others, although I wasn't sure what I could do to protect them. Their powers still worked better than mine did.

The man shook his head, flashing a wide smile. "Don't you love it when everything works out as planned?" He continued to approach us. I backed up, forcing the girls to backtrack with me. The man tilted his head, examining our trio. "The great-grandchildren of Agata and Truda. Who'd have thought I'd be this lucky?"

None of the names sounded familiar to me, but Rebecca's questioning tone from behind surprised me. "You know my grandma?"

The man flashed a grin—his straight pearly white teeth somehow gleamed in the bad lighting. "I know *of* her, little one. She's quite famous in our circle."

I jumped when Rebecca screamed. Savanna reached out to grab my sister, but a soldier snuck up on us and already had her in his arms. Another was going for Savanna. She clung to me, pushing me against the wall, but there was nowhere for us to run. Our capture was inevitable.

It wasn't long until we were all being restrained, but Savanna had other ideas. She shoved her elbow backward into her captor's abdomen, slammed her foot as hard as she could on his foot, but as she was going for his nose with the back of her elbow, he caught her. She was too small for him, her strength no match for his muscle. A sharp silver-plated knife appeared in her other hand, but as she turned to stab his stomach, I was yanked backward just as quickly, cold metal pressed against my neck. The guy who had me cleared his throat. "Drop it or he dies!"

She froze, her blue eyes landing on mine. Her pause in movement was long enough for the guy she was fighting to knock the knife out of her hand and clasp a strange, bangle-like bracelet onto her tiny wrist. The bracelet had spikes on the inside that dug into her skin. Savanna yelped in pain. I could see her opening and closing her hand, attempting to rematerialize another weapon, but nothing happened. The guy who had

Rebecca clasped a matching bracelet on her arm as a precaution. She whimpered.

My neck stung a little as the man pressed his knife through my skin, but it was nothing compared to the pounding in my head. I blinked, trying to refocus my eyes. "Little girl," he said, taunting Savanna, who was still attempting to free herself, "make no mistake, I will kill him."

"You'll kill him anyway!" Savanna snarled. "That's what you plan on doing with all of us, isn't it?"

The man chuckled, the knife at my neck shaking with his laughter. It scraped against my skin. "I'd much rather drag it out first so I can study you, torture you," he said, "but I'm willing to let this one go quickly." He yanked on my hair. "He's fulfilled his purpose. Or, at least, I thought he had." He yanked me back, dragging me away. "Somehow you all seem to still have your powers. No matter." He huffed impatiently. "Those bracelets will do the same."

I struggled against his grip as he dragged me through a door. Yanking my backpack off, he threw me to the ground of an empty dark room. He growled. "I should have known better than to trust you Gypsies." He kicked my stomach as if I wasn't already about to puke. Bending, he clasped the same bracelet onto my wrist. A million tiny needles broke through my skin at once, my wrist growing cold as whatever toxin they injected spread through my bloodstream. Then, once again, he left me alone.

Serena wasn't screaming anymore. I couldn't hear her in the next room. I hadn't heard her since we were caught. I hoped that meant she was still alive, still breathing, and they had just stopped torturing her. I hoisted myself to my feet, banging on the wall that should have separated our rooms. "Serena!" The sound of my fist on the cold metal echoed around me along with my shouts. *Can she hear me?*

I couldn't hear Savanna or my sister either. I wasn't sure where the men had taken them. Savanna may know how to fight, but she was so petite. I didn't think there was a way for her to win a fight against any of those men. And Rebecca, without her powers, was left defenseless.

The room was too dark for me to see. There was a deep thrumming sound coming from above me, followed by the groan of rusty metal moving away from its comfort zone. For a second, I thought someone had crawled through the vents to come rescue me like they did in the movies, but nobody came. That was when I saw it—a cloud of white smoke, barely bright enough to see against the soul-sucking darkness. I pressed myself against the cool, metal wall. This wasn't just any room, I realized. It was a gas chamber.

The man hadn't lied. He *was* going to kill me. I'd served my purpose. I was no longer of use to him. It was actually kind of him to leave me alone in a gas chamber. At least he hadn't sliced my throat in front of Savanna and my sister or left me to die slowly as my disease finished the job for him.

I wondered if the gas would kill me quickly or if I would suffer, choking and sputtering as I gasped for clean air. I thought about what Serena had told me—how four thousand Romanies, some of them diviners, were killed this way in a single day at the Auschwitz-Birkenau death camp. Four. Thousand. People. I guess the Nazis haven't changed much since then. Was it easier for them? To not have literal blood on their hands? Easier for us to die in a room far away from them? A room far away where the only evidence of our deaths could be chalked up to respiratory failure or asphyxiation? Would they bury our bodies—our powers along with us—in the state park above us, or would they dispose of us elsewhere? Maybe they would burn our remains—cremate us beyond recognition—and scatter our ashes haphazardly until all traces of us were gone. No one would be the wiser. Not even the Lawrence Police Department down the street.

They weren't planning to kill us. They were planning to destroy us.

22 // LEAVE IT TO KEVIN TO GET LOST

I wasn't expecting to fall backward. How could I? One second, my back was pressed against a wall—the next, I was stumbling, my surprise knocking me on my butt. I looked up, the yellow lights behind me illuminating the smoky metal room. The gas was still floating in, threatening to overpower me. I skittered back, away from where the wall had been.

"What in the..." a man yelled from behind me, his voice echoing.

I scrambled unsteadily to my feet. *My words exactly*. Quickly, I glanced at the bracelet clasped tightly around my wrist. I had assumed it blocked the wearer's abilities. I'd seen it work on Savanna instantaneously. Why hadn't it worked on me?

"Cut the gas!" another man yelled. I continued to back away, wishing I could make the wall reappear. I hadn't quite freed myself from the threat of my impending doom. My legs hit something solid, and I sprung forward, worried I'd backed into another trap again. Someone moaned. Whirling around to face my opponent, I stopped dead in my tracks. My legs had hit a physician's table, and on it was a barely conscious Serena.

"Serena? Serena!" I shook her, trying to jostle her awake. We needed to run. We needed to get out of there. She didn't look too damaged from the outside, just a few bruises. I was expecting a lot worse judging from all the screaming.

Serena moaned in response, her eyes barely closed. She wasn't hooked to any monitors, nor did she have any needles in her. I placed my index and middle fingers right underneath her jawline, trying to gauge her pulse. The gas was creeping closer, keeping the nearest men from getting too close to us. I coughed. Her pulse was quick, her breathing coming in rapid, wheezing puffs. I was going to have to carry her if we were to escape this large room alive.

The gas was blocking the nearest exit, but I could see several men evacuating through a door on the opposite wall. As I bent to sweep my arms underneath Serena's body, I heard the back exit door slam shut. They had barricaded us in.

"Come on, Serena." I hoisted her in my arms. I was glad she didn't weigh too much, but I still wasn't sure how long I could keep holding her. If we had any hope of escaping, we needed her powers. I carried her to the far side of the front wall, trying to press her against it. "Please, Serena," I said, begging. "We just need to get through the wall."

She moaned again and coughed, red splatters of blood hitting my face. It reminded me of Jesse, how only months ago he had been doing the same as he lay in the middle of the school hallway with a bullet wound in his abdomen. Had she been shot?

I laid her on the ground at my feet, my eyes sweeping her body for blood that shouldn't be there. She didn't look that damaged, but she continued to choke on her blood. The gas was coming for us, the larger space allowing it to take its precious time. I sat there for a second, defeated. Serena wasn't going to get us out.

Glancing at my wrist, I studied the bracelet. Was it not affecting me at all? I'd made an entire wall disappear before. Maybe I could do it again. It wouldn't stop the gas from spreading, but it would buy us some time.

Leaning over Serena's body, I pressed my palms to the cold concrete wall. It disappeared easily. I barely had to coax it. Catching myself as I fell forward, I avoided crushing Serena. I could hear running footsteps heading in our direction. I braced myself.

"Maybe it was this hallway!" Kevin's voice bounced. I relaxed. Grabbing Serena's hands and dragging her body into the corridor, I tried to meet them part of the way.

"Took you long enough," I grunted as Kevin and Kase skidded to a stop from an adjacent hallway.

"I got her." Kase pushed me aside, lifting Serena effortlessly into his arms.

"Watch out for the gas." I pulled up the collar of my shirt to cover my mouth and nose.

A few of our other friends raced up behind Kevin and Kase.

"I got it!" Ursula shouted, pushing past me and holding her hands in the air. A transparent plastic bubble materialized, wrapping around the fumes before she forced it back into the room and formed a temporary wall to block it. I didn't have time to be impressed.

"We have to find Savanna and Rebecca." I looked for the security camera, but it was gone. It had been attached to the wall I had dissipated, which meant they probably didn't see us escape. We could use that to our advantage. Kase studied Serena's face, her mouth especially. "I gotta get her out of here."

"Take the kids with you." I gestured to Mya and Ursula, who both let out a string of protests. Ignoring them, I said, pointing to the bracelet on my wrist, "Whatever you do, don't let them cuff you." Even if it didn't affect me, I couldn't risk it affecting them. It had worked on Savanna, after all.

Ursula placed her hand on my bracelet, causing it to disappear, the tiny needles with it. "See? I can help!"

I didn't tell her removing my bracelet did nothing for me. If she could've dematerialized the excess sugar in my blood, that would've been a different story. I growled in protest, pointing to the semi-limp body in Kase's arms. "You can help Serena. Protect the quarterback at all costs. I will handle your sister." We stared at each other for a second, waiting for the other to give in.

"Fine," Ursula said with a grumble.

Jay-Jay left with them. He was the only one who remembered the way back to the entrance.

The gunfire wasn't echoing throughout the labyrinth anymore. I hoped that meant Frank and Mr. Huckleberry were all right. Kevin and Paige stared at me, awaiting further instructions.

Paige asked, her voice faltering, "They have Rebecca?"

"Not for long." I headed in the direction I thought they had taken Rebecca and Savanna. The hallway spun around me. I tried my best not to clue them in on my suffering. "You guys need to watch my back. Send anyone flying if they get too close." I was tired of backstepping into a hoard of angry supremacists. We walked in silence for several yards, listening intently for any sign of the girls.

We'd made several turns before Kevin broke the silence. "Do you think Serena's going to be okay?"

I was trying not to think about it too much. That was a question for Jay-Jay, but he'd been eerily tight-lipped regarding any of our fates. I wasn't sure if that was because he was trying to keep everybody from freaking out or if he truly didn't know. He could only see absolutes, so maybe Serena's life hung so much in the balance that he hadn't been able to see her outcome. Her chance at survival was probably fifty-fifty. I didn't tell Kevin that, though. I wasn't going to be the one to tell him his sister might die. I'd seen too much death, too much suffering, to burden him with the knowledge of its possibility.

"I think she's going to be fine," Paige said matter-of-factly. "Serena looked like she had passed out."

I forced myself to keep walking, to keep my demeanor indifferent. Paige hadn't seen the blood. I brushed my hand against my cheek where Serena had coughed up a few splatters, trying to remove the evidence as best I could.

It was only moments before all chaos broke loose.

"Savanna!" Mr. Huckleberry's voice repeatedly boomed from several twists and turns back, his rapid footsteps growing closer and closer. Kevin and I shared a wide-eyed look. The others must have reached Frank and him, his eldest daughter unaccounted for. Mr. Huckleberry shouted Savanna's name again. If he didn't stop soon, he was going to give our location away. His voice was panicked, all common sense lost. He bounded toward us, his worry lines increasing as he realized the girls weren't with us.

"Savanna!" he shouted again, close enough to touch. Kevin gasped as he pushed past us. Then, as if he were merely a ghost, he vanished. I groaned. There went Mr. Huckleberry's powers. I wondered when that little inconvenience was going to wear off or if it was a permanent flaw in my abilities.

Further down the hall, Rebecca's loud wail echoed. There was a pause, followed by muffled voices, and then out of nowhere, an explosion. The concrete wall in front of us and to our left began to crack loudly. We stumbled back a few paces before the cracks rapidly grew, the wall exploding in chunks of rock and dust. Paige screamed as some of the bits of gravel rained down on us. Coughing, Kevin and I tried to wave away the thick floating dust. We couldn't see anything through the sea of gray.

"Rebecca, you need to calm down," Savanna said urgently as we blindly made our way through the rubble.

Something grabbed me, shoving my back into a pile of rubble. "You just won't die, will you?" The man who had taken me, who had locked me in a gas chamber, the nameless man who always seemed to be in charge, had his hand clasped tightly around my throat, pinning me against the pile of rubble.

I couldn't breathe or call for help. I was stuck. My hand searched for loose pieces of rock, but throwing them at him didn't make a difference. It just seemed to make him angrier. The dust was still too dense to see through, not that it would have mattered. My vision was growing worse. The fog blinded Kevin and Paige enough to hinder their telekinesis. I wasn't even sure they knew he had me. I could hear them scrambling past us, toward the sound of Savanna's voice.

"I made a promise," the man whispered in my ear, his spit drenching the side of my face, "that I would rid the world of abominations like you." He chuckled evilly. "I made a promise that when the divine are dead, this war will all be worth it—our sacrifices would all be worth it. We would be celebrated as heroes, rising from the ashes as the almighty supreme warriors that we are. When the divine are dead"—his voice grew louder, his grip tightening—"we will be one step closer to ridding this world of evil." I was going to pass out.

A foot flew into my obscured line of vision, slamming into the man's temple. Savanna's voice was full of fire. "Boy, do you have it backward!"

He rolled to the side, losing his grip on my neck. I coughed, breathing in a lungful of dusty air. My vision returned in strange clouds that refused to conjoin in a single image.

Savanna hopped over me, kicking him one last time into unconsciousness. Leaning over my face, she asked, "Are you okay?"

I was still coughing, unable to answer her with more than a simple head nod. Reaching for her hand, I clasped my hand over her bracelet, as Ursula had done for me, and sent it into the void. I blinked as the clouds of vision struggled to stay together.

"Thanks." She breathed, flexing her hand. Testing her abilities, she rematerialized the knife she had lost earlier before making it disappear again.

"What was that explosion?" I was able to ask between coughs. The dust was finally starting to clear, along with my vision.

She was still leaning over me, confused. "I thought that was you guys."

I propped myself up on my elbows and shook my head. "No." My stomach ached with every movement.

Savanna didn't pull away. Her face was inches above mine now. Even given the proximity, her kiss surprised me. It was quick, no time for me to react before she had her arms around my shoulders, hugging me to her.

"They told me you were dead," she whispered.

"I'm a survivor," I whispered back, hugging her tighter. I tried to convince myself that my survival was inevitable, but I could feel my strength waning.

Paige's whiny voice echoed off the remaining walls. "Can you guys, like, stop making out for two seconds so we can get out of here?" The dust had settled, and I could see Kevin struggling to untie the knots of rope around Rebecca's wrists. My youngest sister was hyperventilating, tears streaming down her pale face. Her brown eyes were wild and spastic, refusing to settle on one place.

Savanna and I pulled away from each other and stumbled to our feet. I winced with every movement as we ran to Rebecca as quickly as we could without tripping over the loose gravel. I motioned for Kevin to move his hands away. Gripping the part of the rope he had managed to loosen, I willed it to disappear in my hands. I felt it go, then touched her bracelet, releasing her from its grasp.

She didn't thank me or react in any way to her newfound freedom. We all watched her, waiting for some type of sign. Her breathing started to slow, and her eyes stopped moving, landing on a low space between Kevin and me. I followed her gaze. An unconscious man lay nestled underneath a pile of rocks, his skin covered in dust. His light eyes were open, unseeing, and I gulped at the realization that it was not an unconscious man I was seeing. It was a dead man.

What had caused that explosion? The ground beneath us began to shake, rattling the entire elaborate bunker. Dirt sprinkled in from between the cracks in the walls and ceiling. For a brief second, I questioned the stability of the bunker. I knew little about earthquakes. Were we safe underground?

"We have to get out of here," Paige said. I stood with her, getting ready to run. I vaguely remembered the way back to the entrance. The others didn't move. Kevin's hand was wrapped around Rebecca's ankle. Her eyes were unfocused like they had been the night Ursula was forced to apologize.

"She's doing this," Kevin said through gritted teeth.

"Can you counteract it?" I asked Kevin. I didn't have time to question his claim. Rebecca was proving to be more powerful than all of us. I was pretty sure a normal materializer couldn't conjure an entire natural disaster.

"No," Kevin said, defeated. "I can't seem to mimic her abilities." He let go of her ankle, giving up.

Savanna snapped her fingers in front of Rebecca's face. "Rebecca, sweetie, the bad guys are gone. They're not gonna hurt us anymore. We're safe."

My sister didn't respond, the tremors growing worse. I wasn't sure I could carry her if I needed to. I could barely hold myself upright. I definitely wouldn't be able to do it and run at the same time.

Blood started to drip from her nose, her unfocused eyes suddenly full of fury.

"You have to let us get out of here before the roof collapses," Paige said, trying to talk some sense into her. "Then you can have your fun—bring the whole place to the ground—I don't care, but so help me God, if I die down here, I will haunt your ass!" That seemed to do the trick. Paige wasn't somebody I would want haunting me every minute of every day. She was already annoying enough as it was.

Rebecca got on her feet, testing her balance, before leading the way back to the entrance.

The building was still shaking, making it difficult to keep up, but Rebecca continued at an unbroken pace as we weaved back through the labyrinth of hallways. We didn't come across any more men from the New Order. Besides the rumbling, the place seemed like a ghost town—too quiet. Mr. Huckleberry was pacing anxiously by the exit. I thought he was going to faint with relief when Savanna came into his view.

"Daddy!" She ran to him, his big arms engulfing her in his embrace.

"Baby girl," he whispered, his voice shaky.

I hadn't noticed how wrecked Savanna looked until then. I'd been too focused on getting us all out of there alive. There were long, shallow cuts along the length of her arms and legs. I could see small speckles of blood leaking through the fabric of her shirt. Her left cheek had a slight reddish tinge to it, and a bruise was forming at a spot below her eye. Her elbows were purple, her brown hair unkempt from the action.

Paige and Kevin scrambled to the exit. The hatch was already propped open, waiting for our departure. The park had closed by then, the lights in the visitor's center turned off. Nobody would see us crawl through.

"The others are waiting for us at the park entrance," Mr. Huckleberry said, filling us in as he climbed the ladder. "Frank took Serena to the hospital."

I followed him, Rebecca right behind me. Savanna was already materializing flashlights to replace the ones we lost. We raced out of the building and into clean air. My lungs continued to burn, my heartbeat thrumming loudly. It sounded almost like a shaman's drum.

I was about to follow everyone back to the trail when I realized Rebecca wasn't following me. I stopped running, turning around to search for her. She was heading toward the museum building across the shaking ground.

I chased after her, following her past the buildings and into the park. I nearly ran into her when she froze in her tracks, moving her hands as if she were breaking an invisible stick. My head felt like it was splitting as a shockwave rolled through the park, the ground fissuring in front of us. The earth turned into itself, burying part of the underground lair. Trees from further out bent with the ground, some falling between the cracks.

The shaking stopped.

I squinted into the darkness, the waxing crescent of the moon refusing to cast a brighter glow over the destroyed land. The strength in Rebecca's power was amazing and terrifying at the same time. The scene began to blur in front of me. I could hear horses nearby in their stables, unharmed. Rebecca's knees buckled, and I blacked out.

23 // MY GREAT-GRANDMOTHER IS A FUGITIVE

I heard the voice of an aging Polish woman first. She was trying to disguise her accent, but I could still hear it in the vowels and in the way she overenunciated. "You face a lot of prejudice in the American South," she said, enjoying the attention. "But none like what the so-called Gypsies faced in Europe during the Second World War." She was telling a story—her story—and I listened quietly, patiently, for the rest.

"I was born in southeastern Poland to what some would call a *Polska Roma* family. My family, like many of the *Polska Roma*, did not trust outsiders. They had been hurt too many times by those seeking power and destruction over their people. Romanies are always running from persecution—they did back then, and they do now—wherever they go. I was not surprised when I came to America and found that many here still think of us as outsiders, as beggars, as thieves. *Gadje* often do not understand how they made us this way. They do not understand their role in our suffering.

"I did find one man who thought different, however, and we fell in love, but we never had children of our own. My son, Martin, was born in Kraków before I came to America.

"My family did not travel as much as the other Romanies. We stayed mostly in a village called Szczurowa. The German police came to our village. I was seventeen years old when my family was massacred by them. Some of the—what you call—diviners were able to escape, but I was unable to say goodbye to the place I called home. I was heartbroken. My friend, Agata, became my family, my best friend, my sister." She chuckled and spoke to someone out of my sight. "You remind me so much of her. You have the same fire in your soul."

Her voice grew darker, hollower. "We traveled among villages for a small time. Agata wanted to fight. Her brother, Dobry, would not condone it. He would tell us, 'To burn your enemy's caravan is to burn your future,' but Agata saw no caravan. She saw no proof that the German police were anything like our people, and she wanted them to pay for what they had done to us. I see now how Dobry was right. He spoke in strange ways, but he meant for us to understand that attacking our enemies would only harm us in the end.

"Agata's heart grew cold as we continued to lose more of our people. She saw massacres in the forests and heard of the death camp in Oświęcim. She saw the evil that wanted nothing more than to kill us. She heard of the plot for the 'final solution.' We survived the *Porajmos*, 'the Devouring,' but only because of her wit. Agata has always been resourceful. She knew how to survive on nothing but hatred. I had promised her I would stay with her no matter what happened, and when she lost her way, I stayed with her. We plotted to overthrow the *naziści*, to overthrow their leader, Adolf Hitler.

"I remember that day clearly, although I have wished to forget. It took a long time to travel to Berlin on foot, but we did. I wanted to rest, but Agata called me spoiled—she was too eager to execute her plan of attack. The Germans had lost our country to the Soviets and the Americans were close. Germany was already losing, about to meet their fate, but for Agata, the attack was personal. She wanted to be the one to end his life. Adolf had barricaded himself in a bunker. He was extremely distressed, ready to end his life at any given moment. He did not want to die how Benito Mussolini had in Italy. Instead, he wanted to die in peace. Agata could not believe it. She thought it was a trick. She was as paranoid as Adolf Hitler in that moment. He laughed at us. Two nineteen-year-old Gypsies had come into his bunker to murder him. Eva, his wife, was not so delirious, but she swallowed the cyanide to avoid her murder. That was when Agata took Adolf's gun and shot him.

"She thought she had done good, that she had avenged our friends and families. But, as it is said, 'in the hour of your greatest success are sown the seeds of your own destruction'—it was done. And her success cost her. I no longer recognized my friend, and we parted ways.

"At some point, our names were discovered, and we became known as killers. I fled to America with my son, fell in love, changed my last name, and never saw Agata again. But staying with her before had sown the seeds of my fate, and now generations will flee for what we had done. For that, I am sorry. I put you, my family, in danger."

I opened my eyes to the bright hospital lights.

"Welcome to the party," Ursula said from the foot of the bed, the first to acknowledge my alertness. She had a cone-shaped birthday hat fastened to her dark hair. One of those blowouts that kids always seem to have as favors at their birthday parties was nestled between her fingers.

Mom smiled next to me, squeezing my hand, her knowing, psychic glint back in her eye. Her powers must have returned, her brown eyes unsurprised by my wake.

"What did I miss?" I asked, slowly positioning myself upright. Savanna was sitting in a chair by my feet next to an elderly Romani lady. Rebecca, Paige, and Jay-Jay occupied a bench seat against a wall of windows, their heads all donned with the same party hats. It was daylight outside, but the sun seemed to be setting. I wondered how long I'd been out. Waking up in a hospital wasn't new to me but waking up to a party was.

"Your great-grandma was telling us some war stories," Savanna said, smiling at the elderly woman. "She's an amazing woman."

"Oh, I can't take the credit." The woman smiled in spite of herself, placing her hand on Savanna's arm. "Life always throws us curveballs. It's how we handle them that makes all the difference."

The television in the corner was on, the sound muted. The news was showing bird's-eye view footage of Fort Ben, its greenery ravaged by what the headline was calling a "mysterious" earthquake. The damage appeared vaster on screen than I remembered. I glanced sideways at Rebecca, who shrank back against the window with a guilty expression.

The Polish Romani woman smiled knowingly at my sister. "I grew up with the stories, the folklore, of *boska istota*, divine beings that possess untold power. In one of the stories, there is a mention of the *Wybraniec*, a chosen one, who is more powerful, more compelling, more divergent than the rest. I have never met one before, but I am sure I am looking at one now." She winked. Rebecca smiled.

"There will always be people who will want to control us—harness our powers for great evil. We cannot let that happen," Great-Grandma Anderson said in a grave tone. "Exposure is not worth a single life that could be lost in the reckoning. That is why we hide—why we pretend to be like everybody else. The *naziści* can always come back—can always develop new technologies to harm us. Only with the *Wybraniec* could we stand a chance, but then, why fight at all when we could lead an existence without confrontation?" She drew her gray eyebrows in. "I am unsure what the future holds for your generation. Perhaps you will make waves of change for our people, or perhaps you will all end up as your friend has." My stomach dropped at her last words. Was she referring to Serena? Her eyes glistened as my heart skipped a few beats in the monitor.

A nurse knocked on the open door, chastising the visitors about the large gathering. "Visiting hours are nearly over."

My great-grandmother rolled her eyes, sighing heavily. "I find it best not to annoy the nurses. I am sad to go, but I must get back to my Bruce. Fifty-six years of marriage with that one, and he still hates it when I go out alone. I am glad to have met you all today. I wish it were under better circumstances."

Savanna helped her stand as she balanced herself with her cane. The lady gripped the plastic footboard of the hospital bed and said, teasing me, "Leave it to my grandson to find a friend in the great-granddaughter of my best friend." Savanna giggled, leading her out of the room.

"Dad's waiting for you kids in the lobby," Mom told my sisters while standing up. "I want to talk to my grandma before she leaves."

As they followed her out of the room, Ursula hopped off the bed. "I guess that's my cue to leave."

Soon, only Jay-Jay was left in the room with me. It was silent for a few long moments as he considered what to say. Finally, he spoke, his voice racked with guilt. "I'm sorry I was kind of useless back there."

His apology surprised me. I knew he had been acting a little shady in the bunker, but I guessed knowledge of the future could do that to a person.

"It's not your fault," I said, trying to console him. "Your power is passive. We all knew that."

Jay-Jay sighed, his shoulders dropping. "I wish I could have known more. I thought I *did* know more. But there were so many unknowns. I could only see the absolutes."

"I know." I tried to smile. "I grew up with a psychic mother. I'm used to varying levels of certainty."

"I could have been leading you all to your deaths."

I thought of Serena. Did I detect enough guilt in his troubled voice to assume her fate? Had she not survived? I gulped. "But we all survived, didn't we?" My room had been full of people only moments ago—people who had survived.

Except for the Lindts. I hadn't seen any of them. There was an uncomfortably long pause. Jay-Jay stared at the floor, rubbing his hands nervously. *We had all survived, hadn't we?*

Too much time had passed before he finally nodded his head. His voice thick, he said, "Yeah. You all survived." There seemed to be a much deeper meaning to his words, but I let myself relax at the reassurance that we were all still alive. At least, for now.

"Serena?" I prompted.

He nodded, still staring at the floor, still rubbing his hands. "No visitors allowed," he said. "Her choice, not the hospital's. I heard her mom say she was screaming all night after she woke from the surgery. Massive internal hemorrhaging. Doctor said she's lucky to have survived."

I closed my eyes. I knew that feeling. That feeling that you get when you have survived unspeakable odds, only to wake up not feeling lucky at all. I groaned. "What did they do to her?"

Jay-Jay shrugged, grimacing. He wrung his hands, nodding to himself in agreement to an unvoiced idea, his lips pressing firmly together. I wondered if he had seen it in his vision, if he had known all along how much they would hurt her. I wondered if that was where most of his guilt was stemming from. He couldn't stop it. Her suffering was absolute.

Savanna walked back in the room, and Jay-Jay excused himself. She took a seat in the chair my mom had given up, sliding her hand into mine. Smiling, she said, "Our great-grandmothers were best friends."

I knew what she was getting at. I smiled back, pushing my worries regarding Jay-Jay to the back of my mind. "You think that's fate?"

She leaned forward, her breath tickling my skin. "I think you woke up on my birthday for a reason."

"It's *your* birthday?" I asked, my heart rate accelerating. I recalled Jay-Jay mentioning she had an August birthday, but so much had been going on then, I hadn't had a chance to ask what day it was. She continued to smile, and I knew she was about to kiss me again. I could feel it coming.

"Number fourteen." She giggled.

"Well," I said, then swallowed, "maybe it *is* fate." And *I* kissed *her*, longer than she had kissed me in the bunker. It was the first time I'd ever kissed a girl, and it was better than I'd ever imagined it to be. Our lips danced around the other's, fitting like pieces of a jigsaw puzzle. We could hear my heart monitor beeping quicker.

She pulled a few inches away, laughing. "The nurse is going to kick me out if she hears that thing."

"I don't care."

"Well, I do," she said, sitting back in the chair. Her voice grew sad. "I don't want to leave you." I studied her, staring at the slow-fading scars that ran down her arms. The bruise on her cheek was more prominent as it settled with time. Her elbows were still a purplish blue. Her next words jarred me out of my trance. "You ran from me before. Why?"

I had to strain to remember. So much had happened since then. She was referring to the football game when she had approached me after my apparent altercation with Kevin. I swallowed. "Does your mom have her powers back?"

Savanna nodded. "Yes, but that's not why I'm asking."

"Why *are* you asking?" To me, the reason had been obvious. I had run because I had hurt her mom.

She sighed, resting her head on the edge of the mattress, studying me with her cool blue eyes. "I want to make this work with you. I think Jay-Jay is right about us being destined for each other." Her hand searched for mine, gripping it tight. "But I need to know why you ran, and I need to know you won't do it again, at least, not from me." She held our hands to her chest and said, her voice pleading, "Don't ever run from me."

I thought about what I had told her upon my return. It's what I do. I run. It's an automatic reaction. My sense of self-preservation kicks in. My brain doesn't want to feel hurt, doesn't want to feel pain—so I run. I run from my problems.

It's like how my powers make things disappear. I make myself disappear. I wasn't sure if I could make the promise she was asking me to make. The action was too involuntary. Could I choose not to be that person anymore? Could I choose not to run?

"I'm done running." I'd said it without meaning to, my tongue betraying me once again. My hand trembled in hers, and I loosened it, cupping the side of her bruised face. We'd been through so much in such a short amount of time. We each had our fears. But there was one thing I had learned about Savanna that was more important than anything: she was a fighter. And she would fight for us at all costs. I knew it. And as long as she would fight for me, I would fight for her. My lips trembled with my hand as I made my promise. “I will never leave you.”

EPILOGUE // SERENA

The worst part was that I survived. The second worst part was that Frank hadn't kept his promise. Actually, no. The second-worst part was Jay-Jay almost certainly knew what was going to happen to me—but he didn't care enough to stop it. He'd said nothing when I asked of my fate, but I hoped if they were to kill me, it'd be quick and painless. I shouldn't have thought of the Nazis as merciful people. That was wishful, stupid, moronic. My power was of special interest to Dr. Sauer, and the man was not known to investigate evasively. I would have answered all the questions he asked of me if he had only asked.

Dr. Sauer never spoke directly to me. He was incredibly impersonable. Was he superstitious? Did he think if he spoke to a Gypsy, they would be able to curse him? I *did* curse him, just not with the type of curse he feared.

I don't know how people block painful memories. I wish I could. I remember every detail I was conscious for, every rod through my stomach that should have felt like nothing more than a tickle. I didn't understand how he did it, how he could push an object through my skin with no effort at all, but still jar my insides. I didn't understand how I could stay so motionless either, unable to evade my capture. I'm not sure I want to know the science behind it all. Just thinking about it sends me into a state of uninterrupted panic and fear.

When I woke up in the hospital in the middle of the night, I scared my mother to death. I screamed and I cried and I threw things. The effort tore my stitches. I wanted to die. After what I had been through, it was better than living.

I don't remember many of the days I spent in the hospital. The doctor thought it best to sedate me until I'd healed more. But I don't think I will ever heal from this, and I think the effort everyone put in to save me was wasted. They shouldn't have come after me. They shouldn't have put their lives in danger for me. They should have ignored Jay-Jay's visions and left me to die. By the time they arrived, I had wanted that anyway. I'd begged for it. My mom says I still talk in my sleep—scream, really—weeks after the incident, begging for them to kill me.

I'm rarely left alone anymore, even to use the restroom.

September flew by in a blur, but there was one memory that stood out above the rest. It was raining outside, thundering, when Mya flew into my bedroom, announcing too excitedly that she had "become a woman." I had rolled my eyes, returning my attention back to the book I was pretending to read. After she left, the words on the page started to blur through my tears, my hands shaking with uncontrollable strength. For a second, I didn't know why I was crying. It was something I started doing. All the time.

My conscious caught up with my subconscious, and I threw the book as hard as I could against the opposing wall. My mom heard my scream and came running. And I screamed and screamed as I had in the hospital. Because they hadn't told me what I knew to be true.

"I wanted to wait to tell you when you were in a better place," my mom had said, hugging me to her chest as tightly as she could. "I can see now that was a mistake." She rocked me for hours as if I were a small child, and this realization made me cry harder because I would never get to do the same with my child.

My period hadn't come, and it wouldn't ever again.

"One wants to die
No one knows, only the sky,
Only the river hears our lament.

...

All the birds
Are praying for our children,
So the evil people, vipers, will not kill them.
Ah, fate!
My unlucky luck!"

– *Bronislawa "Papusza" Wajs*

ALPHABETICAL INDEX OF DIVINERS

Burnett, Sage	*[Telekinesis]*
Burnett, Seth	*[Telekinesis]*
Chambers, Bradley	*[Materialization]*
Chambers, Clarinda	*[Precognition]*
Chambers, Paige	*[Telekinesis]*
Chambers, Rebecca	*[Materialization]*
Cornell, Olga	*[Shapeshifting]*
Huckleberry, Macie	*[Power Mimicry]*
Huckleberry, Milo	*[Quantity Manipulation]*
Huckleberry, Savanna	*[Materialization]*
Huckleberry, Ursula	*[Materialization]*
Jones, Jay-Jay	*[Precognition]*
Lantern, Frank	*[Telekinesis]*
Lindt, Hudson	*[Telepathy]*
Lindt, Kevin	*[Power Mimicry]*
Lindt, Mya	*[Telepathy]*
Lindt, Nancy	*[Precognition]*
Lindt, Serena	*[Mass Manipulation]*
Schwartz, Kase	*[Mass Manipulation]*
Schwartz, Rice	*[Telekinesis]*

ABOUT THE STORY

DISCLAIMERS

The Romani people are not superhuman, mythical creatures who possess otherworldly abilities. They are simply people who go about their daily life in as human a way as possible. They possess their own culture, their own ethnic histories, and their own traditions. The term *Romani* is an umbrella term, as there are many names that categorize different sub-groups. This is much like using the term *Africans* to describe those hailing from an entire continent as opposed to the specifics of *Rwandans* or even more specifically, *Tutsi*. It is like using the term *Latinx* to describe a group of people hailing from Latin American communities as opposed to *Mexican* or *Cuban* when describing someone's specific ethnic origins. In this book, Serena uses a more specific term to describe their ancestors. The Sinti are a Romani group primarily hailing from Central Europe. The Sinti were constantly experiencing discrimination throughout their continent and varying countries. They represented a good portion of the Romani people who were captured, tortured, and killed by the Nazis during World War II. In the final chapter, Bradley's great-grandmother relays her experience living through such a tumultuous time. She grew up Polska Roma (Romanies who lived primarily in Poland), living in one of the few Romani communities who had assimilated into Polish culture. The massacre of her hometown in Szczurowa is based on a very real event. There is still a standing memorial in Szczurowa for the Romani families who were killed.

In the beginning and end of this book there are stanzas from a Polska Roma poet who lived during the time of the Second World War. Bronislawa Wajs, who was often called "Papusza" (meaning "doll" in the Romani language) was deemed a traitor by her people for sharing their culture and experiences with the outside world. However, it is her musical poetry that gives us an insight into how the Polska Roma lived in a time of great peril.

This book is not intended to further the stereotype of Romanies possessing supernatural abilities, just as similar fantastical stories are not intended to suggest any human of any ethnicity is a supernatural being. The idea of magic has always been something that has captured the interest of millions of humans across the globe. It is through magic that stories are often told. I use "magic" in this story to capture interests so that more important issues can be brought up under its guise. While the "magic" is simply a work of fiction as well as the characters throughout this story, the rest of the story represents real issues, both in the past and in the present.

I want to also address the depiction of type one diabetes in this story. Because this is a fiction story and because Bradley is not a real person, there may be small inaccuracies when it comes to his battle with type one diabetes. However, this is a very real condition that affects the lives of 1.25 million people in the United

States. It is important to remember that while all people who have type one diabetes can't produce insulin, one person with this disease may experience it slightly different than another. It is important for each person to get to know their bodies and how their bodies react to certain outside influences. One person's symptoms may differ from another. Sometimes those with type one diabetes experience sudden highs and lows in their glucose levels for little to no reason, despite consistently monitoring their blood and taking the necessary measures to keep their levels at a consistent functioning number. What is considered a high or low blood sugar level for one person, may be normal for another.

There is currently no cure for this disease. However, there have been major strides in current research. While we wait for a cure, it is imperative to realize how expensive living with this disease in the United States can be. According to a 2020 article by Robert Preidt posted on Web MD, "Out-of-pocket costs for Americans with type 1 diabetes average $2,500 a year." Of course, that cost is pertaining to those with insurance. Some patients pay more than $5,000 a year in out-of-pocket expenses. Without insurance, insulin pumps can cost around $6,000 and that doesn't include batteries and sensors that constantly need replaced. Continuous glucose monitors are a cheaper option but can still cost over a thousand dollars. In the past decade, insulin prices have also skyrocketed. One vial of insulin in 2020 could cost around 250 dollars. There are several people—both children and adults—who may need your help in covering these out-of-pocket expenses. If you have the means, consider donating money to a person in need or consider donating to an organization working towards a cure.

I hope you enjoyed Bradley's story.

ABOUT THE AUTHOR

For nearly a year-and-a-half, E.K. Barnes owned and operated *Scribe Stash*, a personalized subscription box service for readers and writers, where she also participated in writing and editing book, movie, and product review articles. She has been interviewed by Outlet Publishing Group and Double the Books Magazine regarding her writing endeavors and her work with *Scribe Stash*, respectively. Prior to and alongside this short endeavor, E.K. has written and performed several speeches and presentations across different topics – specifically regarding people, events, and mental health. E.K. is a member of the Independent Author Network. She is a 2014 graduate of Olathe Northwest High School in Kansas and has been a student at Johnson County Community College, MidAmerica Nazarene University, and Southern New Hampshire University.

E.K. comes from a family of creatives – her brother is a musician with dreams of becoming a film composer, her sister has a degree in graphic design, and her parents both hold degrees in music.

She currently resides in Kansas with her dog, Nikki.

www.ekbarnesauthor.com
Instagram:@ekbarnes_author | TikTok: @ekbarnes_author

CPSIA information can be obtained
at www.ICGtesting.com
Printed in the USA
LVHW031025010621
689027LV00012B/1676